The Chandler Legacies

ABDI NAZEMIAN

Balzer + Bray
An Imprint of HarperCollins Publishers

ALSO BY ABDI NAZEMIAN

The Authentics

Like a Love Story

For every friend and mentor I met in boarding school who pulled me from the darkness into the light. You will always be family to me.

Balzer + Bray is an imprint of HarperCollins Publishers.

The Chandler Legacies
Copyright © 2022 by Abdi Nazemian
All rights reserved. Printed in the United States of America.
No part of this book may be used or reproduced in any manner whatsoever
without written permission except in the case of brief quotations embodied in
critical articles and reviews. For information address HarperCollins
Children's Books, a division of HarperCollins Publishers, 195 Broadway,
New York, NY 10007.
www.epicreads.com

ISBN 978-0-06-303932-2

Typography by Michelle Taormina
22 23 24 25 26   PC/LSCH   10 9 8 7 6 5 4 3 2 1
❖
First Edition

This book contains descriptions of sexual abuse, physical abuse, homophobia, and hazing. I tried to portray these issues with sensitivity, but please proceed with caution and care. My hope is that this story will help those who have experienced these traumas to feel less alone. If you need help, there are resources listed in the back of the book.

The easiest person to lie to is yourself.
That's why it's so important to find people you trust.
They'll help you tell the truth.

—Hattie Douglas, *Supplemental Facts*

Prologue

JANUARY 2008

If you had a choice between telling the truth and hurting someone you love or keeping a secret that eats away at you, which would you choose? I think most people would choose to keep the secret. We weren't most people. That's what we would discover in the last months of the twentieth century, those months that changed our lives forever.

Eight years ago, following that turn of the century, I arrived on campus before everyone else to confront Professor Douglas. It had snowed over the holidays, and with no students traipsing across the grounds in their Timberlands, the whole school looked like a cloud. Everything imposing and menacing about Chandler suddenly became innocent and fresh. Like it was a place of new beginnings, which I knew by then it wasn't. Chandler was, and is, a place weighed down by history.

There was so much snow that it even covered the school motto on all the campus benches and buildings.

Veritas vos liberabit.

It's as if nature knew that truth will not, as it turns out, liberate us all. It takes more than truth to liberate. It takes action.

I remember knocking on Douglas's door five times before she finally opened it. Her trademark spiky auburn hair looked more electrocuted than ever. I pulled the pages from beneath my coat and handed them to her. She didn't take them right away.

I followed her apprehensively, setting my massive backpack down. She must have sensed something was wrong, because she suddenly looked at the pages in her hand like they were a ticking time bomb. "So what's it about?" she asked.

"Well, it's personal," I said. She waited for me to continue. "It's about five students who are chosen for a writing workshop by a brilliant professor who . . ."

I never finished that sentence. It was too much to fit into one thought. It's still too much. Maybe that's why we wrote it all down.

Because sometimes stories are the only way to make sense of complicated emotions.

SEPTEMBER 1999

Beth Kramer

If you take the interstate from New York into Connecticut, you might notice the pollution that has started to infest our highways—soda bottles, packs of cigarettes, gum wrappers. You might notice the red of the trees in the fall, the green of them in the spring. If you're very observant, you will probably notice the hidden police cars, covertly stationed near the off-ramps, waiting for speeding luxury cars they can teach a lesson to—Connecticut being the capital of traffic violations.

"Mom, there's the exit," Beth Kramer tells her mom, Elizabeth, pointing to an unmarked off-ramp. Beth and her mom share a name and they're both redheads with freckles, but they share very little else.

"It's so confusing," her mom says. "Can't they just put up a big old sign like normal people?"

"No, because this isn't a place for normal people."

Here's the thing. In 1958, when the interstate was

first built, the Headmaster of Chandler Academy and the Headmistress of Plum School (they were still separate institutions then) petitioned the state for their very own interstate exit. Exit 75. The only catch is that they wanted it to be a hidden exit with no signage. Beth doesn't say any of this to her mom, who hates everything Chandler represents and would bristle at the whole concept of a hidden interstate exit. Her mom would understand, like Beth does, that the whole point of Exit 75 is avoiding townies.

Beth is one of those townies, and yet here she is, arriving for her sophomore year. A second chance at convincing them, and convincing herself, that she belongs here.

Beth's mom takes the unmarked exit and drives down the half mile of New England foliage that separates road from school. There's nowhere to pull off and stop the car until they get to campus. Beth thinks of all the buried secrets in these woods. Trees carved with lovers' initials. Decades of cigarette butts buried under leaves and dirt, because what happens here tends to stay buried.

But anything can be unburied.

As soon as her mom pulls into campus, Beth hauls her giant backpack out of the back seat. "Okay, thanks Mom," she says.

"I could come help you settle in," her mom offers.

"I'm not a third former this time," Beth says. "It would be pretty embarrassing for a fourth former to have her mom help her put a comforter on her bed."

"What's a third former again?" her mom asks.

"It's a freshman. So that makes me a *fourth* former this year. A sophomore."

Her mom shakes her head. "I don't know why this school can't just use the same words as the rest of us."

Beth could say again that it's because this place isn't for normal people, but she doesn't.

"I see other mothers helping."

"Those are nannies," Beth says, half smiling.

"Okay," her mom says with a sad shrug. "I don't know the rules of this place like you do."

Beth throws her backpack onto the ground outside the car. She leans into the car, stretches her body until she's able to give her mom a kiss on the cheek. "Love you, Mom."

"Are you gonna be okay?" her mom says. A loaded question.

She nods instead of answering. She knows that if she engages in this conversation, her mom will use it as one more opportunity to suggest therapy. Okay, she's a little anxious sometimes. But she's not *see-a-therapist* anxious. "Will you be able to find your way back to town?" Beth asks.

"I think so. They make getting out a lot easier than getting in."

Beth slams the car door shut. She waves until her mom's Volvo is out of sight. It stood out like a sore thumb among all the luxury cars. She imagines her mom weaving her way back to the highway. Beth thinks about how she's a little like that hidden exit herself. No one notices her.

And why would they? Look at these kids pouring into campus. New haircuts. Freshly pressed summer dresses purchased from the racks of fancy New York City boutiques. Bright whitened smiles. Stories about summers in the south of France, internships at banks and magazines and movie studios. All the markers of belonging that Beth still hasn't achieved because, well, she can't afford to.

She smiles at the fellow fourth formers she remembers from last year. Amanda de Ravin. Sarah Sumner. Rachel Katz. They all look right past her like she's made of cellophane.

As Beth gazes around the campus, she marvels at how much she knows about it. She's basically a Chandler encyclopedia, her lifelong obsession with the campus having resulted in useless trivia about it filling her brain. Probably taking up space that could be occupied by more important things. She could've at least volunteered to be an orientation guide this year, but she was too scared. Too committed to staying invisible.

In the distance, she sees Sarah Brunson guiding a new family across campus. Her wavy brown hair and forced smile bring Beth right back to rooming with her last year. Brunson wears a rust-and-gold *CAN I HELP YOU?* T-shirt that swims over her fitted jeans. Of course she's an orientation guide. Beth wishes she had that kind of self-assurance.

She wonders if Brunson knows as much about campus history as she does. Like, does Brunson know that the new Math Building was a gift from Moses Briggs, the mutual fund manager from the Class of '64 who swindled countless people out of their life savings? It was supposed to be called the Briggs Building. The name was taken off, but the school still took the money. Does she know that the Main Lawn isn't even real, the school having invested in very expensive fake grass that looks real but can withstand the countless games of ultimate Frisbee and hacky sack that students play?

"Beth!"

Beth looks up in surprise and sees someone waving to her. No, not just someone. Amanda Priya Spencer. Spence.

"Hey, Beth! How was your summer!" Spence asks as she exits the back seat of a Mercedes. Her nanny drives the family car, and Beth can't help but notice that she is wearing the Prada outfit Spence wore to last year's First Huzzah.

Beth freezes, her mind full of questions. How does Spence know who she is? Is Spence just being polite or does she truly care? Should she walk away? Make up an interesting story about her summer?

She does none of these things. Instead, she just stares at Spence for an uncomfortably long time. Spence is probably used to the stares, because her beauty stops people in their tracks.

"Beth!" Spence calls out again as she ties her shiny black hair into her signature high ponytail, a hairstyle duplicated by girls across campus without ever pulling it off the way Spence does. "Hi!"

It's like there are exclamation points after everything Spence says. That's her. Confident. Optimistic. Chosen.

Beth studies Spence like she's studied every effortless Chandler girl she saw in town as a kid. That time at Toppings when three girls in the shortest shorts ordered a single scoop of mint chocolate chip to share, then let it melt as they discussed someone named Tucker's ass when he played lacrosse. That time she and her mom went to Mamma Mia to pick up pizza, and she saw a Chandie girl smoking a cigarette alone in a booth as she furiously underlined *Great Expectations*.

"Oh yeah, fine, I'm sorry," Beth says. "I didn't know you knew me."

Spence laughs. "Of course I know you. You did lights for *A Chorus Line* last year, right?"

"Yeah, I did, that's right." It's not that Beth hid all through her first year. It's just that she chose activities that allowed her to disappear, like being a techie for the school musical.

"Well, thanks for making me look good," Spence says with a beaming smile. Like Spence needs lighting to look good. Please. "So, did you have a good summer?"

"Uh, yeah, fine." Why does it take this much effort to answer a simple question? Maybe because unlike the rest of these kids, Beth stayed in town and worked at Toppings. "I'm sure yours was more exciting than mine," Beth continues in a nervous stammer. "Where were you? St. Tropez? Biarritz? Gstaad?" She pronounces each of these words in a clipped mid-Atlantic accent that makes her sound like a *Saturday Night Live* sketch about Chandies. She observed many things about her classmates last year, and one of these observations is that they mock themselves mercilessly. To belong to Chandler, you apparently need to make fun of its ways.

Spence laughs. "You're hilarious, Beth!"

Okay, she's a lot of things, and hilarious isn't one of them. But Beth can't help being flattered just the same.

As Spence walks away from her, Beth thinks about how much she knows about Spence despite barely ever interacting with her. Like, she knows that Spence's paternal grandfather went to Chandler and played crew, and her paternal grandmother went to Plum and played the lead in *Antigone*. Her maternal grandparents, both doctors, moved from India to New York in the late '60s after a new immigration act was passed. Her father, Class of '78, is now some movie-exec big shot, and her mother is a supermodel and activist. *Still* working as a model despite pushing fifty. Those are the kinds of genes Spence has. Meanwhile, Beth's mom has worn the same elastic-waisted jeans for the last decade, and people regularly mistake her dad for her grandfather because life has worn him down so fast.

She walks toward Carlton House, her fourth-form dorm, trying not to let the Benzes and BMWs and Maseratis intimidate her into feeling bad about herself.

Behind her, she hears Spence greet Henny Dover.

"Hey, Henny! How was your summer!"

Beth's heart sinks a little, suddenly feeling a little less special.

Beth reaches a finger into her scalp, but stops herself. She's vowed not to pull in public. She rushes toward her dorm and falls hard on the pavement, catching herself with her palms.

She looks around, praying no one saw her. But they did. Of course they did. Well, fine—let them laugh. She takes a moment to feel the sting. At least it reminds her she's alive.

"You okay?" Henny asks.

Thankfully, Spence is walking away. Maybe she didn't see what happened.

"Yeah, I'm fine," she says.

"Are you new?" Henny asks. "I'm Henny Dover. I can walk you to your dorm if—"

"I was here last year," Beth says. "We know each other."

"Oh right," Henny says, squinting.

In a way, Henny *not* knowing who she is makes her feel more at ease than Spence knowing. It confirms her core belief about herself: that she's insignificant.

She walks away, chewing on her hair. Her fucking hair. If she could change one thing about herself, it would be the hours she spends thinking about her hair.

Walking to Carlton House, Beth takes in the campus in all its glory. For years, she only saw the campus in brochures, even though it was only two miles away from her home. Those brochures that she pored over didn't even come close to capturing the real thing. And that website. It drains the place of all its magic with its low-resolution images. There's nothing low-res about this place.

She knows most of the girls in her fourth-form dorm from last year. But not a single one is a friend. She may have survived one year as a Chandie, but she certainly didn't make any friends.

At least she'll be living in a single this year. Brunson avoided her for most of last year. And why wouldn't she? Brunson was just pretty and confident enough to fit right in with the other girls. She made friends quickly. Packed her schedule with extracurriculars and social plans, never once inviting Beth along to join. When Brunson and her friends congregated in their room to eat Twizzlers and do homework together, Beth would just put her headphones on and drown them out. Better to ignore them than to be ignored. It wasn't an ideal existence, but it worked.

And then Brunson went and ruined everything by complaining to their dorm parent about Beth's red hair being all over their room. Brunson told Beth that she empathized deeply with hair loss, which was such an odd thing to say, but she also said that she was grossed out by the hairs that found their way into their shared Crock-Pot. In a meeting between the two roommates and their dorm parent, Brunson suggested that Beth wear a hairnet in the room, and the only grown-up in the room said that sounded like a perfect compromise.

A *hairnet*.

HAIR. NET.

Beth said nothing. Just smiled. And then she wore the hairnet as suggested. But not just in the room. She wore it *everywhere*, to class, to tech rehearsal for *A Chorus Line*, to Chapel, to all-school meetings. When people asked her why she was wearing a hairnet, she just shrugged. She didn't need anyone to know why, except for Brunson. She wanted to throw Brunson's petty cruelty back in her face.

In the hallway of her new dorm, Beth runs right into Jane King, who grew her thin hair out over the summer and now wears it in a Spence-like high ponytail. "Oh hey," Jane says. "What are *you* doing here?"

"What do you mean?" Beth asks. "This is my dorm."

"I thought you were a day student," Jane says.

Beth sighs. All she wants is to be one of these girls. Maybe someday to even date one of them. But they'll always see her as a day student, even when she's a boarder. Because she's a townie. It's like they can smell it on her.

"I'm not," Beth says. "I mean, my parents live nearby, but I live here."

"My bad," Jane says.

Beth heads to her room. As she does, she overhears another returning sophomore, Paulina Lutz, whisper to a new sophomore. "Wait 'til you see Freddy Bello. He got even hotter over the summer. Frede-rico Suave."

Beth rolls her eyes and closes the door to her single. With her own room, she'll be free to spread out. No hairnet. She can let the strands she pulls go wherever they want to go.

She can already feel the release as she digs her right hand into the crown of her scalp, her thin fingers searching for the perfect hair to pull out.

Yank.

She stares at the long red hair in her hand. Then blows it away, onto that old, old carpet. Then she digs back in. She marvels at how each strand of hair seems to have its own texture. Some strands are smooth. Some are rough. She finds the roughest one she can and . . .

Yank.

Blow.

Yank.

Blow.

As she engages in her ritual, she thinks about the year ahead. She *has* to be chosen this year. She applied last year, but she didn't even get an interview with Professor Douglas. This time, she has to make Professor Douglas see that she's special, that she can write, that she has something unique to say that no one else does. If Douglas will just let her into the Circle, the other students will finally see that she's more than just another townie. They'll understand that the reason she was given a scholarship is because she's fucking smarter than them. She *earned* her way in.

When she's pulled enough hairs out to satisfy herself, she briefly feels the smooth skin of her scalp. She loves this feeling of freshness. Just new follicles waiting to grow new hairs. Regeneration. Like the school, which always admits new students, her head will always grow new hairs.

She digs into her backpack and pulls out her favorite book. *Supplemental Facts* by Hattie Douglas. It's the only novel Professor Douglas has had published (twenty years ago, hard to find, especially as she does not allow the Chandler Library to carry it). Beth has so many questions, first about the book (Is it autobiographical?), but also about the publishing (Was it hard to publish a lesbian novel in 1979?).

As her submission essay for the Circle this year, Beth decides to gush about this book. She compares herself to the lead character of the novel, a woman who hides a secret lesbian life from her husband in the early 1970s. It is, of course, no secret that the professor is a lesbian, and that she was once married (her ex-husband still publishes, thirteen novels so far, and also four wives). Professor Douglas is, in fact, the only openly gay teacher on campus. Some might count Father Close, the school priest, who quotes Karen Carpenter in every sermon, but he's, well, a priest. Beth's analysis of Professor Douglas's novel is deeply perceptive because she sees so much of herself in it.

And that title, *Supplemental Facts*. She loves that title. She thinks of all the supplemental facts no one knows about her, and she puts them into her essay. Like how it feels to be a townie who insisted on being a boarder. Like the feelings that stir inside her when she watches the way Chandler girls glide through life.

Before putting the essay in a manila envelope and dropping it off in the mailroom, she digs into her scalp and pulls the smoothest hair she can find. She closes her eyes and blows it into the air. This is her small offering to the whims of the universe.

She checks the inside of the envelope obsessively, making sure the essay is there, as if it could disappear into thin air without her watchful eye.

Then she seals the envelope.

Amanda Spencer

"Okay," Spence says as the Livingston girls sit adoringly around her. "Catch me up on everything."

Spence listens as one sixth former tells her about traveling across Asia with her diplomat dad, and another tells hilarious stories about working at the Body Shop. "But who cares about us?" one of them says. "Tell us about Strasberg."

"Oh, it was pretty wild," Spence says. "I got to do scenes in the same theater Marilyn Monroe performed in."

When Spence closes her eyes, she's right back at Strasberg, the acting program Mr. Sullivan helped get her into.

"And I wrote my own scenes," she continues. "I learned so much about like, constructing a narrative and writing dialogue and . . ."

She stops herself when she sees how bored the girls

look. These girls don't care about this. She quickly changes course.

"And you won't believe who was in the audience for my show," Spence says. "Meg Ryan!"

Now the girls perk up. Spence knows that her proximity to celebrity is one of the things her fellow students like most about her. *What was her hair like?* "Very French New Wave." *What was she wearing?* "A black blazer over a tank top, effortlessly chic." *Did she say anything to you?* "I mean, she asked me where the bathroom was."

When the girls are gone, Spence transforms her room. She replaces the plastic trash can with a beautiful porcelain can she bought at Bloomie's. She dumps the cheap soap bar the school gives them and lines up her Clarins products. She hangs the new framed posters she brought with her this year. Last year's Magritte and Escher prints from the MOMA are replaced with a print of Marilyn she found at a memorabilia shop in Greenwich Village. In the photo, Marilyn is reading a book called *How to Develop Your Thinking Ability*, which Spence thinks is lovably hilarious and also a little sad. Next to Marilyn goes the signed and personalized photo of Madhuri Dixit that her mom managed to get for her birthday two years ago. Spence briefly remembers the kids calling Spence Bollywood when she was a third former. It was both the biggest compliment in the world, because Bollywood rocks, and also totally racist. For every kid who knew who her parents were, there was another who would stare at her and ask, "What are you?" She knew what they were really asking, but she would always answer, "I'm Spence," and smile hard at them. Eventually it stuck. She's just Spence now.

Finally, Spence tapes a self-portrait she sketched in charcoal onto the wall. In the portrait, Spence bears a striking resemblance to John Singer Sargent's *Portrait of Madame X*, her favorite painting. Even though it's a portrait of a white woman from the nineteenth century, Spence sees herself in it. She likes how it's a portrait of a socialite who is so much more complicated than her role would suggest.

She opens her journal. She's been jotting down ideas for new scenes and plays in there. She writes down the words *Madame X*. Maybe she'll write about her, the real woman who inspired the painting. She starts a scene about Madame X, imagining herself playing her. Spence knows that if she wants to keep acting after Chandler, she'll need to either write her own roles or move to India. She's not going to be anyone's exotic fantasy or comic relief. She feels grateful for Sullivan's color-blind casting policy as she writes. Because he's the head of the Theater Department, she can play anyone she wants to, be anyone she wants to.

Spence writes the words *THE CIRCLE* in capital letters on a page from her journal, then rips it out and tapes it to her wall next to Marilyn and Madame X.

Once she's settled in, she leaves her room and heads toward Holmby House, a sixth-form boys' dorm on the eastern edge of campus. She walks across the first-floor hallway, taking in the musty scent of that many teenage boys living in such a small space. On one door, she sees the names *Freddy Bello* and *Charles Cox.* Through the cracked door, she can hear them catching up. But she doesn't linger. Instead, she beelines to the end of the hallway, to Sullivan's residence. She knocks on the door.

"Coming!" When he opens the door, he's wearing a blazer over a T-shirt and jeans. His feet are bare. He got a Caesar cut over the summer and grew a goatee.

"Whoa, nice new look!" she teases.

"Oh," he says, running one hand on his chin and another through his hair. "It doesn't make me look stupid? I grew it for a role I played at that summer theater festival I told you about. And I just kept it."

"It doesn't look stupid. It's cool. You look like a Reservoir Dog."

"So," he says with a smile. "Was Strasberg everything I told you it would be?"

"Yes!" she says. "I took acting and singing and dance and improv and also, we wrote our own scenes, which we presented to our families at the end of the summer. Well, to some of our families 'cause my parents couldn't show up at the last minute." She pauses and shrugs. "They were both traveling and super busy."

"You should've invited me," Sullivan says.

"Oh come on. You were at your theater festival!"

"It was in Massachusetts. It's not that far from New York. I would've come."

Spence is flattered he would even consider going all that way to see her. It would've been nice, actually. To have someone there in the audience, cheering her on. A supportive grown-up. Not that her parents aren't supportive, she reminds herself. She knows that with their careers, sacrifices have to be made.

"The past is the past," Sullivan says. "Tell me more. Do they still leave an empty seat in the theater for Lee Strasberg because they believe his ghost sits there?"

She laughs. "Yes, it's so bizarre! They talk about him like he's *alive*."

Sullivan looks wistful as he says, "He may not be alive, but he's immortal."

Maybe it's true. Maybe it's why she wants to be an actress so badly. To be immortal. But it's more than that. When she acts or writes, she doesn't feel the pressure of being Amanda Priya Spencer, daughter of George Everett Spencer and Shivani Lal. When she's someone else, she stops feeling eclipsed by her parents' fame and success. It's such a good feeling.

"You want to come in?" Sullivan asks. "I was just making espresso."

She walks into Sullivan's small Holmby House residence. She pauses to peruse his spinner rack of CDs and his shelf of books. He always exposes her to the most interesting art. "Do you know you introduced me to espresso?" she asks.

"Did I?" he asks, making a cup for each of them.

The espresso machine is loud, so she's not sure he can

hear her say, "It was during rehearsals for *Romeo and Juliet* freshman year. I was tired, so you gave me a sip of your espresso." She can remember how shocked she was by the bitter taste.

"I still regret casting you as Lady Montague," he says. "I should've trusted my instincts and made you Juliet, but a third former playing Juliet would've ruffled a lot of feathers."

She thinks of all the roles Sullivan has directed her in. Prudence in *Beyond Therapy*, Gypsy Rose Lee in *Gypsy*, and Estelle in *No Exit*. But her favorite role by far was last year. Morales in *A Chorus Line*. When she sang "What I Did for Love," there wasn't a dry eye in the house.

Sullivan puts their coffees down and motions for her to sit. He only has one couch in his place, and she sits on one end while he takes the other.

"So, can I talk to you about something?" she asks.

Sullivan nods. "My door is always open for you."

"Well, I was thinking . . . I'm so excited for your student scenes class this year, because writing was my favorite part of the summer . . ."

"I'm glad," he says.

"But I was also thinking that maybe if I apply for the Circle, you could . . . put in a word with Professor Douglas?"

Sullivan does that thing he always does when he's thinking. He takes his glasses off and closes his eyes. Scratches that space between his eyebrows.

"The Circle," he whispers.

Yes, the Circle! she wants to yell, because that's how bad she wants in. There are many ways to be chosen at Chandler Academy, but the Circle is the ultimate, and Spence feels pressure to live up to her parents' shining example. She's proven she's good enough to be cast in school plays even when she's up against child stars from must-see TV shows. She's proven she's good enough to sing with the Sandmen, the confusingly named coed a cappella group—the name having withstood the merging of Chandler and Plum in 1987—even when she's competing against opera singers who have duetted with Pavarotti. Now she needs to prove that she's good enough to be in Professor Douglas's Circle.

"You don't think she'll let me in?" she asks.

"No, no, it's not that," he says.

"You don't think I'm a good enough writer? Because we wrote our own scenes all summer."

Sullivan smiles. "I'm sure they were great."

"Then why are you hesitating?" she asks. "If you don't think I'm good enough for the Circle, just tell me so I don't waste my time."

"I've never underestimated you," Sullivan says warmly.

Spence feels herself calming down. "No, you haven't," she says. Then, in a jokey tone, she adds, "Except when you cast me as Baby June when I was born to play Gypsy."

"You played Gypsy in the end."

"Only because that senior you originally cast was expelled for doing cocaine before the tech rehearsal."

Sullivan shakes his head. "I told you then and I remind

you now. Drugs and alcohol are the enemies of creativity. Please stay away."

"I will," she says, rolling her eyes. "So . . . the Circle. Will you help me?"

He sighs. "I just wouldn't want the Circle distracting you from your last year of theater here."

"It won't, I swear. On the bright side, I completed all my math and science requirements last year, so my classes will be a breeze."

"The school let you stop taking math *and* science?"

"I mean, Dean Fletcher called my dad in Hungary and told him I wouldn't get into college if I went through with it. And when that didn't work, he called my mom at Lake Como. My parents scheduled a conference call with me to tell me how important it is to be well-rounded, and I told them that I don't care about going to college anyway, unless it's like, Juilliard. I already know what I want to do with my life." Spence hears herself talking way too fast, like she does when she's excited. There's so much more she wants to say, like how she could never break from tradition like this if her mom hadn't already broken down barriers for her. But she stops herself.

"I'm glad you're committed to acting." He nods approvingly. "You're the most talented student I've ever had."

"Oh," she says. "I mean, wow."

Sullivan left a successful career as a playwright to teach at Chandler. He's taught here for eight years. Not forever, but that's a pretty big deal when one of his former students, Avery Lamb, Class of '95, already has a Tony.

There's a framed photo of Avery and Sullivan staring at her now.

Sullivan crosses one leg over the other, shifting a little closer to her.

"But it's not just acting I'm committed to. Writing too. I promise I won't be distracted from theater," she says. "If anything, this will make me an even better actress because writing is like digging even deeper into psychology, right? Into understanding other humans. Which is also what acting is. You taught me that."

"That's true."

Spence is more convinced than ever that being a star means writing her own parts. And she needs Douglas to make her an exceptional writer. But first, she must be selected. And Douglas tends to select the most offbeat students. Spence needs Douglas to read her submission with an open mind, to see that she's more than just another spoiled legacy kid. She needs Douglas to understand how willing she is to work hard and push herself.

"So . . . will you put a word in with Douglas?" she asks.

Sullivan nods.

"Yes!" she says, clasping her hands. "I really appreciate it."

She stands up and heads to the door. Pausing, she debates giving Sullivan a hug, but that feels weird, so she shakes his hand.

"Mr. Sullivan," a male voice calls out.

Spence turns and sees Freddy Bello and Charles Cox

are at the door now, right next to her.

"Oh," she says. "Hey, guys. You're living in Holmby House this year?"

"Affirmative," Charles says.

"Well, you've got the coolest dorm parent," she says, smiling at Sullivan.

Sullivan blushes but says, "I don't love that term. You kids already have parents."

"It's just that *residential faculty advisor* is a real mouthful," Freddy explains.

"Speaking of cool," Sullivan says. "What's that music?"

She hears a melancholy voice she doesn't recognize coming from someone's room. "Elliott Smith," Freddy says.

"I'll have to borrow that CD." That's the thing about Sullivan. He doesn't just expose kids to art. He wants to know what they're listening to as well. She likes that about him.

"Mr. Sullivan," Charles says, "we think there may be rats in the walls."

Sullivan grimaces. "Really?"

"There's a really gross smell in the common area. And we hear like, teeny little footsteps."

Charles leads Sullivan to the common area, but Freddy lingers behind. "Good to see you again," he says.

Freddy stands in front of her, his arm raised and resting on the wall. He looks ridiculously good. Not that she's interested in him that way. She doesn't need one last Chandler boyfriend distracting her. She promised herself

27

she wasn't doing that this year. For one thing, she'll be graduating and would inevitably have to break up with whoever she dates. For another, high school guys have proven to be reliably immature and only interested in one thing.

She notices that Freddy is holding a copy of the *Chandler Legacy*. On the front page is an article about Professor Douglas stepping down as head of the English Department after two decades.

"Kind of wild that Douglas is stepping down, right?" Spence asks.

"Yeah," he says. "She was head of the English Department longer than we've been alive."

She nods. "Time is weird."

"Deep thoughts," he says playfully.

Spence reaches over to grab the paper from him, then swats him with it. She reads a quote from Douglas aloud. "'I want to focus purely on teaching again,'" Spence reads. "'And of course, on the Circle.'" She hands the paper back to him. "I was thinking of applying this year."

Freddy's face brightens. "Really? To the Circle? Me too."

"You?" Spence asks.

Freddy flinches. Spence wishes she could take it back. It's not that she doesn't think he's smart enough. It's just that he's an athlete. Pole vaulting, of all things. That must keep him pretty busy.

"I should go settle into my room," he says.

"You and Charles Cox again, huh?" Spence asks.

"Yeah." Freddy blows a strand of hair out of his eyes. "If it ain't broke, why fix it, right?"

"I guess," Spence says. She thinks about the things that don't appear broken that she'd love to fix. Like her inability to fall in love. Everyone on campus gossiped endlessly about the reason she broke up with Chip Whitney last year, concocting absurd stories. But the reason was simple. She just didn't love him. And she suspects she just might not be capable of feeling that for anyone.

"You living with someone this year?" Freddy asks.

"No, I got a single," she says. "I'm too fastidious for a roommate. They all hate me for cleaning up after them. I guess I'm weird." She shrugs.

"Well, you use the word *fastidious* in everyday conversation, so yeah, you're definitely weird."

"Shut up," she says, smiling. "At least I'm clean. You guys have barely moved into this dorm, and it already stinks. No wonder you have rats. Take a shower."

"I heard some rumors about the length of your showers from some of the girls last year. And apparently, all the girls want to borrow your fancy products or something."

"Not fair," Spence says. "I don't know anything about your shower habits."

An uncomfortable energy fills the air as she imagines him in the shower.

Freddy catches her eye and his face flushes. "I'll uh, see you later," he says, and strides off.

Spence leaves the stink of Holmby House. In the common room, Sullivan and all the senior boys search for the rats.

She pushes her way into the fresh air and starts to plot what she'll submit to Douglas. Whatever it is, it has to be submitted before Labor Day, and handed into Douglas's mailbox between 5 p.m.–8 p.m. The timing is, as with everything about Douglas, crucial. Because 6 p.m.–8 p.m. is the only truly free time Chandies have. It's when they can go to the student social center to play Ping-Pong or foosball or watch *Friends* or go to the Tuck Shop and eat grilled cheese and curly fries and gossip.

Spence is willing to skip all that to turn in a handwritten scene from an untitled play in progress. She'll finish that Madame X scene. She'll make it great. She has to be invited to the second round. If Douglas meets with her, she'll see that Spence has things to say.

Ramin Golafshar

"Can I help you?" a girl with long, wavy brown hair asks. Ramin and his mother stare at the Chandler map, trying to find his dorm. Ramin studied this map before arriving, and yet he's still lost. He looks up. The girl wears a rust-and-gold T-shirt that reads *CAN I HELP YOU?* in big block letters.

"Um, we're looking for Wilton Blue Basement," Ramin's mother says in her heavily accented English.

The girl's bright smile becomes a comic grimace. "Oh, that's way up there." She points to a hill. "You need to climb the hill, go through those trees, and then you'll see the sophomore boys' dorms."

"Okay," Ramin's mother says. "Thank you."

"I'm Sarah Brunson, by the way," she says. "I'm in your class. Everyone calls me Brunson. Basically, half the campus is an Amanda, Sarah, Jennifer, Matt, or Ben, so if you meet anyone with one of those first names, it's a safe bet to call them by their last names, or some abbreviated version. You get it, right?"

"I get it, Brunson," Ramin says dryly.

"Wait, I'm so rude, what's your name?" she asks Ramin. Then she adds, "I'm guessing it's not Matt or Ben or Jennifer."

He says his name, but pronounces it like an American. "Reh-min" instead of the far more beautiful "Rah-meen," and he feels so stupid for letting this girl just give him a whole lecture about *her* name, while he couldn't even tell her that the first syllable in his name rhymes with *Shah* and the second syllable with *queen*.

"Well, Ramin," Brunson says. "Let me tell you. The Wilton Blue Basement isn't as bad as people say it is. Don't believe the rumors, okay."

"What rumors?" he asks nervously.

"Oh, you know . . . ," she begins, and he wants to tell her that he *doesn't* know, which is why he asked. But he doesn't, and she continues. "It's just that being an incoming Chandler sophomore boy is legendarily difficult."

"Oh." Then he asks, "Because most of the kids know each other from freshman year?"

"We call freshmen third formers here, just so you know. It's all so confusing when you first arrive."

"Okay, thanks," he says, impatient to get to his dorm.

"Anyway, starting school when everyone knows each other is definitely hard," Brunson says. "But the reason being a sophomore boy sucks is 'cause the sophomore boys' dorms are all the way up there." She points to the hill again. "When Chandler merged with Plum, they turned what they kept of the Plum campus into dorms for the sophomore boys. It's not fair, if you ask me. You're so far from food and light and modern architecture. But hey, you have much better housing to look forward to when you're a fifth and sixth former."

He forces a smile.

"Plus," she continues, "it's an excuse to escape your dorms by doing lots of extracurricular activities. I'm a fourth former too. That's a sophomore."

"Yes, you told me," he says, feeling patronized.

"Anyway, living in a crappy dorm can be a blessing. The less time you wanna spend in your room, the better. It'll inspire you to do tons of activities. I'm a peer counselor and a writer for the *Chandler Legacy* and on the yearbook committee and—"

"Brunson!" She's mercifully cut off when another girl waves to her. Then another. He thinks of all the ways they could butcher his last name if given a chance.

"I think we're going to go now," he says, but Brunson isn't paying attention anymore. She's discussing a senior's unfortunate archery accident with a group of girls.

"Wait, seriously?" she says to the girls. "Good thing he didn't sign up for riflery!" Then she sees a timid new student and without missing a beat, she asks, "Can I help you?"

Ramin uses the map to lead his mother toward the hill that Brunson pointed them to. As they walk past all the gleaming buildings students take classes in, he plays tour guide for his mom. "That's the Harbor Arts Center, the Oxford Dining Hall, the Beckett Science Center, the Jordan Center, which is the gymnasium, and it has an ice rink!"

"How do you know all this?" his mother asks.

"I studied the website," he says. "Oh, there's the Chapel."

The walk from the Main Campus up the hill takes him and his mother about ten minutes. They pass girls on the lawns, sitting in clusters, eating muffins and soaking up the sun. Boys throw Frisbees and kick some little woven ball into the air. They seem like they don't have a care in the world.

Ramin and his mother arrive drenched in sweat, because it's steep, and because it's the unbearably hot first weekend of September. When they reach the top of the hill, Ramin can feel the stark difference between the two parts of campus. The Main Campus is a spectacular assortment of buildings, some of them almost a hundred years old but newly remodeled, and others built recently by a Nobel Prize–winning architect. Old or new, each building on Chandler's Main Campus is blinding in its scale and grandeur. Green lawns are everywhere, joyful people atop the fake grass. The sun shines down there. But up here, where he will apparently be living, everything is dark. The trees don't allow much light.

He sees a sign that reads "WILTON BLUE."

"There it is," he says, motioning to the stairs that lead to the basement.

His mother shakes her head disapprovingly. "How can you live in the basement?" she asks. "There will be no light."

"Stop it," he begs her. "You always insist on looking at the negative side of everything. Can we focus on the positive?"

"Well," she says, taking his hands in hers and kissing them, "I'm positive about how proud I am of you. Your father and I wouldn't even have known this school existed."

Ramin feels his heart sink a little at the mention of his dad. He's always looked up to his father, who never failed to take care of his family in an unstable country. But Ramin wonders if he is secretly happy that his only child moved all the way to America. At least now his dad won't be faced with the source of their family's shame anymore.

"You found this place," his mother continues, impressed with her surroundings. "You convinced us to let you apply. And now you're here."

He quickly pulls his trembling hands away from his mother's grasp. He doesn't want to think about why he had to escape his life.

"I can go in on my own," he says.

"I want to see where you live. I want to help you make it a home."

"It's not a home." Tears form in his eyes. His heart

starts to break. He *has* to say goodbye to her out here. Where the other boys can't see him. He can't let a whole new set of classmates see him cry as he hugs his mother goodbye.

"Okay," she says. "Then this is goodbye for now."

He nods sadly.

She kisses each of his cheeks, then holds him tight. Like she's afraid to let go. He can feel her anxiety. The men in her life tend to die when they leave her. Her father, dead in the Revolution. Her brother, dead in the war with Iraq. It's no wonder she's anxious. His mother must sense his fear as he clutches his ex-boyfriend's wool sweater on this sweltering day. He had to wear this sweater, though. He needed to be draped in Arya today, even if Arya broke his heart. And his mom has to know it was Arya's sweater, because she buys all of Ramin's clothes and she never bought this.

"Don't worry, you can do this," she says softly, reading his hesitation.

What was he thinking applying to a place like this, bringing all his pain with him to a place of sunshine and privilege? He'll never fit in. He'll be back in Iran within months. He can't possibly be like these boys zipping past him, all smiles and potential.

"I don't know," Ramin says, clutching at the bottom of the sweater.

The summer breeze seems to blow the scent of the only love Ramin has ever known up from the sweater across the whole campus. That sweater. It's one of the only things he has left of Arya. This and their beloved books. He closes his eyes and says a silent prayer that Arya's scent never disappears from the sweater.

When he arrives in the basement, he's so glad his mom didn't see it. Dark and windowless, it would only play into all her hovering and fretting. His mom worries about everything, engaging in strange superstitious tics that embarrass Ramin. He knows she can't help it; it's a reflex for her. At the mere mention of death, illness, or bad luck, she bites each of her hands and pretends to spit on the floor. And while he loves his mother more than he loves just about anything else in the world, the last thing he needs as his first impression at Chandler is his mother pretend-spitting all over his room. It's bad enough that he's an incoming fourth former, entering school when most of the other kids have already known each other, built friendships and allegiances. It's bad enough that his roommate is Benji Pasternak, who wrote to him over the summer on monogrammed stationery postmarked from Cap D'Antibes, where Benji was spending the summer with his own mother, who won the Oscar last year for producing that movie about the Iranian hostage crisis, which is an unfortunate coincidence.

He finds his room easily. It has two cutout stars on it, one with the name *Benji Pasternak* and one with the name *Rameen Golafshare*. Yes, they misspelled both his first *and* his last name. He debates pulling out a pen and correcting it, but he doesn't have the energy.

He goes inside. Benji has clearly arrived already, because his stuff is everywhere. He's chosen the top bunk, placed a steel-gray comforter on it. There's a lacrosse stick by the door. There are posters on the walls: the Dave Matthews Band, Jimi Hendrix, and a movie poster for *Hostages*, his mother's Oscar-winning movie. In the poster, the Colombian singer who stars in the movie wears a chador, leering at the viewer. If Arya were here, they would be laughing about this. But somehow, without Arya by his side, there's nothing funny about it at all.

Ramin sits on the bottom bunk and zips open the side of his suitcase that houses his books. The books they read to each other. He digs through them until he finds the one he's looking for. Arya's mother's Hafiz poetry book.

Because the woman I love lives inside of you.

The word *woman* has been crossed out, replaced in Arya's handwriting with the word *man.*

I lean as close to your body with my words as I can.

And I think of you all the time, dear pilgrim.

The word *pilgrim* crossed out. Replaced with Ramin's name.

Because the one I love goes with you. Wherever you go, Hafiz will always be near.

Hafiz crossed out. Replaced with his name. *Arya.*

Ramin's eyes throb. He touches the words on the page, thinking about how words are what got him out of Iran. He followed American news stories about Iran, and he knew the narrative America liked. America wanted to be his savior. And he wanted to survive. That worked out nicely. So he wrote an essay that detailed everything he went through, every awful detail. He applied to twelve boarding schools and was accepted to three. But only Chandler gave him the scholarship money he needed.

He holds the book close, his eyes tracking Arya's handwriting from right to left. So beautiful. His penmanship like calligraphy. He can still taste the moment Arya crossed these words out and replaced them with his own. They were naked. They were by the lake. Their lake. They were in a place that was only stars and sky and air. A place untouched by man's violence.

He quickly hides the book when the doorknob turns. Benji sweeps in, blond hair and long limbs. He holds one of those weird woven balls.

"Hey!" Benji says, kicking the ball in the air as he talks. "Nice to finally meet you."

"You too," he says, smiling.

"Okay, please pronounce your name for me 'cause I wanna get it right," Benji says, still kicking that ball.

Ramin has a silent debate with himself. Does he teach Benji to pronounce it correctly, or the way that's easy for Americans? He chooses the easy way.

Benji repeats it four times. "Ramin, Ramin, Ramin, Ramin." Then, big smile on his face, he says, "Got it. Honestly, I like the name. Better than being named after a fucking fictional dog."

Ramin laughs, even though he doesn't know any fictional dogs, or real ones. Most people don't have dogs in Iran.

"I hope it's okay I took the top bunk," Benji says. "Bottom bunks make me claustrophobic."

"Oh sure," Ramin says, eager to please.

There's a long silence between them. He wonders how he'll fill the time with Benji—what will they possibly have in common?

Desperate to fill the empty space, Ramin points to the *Hostages* movie poster. "I loved that movie," he says, hoping Benji doesn't ask any follow-up questions because of course he hasn't seen it, and hopefully never will.

"Oh wow, that's amazing," Benji says, "because there was a backlash from a bunch of Iranians. Or Persians. Or whatever you want me to call you. What do you want me to call you?"

"Call me whatever you want," he says.

"I'll have to tell my mom you liked it," Benji says with a smile. "I don't know why people had such an issue with the Iranian woman being played by a Colombian singer. What's the difference if you look the same, right?"

"Right." Ramin forces a smile, hating himself for it.

"Plus, she's so hot, right?" Benji says.

"Right," he says again, hating himself even more.

That night, he follows Benji into the common area, where the Wilton Blue Basement boys—like every dorm on campus—sit in a circle and do their introductions. Mr. Court, the very old and hard-of-hearing residential faculty advisor, leads the conversation.

"Okay, kids, let's introduce ourselves and share one

fun fact. I'll start. I'm Mr. Court. I know you kids like to call your residential faculty advisors your dorm parents, but I'm too old for that."

"He's our dorm great-grandparent," Benji whispers to Ramin, who's too distracted by the words *fun fact* to laugh.

He can't think of a fun fact about himself. *Hello, my name is Ramin and my boyfriend broke my heart. And where I live, I could be killed for being who I am. And my name is misspelled on the door of my dorm room. And my roommate's mother won an award for making a racist movie about my people.* All these facts merge into one overwhelming emotion, like a dark growing cloud over him.

"How about we start with our prefects?" Mr. Court says.

"Hey. I'm Toby King," says a huge guy with a crew cut and muscles that bulge out of his clothes. "I play lacrosse and football, just like my man Seb." Toby gives Seb a high five. "Oh, and don't ask me for my dad's autograph, okay?"

"Who's his dad?" Ramin asks Benji.

"Uh, Toby King is Toby King's dad." Off Ramin's blank look, Benji adds, "The football player. The Nike spokesperson. The philanthropist."

Ramin nods, pretending he knows, but American football doesn't travel all the way to Iran.

The next prefect introduces himself. He's even bigger than Toby, and he doesn't wear a shirt. "Hey, I'm Seb Parker. I'm a PG, so I'm new just like some of you.

Although I was here as a third former, then went to Montgomery the last three years, and now I'm back."

"What's that? Speak louder," Mr. Court says.

Seb raises his voice loud. "I said I'm new like some of them, but—"

"Oh!" Mr. Court says. "Raise your hand if you're new to Chandler."

Ramin is the only one who raises his hand. Great. He wants to ask Benji what a PG is, but Benji's busy laughing about something with a kid in a polo shirt. So Ramin turns to the kid on his other side, a Japanese boy with longish hair in the front, wearing a David Bowie T-shirt. "What's a PG?" he asks.

"It's a post-graduate year," the kid explains. "Usually, athletes with crappy grades at their last school do a PG year here so they can get into a better college."

Well, no wonder Seb looks so old. He should be in college.

The boy beside him goes next. "Hi, I'm Hiro Fukuda. I'm from Tokyo. Oh, I'm allergic to nuts."

"Hi, I'm Ramin Golafshar, and I'm, um, from Iran."

"Hey, I'm Benji Pasternak, and I'm the hacky sack champion of the school."

Once Mr. Court has made each student repeat themselves because he can't hear them, the students start testing his hearing, having fun with the circle game.

"I'm Matt Mix, and I'm hung like a horse."

"What's that?" Mr. Court asks.

"I'm Matt Mix, and I love lacrosse."

42

The kids laugh, all except Ramin and Hiro, who eye each other like they're trapped inside the same version of hell. Matt Mix high-fives a few other boys.

That night, after all the other boys have gone to bed, Ramin sneaks out of his room. It's against the rules to leave the room for anything other than a bathroom visit, and that's exactly what he has planned. He's way too scared to use the bathroom in front of all these other boys, and even more scared of showering in front of them. The showers don't even have curtains for privacy. Just a row of jets and some bars of soap. The hallway is dark and empty. He makes his way to the bathroom and pushes open the swinging door. Four stalls. Four urinals. Six showers. All meant to be shared by twelve fourth formers and two prefects. Unless you're so afraid to share the space that you wake up in the middle of the night to use the toilet and shower.

He enters the bathroom holding his towel, thrilled to find it empty. He gets under the shower jet, finally cleaning himself off. He closes his eyes, breathing in the steam. He thinks back to the showers he took with Arya, who loved to lather them both up until they were one soapy blob.

After he finishes, he wraps a towel tightly around himself. Before going back out into the hallway, he peeks out to make sure it's empty. It is, but when he walks toward his room and reaches for his doorknob, he finds a sticky substance on it. He pulls his hand away in shock.

Smells it. The scent is unmistakable, a smell he knows too well from pleasuring himself, and pleasuring Arya.

His heart starts to race. He knows firsthand the brutality of boys, but he thought he was escaping it by coming here. But now he's faced with a stinging new reality. That bullies are everywhere. Disgusted, he wipes his hand onto his towel. Then he looks around the hallway, but no one is there.

He can't sleep that night. He stays up reading their poetry books, those verses they spent hours reading to each other. Those verses were their love language to each other.

Ramin lies low on Sunday, his head buried in his books. He writes a letter to his parents, letting them know everything is fine. The next day is Labor Day. Ramin and the Wilton Blue Basement boys head to the Harbor Arts Center for the first all-school meeting of the year. The buzz of the room is deafening as students pour in, teachers trying hard to get them into their seats. He ends up sitting in between Hiro and Benji again, which is fine by him. Better than sitting next to one of those humongous prefects who look ten years older and a hundred pounds bigger than him.

Headmaster Berg takes the microphone first and quiets the crowd with a loud, "Welcome, Chandler community. As you all know, our fine school was established at the turn of one century, and we're approaching the turn of a new century. In one year, Chandler will be one hundred years old. Not bad, huh?" The crowd cheers. "I'm feeling great about this year, and I hope you are too. We have lots of exciting announcements coming up today, but first, please rise for the school song, which will be led by our very own Sandmen." The school stands.

Six students—four boys and two girls—take the stage and begin to sing the school song, which Ramin knows because it plays when you enter the school website. He sings along quietly at the start, enjoying the feel of his voice disappearing. *"To our green and hilly campus,"* he sings. *"Where the truth shall liberate us. Wear your rust and gold. Sing it loud and bold."*

He's not singing it loud or bold. But Sarah Brunson, that girl who wore the *CAN I HELP YOU?* T-shirt and warned him about the torture of sophomore boys' dorms, certainly is. She's in the row just behind him, and her out-of-tune voice booms. *"When you hear this cheer, answer proud and clear!"*

Onstage, the Sandmen move closer to the audience for the call-and-response part of the song. *"Oh Chandler,"* they sing.

"My Chandler," the audience responds.

"Oh alma mater," they sing.

"My alma mater," comes the crowd's response.

Something about the call-and-response frees him. He realizes that in this cacophony, his voice will disappear whether he joins in or not, so he may as well sing out. Which he does for the rousing finale of the song, *"We belong to you. And only you. And always you. Fore-e-e-e-ver."*

The whole school pauses for three breaths before cheering, *"Forever!"*

When the song ends, he takes his seat along with the rest of the crowd. He's mesmerized by the girl who takes the microphone now. She was one of the members of the singing group, but she stood out from her fellow singers. There's a gleam to her eyes and a radiance to her smile that's hard to look away from. "Hey, everyone, I'm Amanda Priya Spencer," she says. Ramin smiles when she says her name, loving the ease and pride with which she owns her identity.

Half the crowd starts to hoot "Spence, Spence, Spence" at her, which she seems to enjoy. "Okay, calm down everyone, I know we're excited to party like it's 1999 this year, since it *finally* is 1999. Which is why I'm here to invite you to party with us, the Sandmen." Spence waves her arm toward her a cappella group, and they all take a bow. "We have two open slots this year, and all we want is the best singers. And please, ladies, don't be discouraged by the fact that we're called 'the Sandmen.' The name is a relic from the days when Chandler was an all-boys school."

At the mention of the school being open to only boys, a group of boys boo, Seb and Toby included. Some of them chant, "Girls, girls, girls."

"I've loved being a part of this amazing group," she says, ignoring them. Then, putting on a British accent, she adds, "A splendid time is guaranteed for all."

The boys don't stop chanting, though. Hiro leans in

close to Ramin and whispers, "Prep school boys are like cavemen. It's like evolution stopped here."

Onstage, Spence doesn't let any of it rattle her. "So come audition. Come on, sopranos, come on, baritones, come on, tenors. Come one, come all."

"I'll cum on her," Seb says, and most of the boys laugh.

"Not if I cum on her first," Toby says.

All the Wilton Blue Basement boys laugh, except for Ramin and Hiro. Ramin shudders from the menace of their laughter. He thinks of last night, of the cum on his doorknob. It feels like a nightmare, like something that can't possibly be true.

From behind them, Brunson leans in and speaks up. "You guys are fucking gross," she says. He smiles at her, silently thanking her. Maybe he was wrong about her yesterday.

The all-school meeting keeps going after that.

The school priest, Father Close, delivers a sermon about being open to new experiences this school year. "To quote the great Karen Carpenter," he says. *"There is wonder in most everything I see."* Ramin clocks his flamboyance with fascination.

A teacher named Mr. Sullivan announces that the winter play will be *Angels in America*.

"The gay play?" Toby asks, and the boys laugh again. Ramin looks at the floor, wishing he could escape this moment and also wishing he could know more about this gay play.

A teacher named Mrs. Song announces that the

History Department has organized two spring trips—one to Rome and one to Cairo—and that slots are limited and open to sixth formers only.

"Fuck me," Toby says. "Italian girls are so hot."

There are announcements about athletics and student clubs and new teachers. Ramin wants to focus on the dizzying options being presented to him, but he can't because Seb and Toby seem to use every announcement as an opportunity to make comments about girls being hot or boys being gay.

In the late afternoon, he shows up for his first work study. Each student has one, even the ones whose parents donate buildings to the school, and they begin the day before classes. He's assigned kitchen duty. He enters the kitchen, the smell of it making him feel nauseous.

"Here you go," a deep voice says to him.

Ramin turns around to find a tall boy with long dark hair holding an apron out to him. His breath stops.

"Take it," the boy says.

But he's frozen. Stunned. It's not that this boy looks like Arya, not exactly. He has a bigger build, longer hair, a rounder nose. But his eyes. Those brown eyes. They have the richness of Arya's eyes, the spark that made him want to dive inside Arya.

"You okay?" the boy asks. "I know kitchen duty can be a little shocking at first. It's pretty much the worst work study." In a stiff voice, he adds, "But it builds character."

Ramin laughs. He's back in the moment now. He takes the apron.

"I'm Freddy, by the way. Freddy Bello."

"Do people call you 'Bello'?" Ramin asks nervously.

Freddy laughs. "No, the whole last-name thing is reserved for people with generic first names. I'm the only Freddy on campus, though it's actually Frederico."

"And I'm the only Ramin."

"Cool," Freddy says. "Well, nice to meet you, Ramin. Good luck in the kitchen. It's not that bad. Just dump all the uneaten food into those trash cans, and put the plates and silverware in the bins on the conveyer belt. Then go home and take a shower."

Home? That basement is not his home.

"Nice to meet you, Freddy," he says. *Freddy.* It's such an optimistic name. And *Bello* literally means "beautiful." The name *Arya* reminds Ramin of the sad operas his mom likes to listen to. Maybe he's moving from sadness to optimism.

As Freddy walks away from him back into the main dining area, Ramin stares at him and then quickly looks away, like he's been caught. He knows too well what this illicit act could cost him. The kitchen manager, a beefy man with tattoos covering his arms and neck, approaches and gives him the same instructions Freddy did.

Ramin takes the students' trays and throws the food into the garbage, then places the trays and plates and utensils in different bins on two conveyor belts. He does this for one hour, until he's allowed to eat.

In the main dining hall, the options for the day are accompanied with allergy and calorie information. He stares at the options: *Chicken Parmesan, 500 calories, contains dairy, wheat, and poultry.* He catches the eye of Spence, who's talking to Freddy as he fills his plate with seconds.

"Cool, right?" she asks Freddy as she points to the menu. "I petitioned the school last year to add a calorie count and ingredients to the food. It really helps when people have allergies."

With a smile, Freddy says, "Very useful. I had no idea Chicken Parmesan had poultry and dairy in it."

"You're such a jerk," Spence says, but it's clear she doesn't mean it.

"What's the soup today?" he asks her.

"Oh, you know," she says. "The soup's always just yesterday's leftovers in hot water."

"Appetizing." She's called away by a group of other girls who yell, "SPENCE! SPADES!"

She heads to a table of girls dealing cards, and Ramin stares at Freddy, who lingers behind and fills his own tray with food. He wonders if Freddy will ever look back at him, but he doesn't.

Ramin piles some chicken and rice onto a tray and searches for an empty table at the front of the room. At one table are Spence and her girlfriends, playing cards instead of eating. At another are Freddy and a few boys, eating instead of talking. Among the boys are Toby and Seb, which fills him with a deep disappointment. Freddy can't be like these guys, can he?

He sees an empty table and is about to sit when Toby gets up and stops him. "Senior section," he says.

"Oh." His hands shake, hard enough that some of the soda on his tray spills. "No one was sitting here, so—"

"Senior section," Toby repeats. "That means only seniors sit here. Are you in the sixth form?"

"No, I'm a new soph—"

"I know who you are, for fuck's sake. I'm your prefect. Learn the rules."

"Cool it, Mussolini," Freddy says to Toby, and Ramin breathes a sigh of relief. Maybe Freddy's different.

Ramin grabs his tray and scampers away to the back. Behind him, he hears Toby slap the back of Freddy's head and say, "I see someone was paying attention in Song's World War II class last year."

He sits at the only other empty table he finds. He's halfway through his very bland chicken when a woman in a leather jacket and blue jeans sits next to him. "Ramin Golafshar?" she asks, and Ramin is struck. Not by her aura, or her spiky hair, or her leather and denim and motorcycle boots, all of which are striking. But by the fact that she's the first person to pronounce his name perfectly. "You are Ramin Golafshar, right?"

"I am," he says. "Sorry, am I not supposed to be sitting here?"

She laughs. Her laughter is deep-throated and generous. "Well, technically, this is the faculty section, but we won't kick you out for sitting here if you want to. We're not as serious about protecting our territory as the seniors are."

"Thank you for that," he says, relaxing a little.

"The food's terrible, isn't it," she says, not as a question.

He laughs now. She's the first person he's found any common ground with since he's arrived. "It's definitely not my mother's khoresht gheymeh."

"I love khoresht gheymeh," she says. Ramin can't believe she's even heard of it. "I have a Persian friend who used to make it for me. She would get the French fries from McDonald's and layer them on top of the stew. I'm sure your mother doesn't do that."

Ramin laughs. "Well, no. It would be impossible since we have no McDonald's in Tehran."

"A fair point. I'm Professor Douglas, by the way. Hattie Douglas. Most people just call me Douglas."

"I'm Ramin," he says, then quickly adds, "Oh, you knew that already. Sorry, how do you know me?"

She pushes her tray of food aside. "I'd like to discuss your admissions essay with you."

"Oh." He wants nothing less than to discuss that essay. He wrote it because he knew it would help get him into a place like this. But he never wants to relive or talk about what's in it.

"As you may know, I was the head of the English Department until just this year. Managing other people was thankless work. Now I can focus on the Circle, which you may have heard of."

"The Circle?" he asks. "I don't remember it. I read the brochures and the blue book, and I was at the all-school meeting this morning, but—"

"Oh, we don't publicize the Circle in those ways. It's not that kind of experience. But students usually talk about it, so I thought maybe you'd know by now."

"No one really talks to me," he says, which isn't entirely true. But it's definitely how he feels.

"It's a lot less mysterious than it sounds," she says. "It's a writing workshop, but often it becomes more than that. It becomes, well, a family. But first and foremost, it's about writing and self-expression. I could tell from your admissions essay that you're a very special writer, and that you have a lot to express."

He smiles. He was nervous she would ask him to talk about his past, but instead she's offering him a future.

"That sounds amazing." He's shocked at hearing the word *amazing* come out of his mouth. He heard Benji use it and it sounds nothing like him, but maybe he's changing.

"Students must submit a piece of writing to be considered for the Circle, but if you're open to it, I'd like to consider you based on your admissions essay."

"Of course. Thank you." If his sticky doorknob last night was a nightmare, then this is a dream. The chance to write, and to make friends. It's everything he wants.

"Will you tell me your date, time, and place of birth?" Professor Douglas asks.

He's a little confused by the question, but he answers

as best he can. "March third in Tehran. But I don't know the time I was born. I've asked my mom before, and she says she doesn't remember. It was the morning, though."

"That's okay. It's enough to know you're a Pisces."

He smiles. "I had a friend who was very interested in astrology."

She leans in as she asks warmly, "The friend you wrote about in your admissions essay?"

He nods. Talking to Douglas is the most at ease he's felt since arriving on campus. He hopes desperately that this won't be the last time.

"Check your mailbox tomorrow afternoon after your first day of classes," she says. "And please, no matter what I decide, don't stop writing."

He looks around at the dining hall. All around him are bright eyes and happy voices. On the walls are wooden plaques with the names of students who have achieved great things. Athletics honors and arts achievements. He came to this school to be free, and in this moment, for the first time, he thinks that may actually happen.

Sarah Brunson

"Let's play hide-and-seek," Madame Ardant's three-year-old boy demands, tackling Brunson down to the ground with a hug. This is how she's usually greeted when she shows up for her day-care work study. With hugs and cheers from a roomful of toddlers who love her. If there's one thing she's good at, it's hanging out with little kids. She'd better be, since she pretty much raised her sister.

Before she can respond, Mr. and Mrs. Plain's little girl joins the huddle and says, "Teatime! Teatime!"

She laughs. "I have an idea," she says. "Teatime hide-and-seek." She pulls out the miniature wooden tea set that looks as old as the school and explains the rules of the game as she pours imaginary tea for the kids. "Now, be very careful as you find your hiding spot," she says to the rapt kids. "This is oolong tea, it's very special." She extends the *ooh* sound in *oolong*, and the kids all repeat the word in delight.

She feels light and happy. The first day of classes went spectacularly well. As a returning fourth former, she was able to choose her own classes and teachers, and she got into all her first choices. This wasn't a surprise to her, because she chose the hardest classes. She's not like those other kids who seek out teachers who give easy As. She's taking American Studies with Colbert, World War I with Song, and Trigonometry with Shilts.

When she's done entertaining the kids, she's filled with their innocence and joy. Next, she heads to the offices of the *Chandler Legacy* on the second floor of the Humanitas Building, where English classes are taught. The hallways of the building are lined with quotes from books that are required reading for Chandies. "All animals are equal but some animals are more equal than others," from *Animal Farm*. "Let me not die ingloriously and without a struggle, but let me first do some great thing that shall be told among men hereafter," from the *Iliad*. "I don't like work—no man does—but I like what is in the work—the chance to find yourself," from *Heart of Darkness*.

As she passes by quote after quote, she notices something she's never thought about before. Every book quoted is by a white man. Every book that's required reading for incoming Chandies is by a man, almost every single one white. Sure, there are teachers who manage to add a female author here or there. Douglas certainly does. And yes, every student last year read Maya Angelou before she came to speak for Diversity Day. But that was a one-time thing. Brunson dreams of a day when these walls are lined with quotes from women like her. If she gets into the Circle, that might just happen. It could be the start of the rest of her life.

And if she doesn't get in, then she'll keep taking advantage of every possible opportunity the school offers her. Her dad is still paying off her mom's medical bills, and even though Brunson has *a lot* of financial aid, this school is still the most expensive thing they've undertaken that's not cancer. If Brunson is going to bankrupt her parents *and* miss her sister's birthdays, she has to make the sacrifice worth it. And truth be told, filling her schedule with nonstop activities and classes is the only way she knows to avoid the torrent of emotions inside her.

She enters the offices of the *Chandler Legacy*, where six Chandies are arguing about bell-bottoms, of all things.

"I'm sorry, but I refuse to acknowledge the trend, let alone write about it," Brodie Banks, the paper's most prolific reporter, says. "Not to mention that a girl should be writing the fashion stories, not me."

The paper's editor, Amanda Barman, points at Brunson with a ruler. "Fine, then Brunson, you're writing it."

"Writing what?" she says, fishing a notebook and pen out of her backpack.

"A piece about this new seventies trend that's sweeping across campus."

Brunson lets out a heavy sigh. "Seriously?"

"Oh wait," Barman says. "Is that the sound of a disgruntled fourth former I hear? 'Cause I have a whole bunch of new kids who want a byline in the *Legacy*."

"I'll write it," she says. "But I mean, it's not that much of a trend. It's just a few theater kids who like to dress like extras from *Saturday Night Fever*."

"Whatever," Barman says. "Do you have something better to pitch me?"

Nothing comes to her. Anyway, this is what the *Legacy* is. A newspaper full of ridiculous puff pieces written and edited by kids who just want to list journalism as an extracurricular on their college applications.

When Brunson is done with her work, she finds Amanda de Ravin, Rachel Katz, and Jane King outside the Student Social Center, rating boys in the school yearbook.

"Guys, we should head to the mailroom, right?" Brunson asks, totally uninterested in rating boys. Maybe if they were rating girls, she would allow herself the distraction. "The letters have to be out by now."

They all applied to the Circle and were all interviewed by Douglas. They enter the mailroom and walk past the huge corkboard with postings about activities and dances and student radio shows and student clubs and *Angels in America* auditions. A big banner above the corkboard reads, "Get Your Rust & Gold Ready for Lowell Night. October 16. Let's Eat Those Purple People!"

"Mine's empty," Katz says, peering into her tiny metal mailbox.

"So's mine," Rav says.

"Me too," Jane says.

Seeing her own empty mailbox, Brunson says, "Okay,

don't panic, guys. Maybe the mail just hasn't been delivered yet."

The four girls head to the main desk of the mailroom. "Hello!" Jane says. "Anyone there?"

From within the mailroom emerges Beth, holding a stack of catalogs and letters. "Oh hey," she says quietly when she sees the girls.

"We're just wondering if Professor Douglas's Circle invitations have been distributed yet," Brunson asks, forcing a smile.

"I can't tell you that," Beth says. Attempting a joke, she adds, "Tampering with the mail is a federal crime."

"Can you at least tell us how many people got in?" Brunson asks desperately. "You know what the invitations look like, right? They're cream-colored envelopes with red seals. I saw one last year."

Looking down at the stack of L.L.Bean and J.Crew catalogs in her hands, Beth just says, "I haven't seen them." There's a moment of tense eye contact between them, and then Beth mumbles, "I should get back to my work study now."

Beth leaves the girls and goes back to distributing the mail.

"Well, I did the math," Brunson says to Katz, Jane, and Rav. "The average number admitted to the Circle is four. But in '95, only two students were allowed in. The maximum was twelve students in '97, but apparently, that was unruly and Douglas said she'd never let that many in again."

Katz shrugs. "I hate the mailroom. It's so stressful."

She's right. The mailroom is pure stress—students hoping for care packages from parents, or awaiting love letters from their summer romances, or waiting to find out which of the Ivies they didn't get into, or deciding what color L.L.Bean sweater to order. They always seem to settle on hunter green, so why do they spend so much time flipping through the catalog pages anyway? Brunson clings to her own hunter green L.L.Bean sweater as she has this thought.

She and her friends spend a half hour in the school store next to the mailroom, browsing the Chandler shirts and mugs and school supplies. Students make their purchases with their Chandie Code, because there's no money on campus. Just a code you use that gets added to your parents' bill. Brunson doesn't make purchases at the school store. The last thing she wants is her parents having to pay *more* for her to be here. Not that using another student's code would be that hard. Most Chandler parents probably don't even look at their bills. But Mary Crane got caught doing that last year, and she was swiftly expelled. Stealing is one of the few offenses that result in immediate expulsion, no questions asked.

When enough time has passed, they head back to the mailroom.

"Still empty," Jane says.

"Same," Katz says.

"Maybe she still hasn't decided?" Rav asks.

But Brunson sees a letter in her mailbox, and her heart

swells with pride. She unlocks the box, and pulls it out. Yes, it's a cream envelope. It has a red wax seal. "You guys," she breathes. "You guys, holy shit."

"Brunson, you did it!" Jane squeals, genuinely happy for her.

She's careful not to break the seal as she opens the letter. She already knows she'll keep this the rest of her life. She did it. She can't wait to tell her parents and her sister. She misses them so much, and hopes they understand what a big deal this is. She briefly wonders if Beth is the one who put it in her mailbox. And if Beth reassessed her when she realized Douglas chose her.

"Wow," Brunson says. "Look." She lets the girls read the letter. On cream-colored stationery, it reads, *Welcome to the Circle. We will meet this Sunday at ten a.m. MacMillan first floor. Please bring a notebook and a pen (not a pencil).*

"Not a pencil!" Katz says with a sad laugh that makes it clear she's disappointed she wasn't invited. "Who wants to drown their sorrows over curly fries at the Tuck Shop?"

The three girls head to the Tuck Shop to fill their insides with grease. Meanwhile, Brunson lingers in the mailroom, searching for other students holding cream envelopes with red seals. She quickly spots Amanda Spencer holding one. She didn't know Spence was a writer, but it doesn't surprise her that Spence would be brilliant at whatever she chooses to do.

Then she sees Freddy Bello ripping the envelope open. She squints in surprise. She always thought of Freddy as more of a jock than an intellectual. But okay.

And then Brunson sees Beth, and her heart sinks into her stomach. She thought she could escape her whole miserable first year at Chandler, but being in the Circle with Beth will make that impossible.

She watches as Spence, Freddy, and Beth come together, showing each other their letters. Spence also holds a care package.

"Wow, so it's the four of us," Brunson says, avoiding Beth's eyes as she approaches them nervously.

Then Ramin approaches, also holding a letter. He says nothing, just stands there awkwardly.

"Five of us," Freddy says. "Hey, Ramin. Remember me? Freddy."

"Yeah, I remember." Ramin waves. "Hi everyone."

"Hello again," Brunson says to Ramin. "Wow, good for you for getting in. It's pretty rare for new kids to get into the Circle. Most of them haven't even heard of it. How did you even know about it?"

"Oh, I didn't," Ramin says.

"Wait, so how did you get in, then?" Spence asks.

"The professor read my admissions essay," he explains. "And just . . . invited me, I guess."

"Wow," Freddy says, impressed. "That's dope. You got in on your first try, and you didn't even apply."

"What was the essay about?" Brunson asks, curious.

"Way to invade someone's privacy," Beth tells her. "Do you want everyone knowing what *your* admissions essay was about?"

Brunson thought her question was innocent, but

now she's flushed with embarrassment. Brunson *doesn't* want anyone to know what her Chandler admissions essay was about. Talking about her mom's illness is just too painful.

Before Brunson can apologize to Ramin, Spence asks him, "Did she even interview you?"

"She talked to me at the dining hall yesterday," Ramin answers. "It was strange. She asked when I was born. Even the time of day."

"She asked me the same thing," Spence says. "She said I have a cluster of water signs, which is probably why I can access my emotions so easily."

"She said I'm a water sign too," Freddy says. "Pisces."

"Scorpio," Spence says.

"Cancer," Brunson says. "Also water."

"Me too," Beth says.

"I wonder if that's how she chooses us," Brunson wonders aloud.

"Yeah, not because we write well," Beth says with a laugh.

Brunson wants to correct herself, but she's too rattled by the way everything she says seems wrong to Beth. Maybe Beth is still hurt about their strained relationship last year, and that horrible comment Brunson made about her hair. Brunson wishes she knew how to apologize and make it right, but she's not good at apologies or conflict.

"So what's in the care package?" she asks Spence, desperate to change the subject. Then, before Beth can say anything, she adds lightly, "Ignore the question if it's an invasion of your privacy."

Beth bites her lip.

"My parents probably sent me some clothes to make up for the fact that they didn't come home to see me off," Spence says as she tears the box open. She pulls out some light pink tissue paper to reveal two gorgeous designer dresses.

"Wow," Brunson says. "Dior?"

"Gaultier," Spence says. And then, as if she's embarrassed, she adds, "I'm sure my mom got the dresses for free." Spence goes to throw the box in the trash when something falls out of it, the latest issue of *Vogue*.

Brunson and Freddy both crouch down to pick up the magazine at the same time. She beats him to it, staring at Spence's mom on the cover, wearing a tight red turtleneck.

"Oh wow," Brunson says. "Your mom is just stunning."

"I agree." Spence smiles, taking the magazine from her.

"It must be weird to have a famous mom," Brunson says, thinking of how her mom is the opposite of a famous model.

"It's all I know, so it's not weird to me." There's a hint of sadness in Spence's voice when she adds, "The weird part is how often she's in a different time zone, but we talk as often as we can."

When she's at school, Brunson's mom calls her once a week, on Monday evenings. She makes a point of asking about her classes and her friends and her activities. But

Brunson doesn't say any of this. She doesn't want to make Spence feel bad. Which is really strange. The girl with the mom who battled cancer for a decade doesn't want to make the girl with a supermodel mom feel bad.

"Anyway, can we talk about something else please?" Spence asks.

"Want to talk about how you didn't think I would get into the Circle?" Freddy asks Spence, a teasing smile on his face.

"What?" Spence says. "I never said that."

"You were shocked I was applying," he says.

"Well, yeah, because you're an Olympic gold medalist, not because you're not good enough."

"Silver." He smiles. "And it was the juniors."

"Yeah, well, still pretty impressive. Anyway, we're obviously all good enough. We're here."

Brunson looks at Beth, wondering if she thinks Brunson's good enough.

"How was your first day in the kitchen?" Freddy asks Ramin.

"Okay, I guess," Ramin says.

"We're kitchen buds," Freddy tells the group before raising his hand up for Ramin to give him a high five.

Ramin just stares at Freddy's hand.

"High five," Freddy says with a laugh. "Kitchen kids are bonded for life."

Ramin gives him a high five, then asks Freddy, "You're not part Persian, are you?"

"Nope," Freddy says. "Why?"

"Oh, it's just that you look a little like someone I knew back home, in Iran."

"Born and raised in Miami," Freddy says. "My mom's from Brazil. My dad's from Cuba. And please don't ask me to get you cigars."

"Please tell me people don't do that," Spence says.

Freddy starts listing the names of boys who have asked him to get them Cohibas, usually as Christmas presents for their dads.

When Freddy's done, Ramin says, in perfect Spanish, "At least no one has asked me to bring them a rug next time I go home."

"Wait," Freddy asks in English, "how is your Spanish so good?"

"My dad made me learn five languages," Ramin replies. "He says that you never know when a country or a civilization will fall, so you need to be prepared to talk yourself into a new one."

"I'm so jealous," Spence says. "If I spoke Spanish, then I could be in the Spanish plays that Señora Reyes puts on in the Chapel. I heard she's doing Lorca this year. Like, could you imagine? Doing *La Casa de Bernarda Alba* in the original language."

"But you're obviously going to be the lead in the winter play," Beth says. "I haven't seen *Angels in America*, but I doubt Sullivan would've picked it if there wasn't an amazing part for you."

Brunson feels her body tense. In another world, she would love to audition to be in that play. She loves it. But

66

her rapid heartbeat tells her she can't be in this play. She can't be in any play.

The Chapel bell rings.

"I have to go," Spence says. "Sandmen rehearsals are upon us. We need two more singers, if any of you can carry a tune."

"Negative," Freddy says.

Brunson wishes she could sing. It would be a chance to add one more activity to her schedule, and also hang out with Spence. But she can't, so she says, "I have to go too. Peer counseling."

"Is that a work study?" Ramin asks.

"No, day care's my work study," she says.

"Oh, you're so lucky," Spence says. "That sounds fun. I have mailroom again."

"Wait, I have mailroom!" Beth says. "I'm headed back there right now."

"Mailroom buds," Spence says in a dead-on imitation of Freddy that makes everybody laugh.

Beth raises her hand, and Spence gives her an enthusiastic high five. Brunson wonders where *this* Beth was last year, when she always had her headphones on and barely uttered a word to her. Then she thinks that if Beth can leave behind the person she was, maybe she can too.

"Well, I'm meeting some guys to play ultimate Frisbee on the front lawn," Freddy says. Turning to Ramin, he says, "You're welcome to join."

Ramin quietly says, "Oh, I, uh . . . I don't know what that is. And . . . I know you're friends with my prefects and, uh, they're not very nice."

"Who are your prefects?" Freddy asks.

"Toby King and Seb, uh, I can't remember his last name. He's doing a PG year and he's . . . big."

"They're not my friends," Freddy says, like he's thinking it over. "Not really."

"Anyway, I should go study," Ramin says, leaving. Spence and Freddy head out next. Until Brunson is left alone with Beth.

"So this is weird," Brunson says.

Beth chews her hair as she says, "Yeah."

"But it doesn't have to be." Brunson knows her smile feels forced.

"Definitely not."

Brunson ties her hair into a bun. "Well, guess I should get to my shift."

"Yeah, I'm going to go back to the mailroom." Beth waves awkwardly as she walks away.

There are only two people Brunson wanted to avoid sophomore year: Beth is one of them. Now she'll have to try even harder to avoid the other one.

Brunson heads across the Chapel lawn toward the infirmary for her peer counseling shift.

"Brunson, cute top!" says Laurie Lamott, one of her fellow members of the student judiciary.

"Thanks, Laurie. You too."

"Is it true you're in the Circle? Word is you were holding one of those sealed envelopes in the mailroom."

"I'm in. Crazy, right?" She smiles, playing the role of the overachieving, nonthreatening popular girl she wants to be.

In the distance, she sees Professor Douglas talking to Headmaster Berg. Brunson catches Douglas's eye, but Douglas only nods in acknowledgment before turning her attention back to Berg. They're whispering, but the heat of their conversation is evident in their body language. Hands are waving in the air. Fingers are pointed.

She thinks about the article she wrote last year for the school paper about how every Chandler headmaster has had a one-syllable last name, and how small the odds of that are. *Searing journalism,* she thinks to herself. But this year will be different. She came to this school to matter, and members of the Circle matter.

When the headmaster walks away from Douglas, the professor walks over to Brunson, who realizes she's been staring at them for at least a few minutes.

"Well, how do you feel?" Douglas asks, eyeing the letter in Brunson's hand.

"Excited," she says. "And scared. I guess I was the right astrological sign, huh?"

"And you wrote a beautiful essay," the professor says.

Brunson smiles. Last year, she swiped *Supplemental Facts* from Beth's desk and read it during one of her many sleepless nights. That novel was the first time she saw herself on the page. It scared and exhilarated her. But she didn't write about *that* part of the book; she wasn't ready to. She wrote about another part of the book that feels seared into her memory, the protagonist's relationship to her sick mother. The way the protagonist cares for her. How she finally tells her mom in the hospital that she loves another woman, but her mom is too medicated to respond. Brunson didn't mention her own sick mom in the essay, but she knows she wrote about illness with more depth than most girls her age could manage.

"Cancer," Brunson says in a whisper. "It's my astrological sign, and also what I wrote my essay about. Funny, right?"

"I'm not sure *funny* is the right word for cancer," Douglas says with empathy.

"I'm so sorry," Brunson says. "Your mom . . ." She stops herself before she asks the complete question.

"Colon cancer," Douglas says, matter-of-fact. "It all happened very fast."

"Did she read your novel?"

Douglas shakes her head. "I wish she had." Brunson senses a hint of sadness in Douglas's voice, emotion knocking at the steel doors of her façade. "I had only written a rough draft when she was diagnosed, and I don't like showing anyone rough drafts." She can hear the regret in the professor's voice. It mirrors her own regrets, like how she hasn't told her own mother anything, at least not anything that matters.

"I'm sorry," she says.

Douglas just utters, "It was a long time ago," but Brunson can tell that's not how she feels.

"Yeah," Brunson says.

There's an awkward lull. "I have to get to peer counseling," she says. "But seriously, thank you. I won't let you down."

"I'm not interested in that." Douglas looks her in the eye. "Just don't let yourself down."

Brunson takes over the peer counseling shift from Rachel Katz when she gets to the infirmary. "Anyone show up?" she asks Katz.

"Nope," Katz says. "Has anyone *ever* showed up for you?"

"No," Brunson says. "I guess not." The thing is, no student in crisis ever comes to another student for counsel, and she gets why. Even though peer counselors are meant to keep everything confidential, they're still other students. And people gossip. Why would students open up to each other when the whole school could find out? Especially when the school has an actual professional counselor, Dr. Geller, who Brunson knows from experience is really good at what he does.

But being a peer counselor will look good on college applications, so she does it. She spends her peer counseling shift writing that silly article about bell-bottoms and bowling shirts. She sketches it out, and figures that tomorrow she can get a few quotes from the handful of kids who have fallen victim to the trend.

When her shift is done, she finally walks home to her new basement room in Mrs. Song's campus house. Unlike the majority of teachers, Mrs. Song isn't a dorm parent. It's just her and her daughter in a beautiful house, and every year, one lucky student gets to live in the basement. Brunson is one of five students on campus who have opted out of dorms altogether this year. They're called "Host Students" because teachers host them in their homes. Mrs. Song and her eleven-year-old daughter, Millie, aren't exactly her new roommates, since they sleep two floors above her, but they're nice, easy company at the end of a full day. And as a bonus, there's always homemade kimchi and bibimbap in the Song fridge. Though truth be told, anything would be better than the unspoken tension of her freshman-year living situation.

"Scrabble?" Millie says when she barges into the basement.

"Only if you promise not to beat me too bad," Brunson says, smiling.

Without missing a beat, Millie sets up the Scrabble board. Brunson sits up. She began the day playing with kids, and now she's ending it playing with a kid. Nothing makes her happier.

On Sunday morning, Brunson tries on every possible permutation of tops, bottoms, socks, and shoes before choosing a simple combo of midnight-blue T-shirt, black jeans, and clogs. She doesn't want to look like she's trying too hard to impress the Circle.

The next decision is whether to arrive early, on time, or late. If she arrives early, she risks the awkwardness of being alone with Beth if she's there, and she can't have that. If she arrives late, she risks offending Douglas. That's definitely not okay. So she walks to MacMillan and hides behind a tree. She watches all the Chandies out on the lawns, kicking hacky sacks, sun-tanning, reading Homer and Shakespeare and Orwell. Someone on the third floor of MacMillan has her window open, and Cat Stevens's voice flows out from her room onto campus.

She enters MacMillan, but waits until the Chapel bell rings ten to knock on Douglas's door. To her surprise, she's the last one there.

"Ah," Douglas says, opening the door and welcoming her in. "We're all here now."

"Oh sorry," Brunson says. "I thought I was on time."

"You are." Douglas turns to the rest of the group now. They're all standing awkwardly in Douglas's living room. There are only two chairs, and none of them want to claim one first. "You can all sit, you know. You're not in a museum." Douglas sits in one of the chairs.

Freddy sits on the floor first. Spence next, then Beth, then Ramin. Brunson, last to arrive, is also last to sit. She stares at the empty chair. If she sits in it, she'll be seated higher than the other students. If she doesn't sit in it, there'll be one strangely empty chair in the room.

"I guess I'll sit on the floor too," she says as she takes a seat as far apart from the others as can possibly be, separated by the mess of books on the floor. Brunson has to move a tattered copy of *Giovanni's Room* so there's room for her. She lays her backpack on her lap, hoping it'll dull the gurgling sounds her nervous stomach is making.

"Welcome to the Circle," Douglas says. "I'm very excited about this year's group. You're all water signs, so I suspect you'll get along swimmingly."

Beth is the only one who laughs at the corny joke.

"Let's begin by discussing what the Circle is and what the Circle is not. Why don't you kids tell me things you've heard about this group, and I'll tell you if they're true or false?"

No one speaks.

"Last year, I picked a group of fire signs, and they couldn't stop talking," Douglas says. "I see things will be different this year. Amanda Spencer or Freddy Bello, as our seniors, why don't you start?"

"Well, it's a writing workshop," Freddy says.

"True," Douglas says. "I'm sure that's not the only thing you've heard."

"My freshman year, one of my prefects said it was a Satanic cult." Spence laughs as she says this.

"False. And thank you for being honest." Douglas smiles slyly before she says, "But maybe it's a coven, because creativity is a form of witchcraft. Emphasis on the *craft*."

"Okay, I'll keep going," Spence says. "I also heard that maybe it's all a cover for you to convert people to the Church of Scientology."

Douglas raises her eyebrows. "I haven't heard that one yet."

"I think it's because Tom Cruise was gonna be in the movie of your book."

"A movie that never got made and a man I never even met," Douglas says. "But if you're worried about being converted, please look around my bookshelves for L. Ron Hubbard."

Brunson eyes the wall-to-wall books. Built-in bookshelves are everywhere, and overflow books are stacked all over the floor, mountains of books that sometimes bend toward each other like leaning towers.

"Okay," Douglas says. "So we've established that this is not a cult of any kind and not an arm of the Church of Scientology. And we also know that it's a writing workshop. What else is it?"

"It's a safe space," Beth says, looking right at Brunson as she says this.

Douglas practically leaps out of her chair when Beth says this. "Aha," Douglas says. "Elaborate, Beth."

"Oh," Beth says. "I mean, I don't know. It's just a place for us to be . . . safe."

Ramin looks like he wants to say something, but he doesn't, so Brunson jumps in. "It's a place for us to explore who we are without worrying that we'll be wrong or that we'll be gossiped about or . . ." She drifts off, staring at Douglas for some sign that she's on the right track. But Douglas doesn't give her an encouraging *aha* like she did for Beth, so she deflates mid-thought.

"I like what you just said." Douglas crouches down next to Brunson, so they're at each other's eye level. "Exploring who we are. What's the best way to explore who we are?" There's a long silence, which Douglas fills by saying, "This isn't a room that cares about right or wrong answers. Say what comes to you. How do you explore who you are?"

"Writing?" Ramin asks nervously.

Douglas leaps back up and points to Ramin. "Writing. Tell me more, any of you."

"Well, anything we write is a reflection of who we are," Spence says. "Kind of like how a painting says more about the painter than the subject."

"Ah," Douglas says. "So in a way, even fiction is non-fiction, because it reflects the author's truth."

Brunson thinks of the ridiculous article she just turned in about the disco fashion trend on campus. It in no way reflected her reality or explored who she is. She doesn't want to contradict the group, but she finds herself saying, "*Good* writing explores who we are. *Authentic* writing. But not all writing is good and authentic. Like, I just wrote the stupidest article for the *Legacy* about kids dressing like the Bee Gees. It doesn't reflect who I am."

And now, finally, Douglas turns to Brunson and gives her a boisterous "Good," before adding, "So that's why we're here. Not just to write, but to write from our hearts and our souls. Now we're getting somewhere." Douglas paces the room as she speaks. "You're going to be doing a lot of writing. You'll be writing in our sessions. You'll be writing outside of our sessions. You'll be writing so much that you'll be woken up in the middle of the night by ideas, by sentences you suddenly know how to fix, by images that demand to be transformed into words."

Brunson watches as her fellow members of the Circle look at each other and away from each other. She could probably write a whole story just about these gazes and what they mean. Or, more specifically, what she *thinks* they mean.

"We'll start writing right now. I assume each of you brought a notebook and a pen."

Brunson pulls a notebook and pen out of her bag, as do her fellow Circle members.

"Before we get creative, I'd like each of you to sign our Circle Honor Code," Douglas says. "Please write these words in your own writing, then sign and date it. *I commit myself to creativity and self-exploration. I also commit myself to respect for my fellow students. I understand that anything that happens in the Circle stays in the Circle.*" Douglas speaks slowly so everyone can get the words down. "Okay, now sign, date, and give me your papers." Once Douglas has collected everyone's Honor Codes, she asks, "Why do you think I specified that you bring a pen and not a pencil?"

The students all look at each other.

"You water signs are really reticent to speak, aren't you? Sarah, why do you think I hate pencils?"

"I, uh . . ." Think, Brunson, think. "Because you don't want us erasing our work as we go."

"Fantastic. Thank you. And Amanda, why don't I want you erasing work as you write?"

"I guess you don't want us getting stuck on one word or one line," Spence says.

"Self-editing is the enemy of creativity," Douglas says. "There is always time to edit and rewrite. In fact, that's when all the best writing happens. But you can't edit and rewrite something that doesn't exist. And trust me, your writing won't exist if you edit as you go. You need to let go. It's the same with any endeavor. You practice, practice, practice, but when it's time to do the task, you let go of everything and trust yourself. Isn't that right, Freddy?"

"Oh, I don't really know," Freddy says. "I'm so new to writing. I'm just an athlete."

"*Just* an athlete?" Douglas repeats. "Writing is athletics. It's playing an instrument. It's something that requires endless practice, and then the ability to let go. I assume you've spent countless hours practicing your pole vaulting, Freddy."

He nods.

"But I also assume that when it's time to compete, you need to put all that out of your mind and trust your instincts."

"Yeah, I guess."

Douglas turns to Spence. "Amanda, I assume the same is true for acting. You rehearse and rehearse, but on the night of the show, you trust that the lines will come to you, and you let the emotion take over."

"Yeah, that's exactly what it's like," Spence says.

"Okay, well, writing is the same. You're going to be writing more than you ever have. You'll get your practice in. But when I ask you to write, I don't want you to stop, or question what comes to you, or cross anything out. That's why we write in pen." She takes a breath. "Now, each of you submitted a piece of writing to me. Your writing was, on the whole, vibrant and moving. That's why you're here. But today, I'd like you to rewrite what you submitted to me from scratch. The goal isn't to turn in a carbon copy of what I already read. It's to see where the journey takes you the second time around."

Brunson nervously shifts her weight. She wraps her arms around herself. She's so focused on doing everything right that she has no idea how to approach rethinking her own work.

"I like to write to music," Douglas continues. "So I'll play one of my favorite records for you now. I'll give you an hour, which is a long time when you're focused."

Douglas goes to her record player and puts a record on. Tori Amos's *Little Earthquakes*. Of course Douglas still plays vinyl. Everything about her place feels nostalgic for another time. Brunson heard some girls playing this CD last year, but the words hit her differently this time. *Just what God needs*, Tori sings, *one more victim*. Brunson wants to be inspired, but nothing great comes. She uses most of the time to look around the room. Douglas looks like she's in a meditative state as she scribbles in a notebook herself. Spence lies down on her stomach, her legs crossed in the air as she writes. Freddy has thrown a Chandler sweater over his head, so no one can see him writing. Ramin sits atop a pillow, slouched over. And Beth chews both her hair *and* her pen as she writes.

The first song leads to the second, and the third, and

when Side A of the record stops, Douglas tells them to keep writing as she flips the record over. *Give me life, give me pain, give me myself again,* Tori sings on the last song of the record.

Finally, the last song ends, and Douglas puts her own notebook down and stands up. "Pens down. You can turn in your writing now."

Brunson stares at the words she managed to get down. Douglas told her not to disappoint herself, but that's exactly what she's done. She takes no pride in her work as she joins the others in ripping pages from their notebooks and handing them in to Douglas.

"I'll give these back to you next week," Douglas says. "Until then, I want you all to get to know each other. This can be a hard place for students. You've all left your families. From here on out, I want you to be each other's family. Okay?"

Brunson mutters an "Okay," but she's not sure how Beth can ever be like family to her after last year.

She thought the Circle would be life-changing and transcendent. But after one session, she starts to wonder if it'll be just like the *Chandler Legacy* and peer counseling and yearbook. Just one more meaningless extracurricular to impress college admissions departments.

Maybe Chandler is just a pit stop before her life can really begin.

Freddy Bello

"If a guy has his left ear pierced, it means he's gay," Seb says. Instinctively, Freddy runs a hand under his mane of hair and clutches the small stud in his left ear.

"It's the right," Bud Simonsen says. "Definitely the right."

Freddy doesn't know why he's biking into town with these guys anyway. Spending time with them is always the same. They argue over which Chandie girl is the hottest, which Chandie guy is the gayest, and if they can't agree, they tackle each other to the ground until one of them begs for mercy. Maybe that's why being in the Circle means so much to him. It's a chance to prove he's more than a jock who can vault himself into the air and objectify girls.

"Dude, it's the left," Seb says again.

"No way," Charles counters. "It's the right ear. If the right ear is pierced, it means he's gay." Charles smiles at Freddy when he says this. As his roommate, Charles knows that Freddy pierced his left ear over the summer, so this is Charles defending his friend. Not that being gay is something that needs to be defended. Not that Charles even knows that Freddy likes both guys and girls, but that he doesn't date anyone because he promised his parents he would stay focused on his schoolwork and training. The last time he screwed up a competition, it was because his heart was recently broken. That can't happen again.

"It's. The. Left," Seb says more aggressively, pushing Charles hard enough that he falls off his bike.

"Fuck you," Charles says as he hops back on and catches up with them again.

There are five of them heading into town. Freddy and Charles are joined by Toby King and Bud Simonsen. And Toby brought along Seb Parker.

Toby, who's a few feet ahead of the group, turns around and asks, "What I wanna know is what it means when a guy pierces *both* ears?" They don't even need to answer the question, because the answer is so obviously horrible that it sends them into fits of laughter.

"Maybe earrings are like handkerchiefs," Bud says. "You know gay guys wear certain color hankies in the left or the right pocket depending on what they, uh . . . like to do in bed."

"For fuck's sake," Seb says, "*Why* would you know that?"

Charles immediately comes to Bud's defense. "Bud's

mom is Melody Simonsen, the fashion designer. He was raised around gay guys."

"You know who else I was raised around?" Bud asks. "Supermodels."

"Oh fuck," Seb says. "Have you seen Cindy Crawford naked?"

The guys all discuss the hottest models, followed quickly by a discussion of the hottest girls on campus.

"Spence is the shit," Bud says.

"Is her mom the Indian one, or her dad?" Seb asks.

"Does it matter?" Freddy says, thinking about how he overheard a few girls last year talking about him as a "Latin lover" and felt himself cringe.

"He just asked a question," Toby says. "A pretty stupid question since George Spencer is a Chandler legend and Shivani Lal is a supermodel."

"There are no stupid questions." Seb shakes his finger as he says this.

"Her mom actually modeled for my mom," Bud says. "She's gorgeous. But Spence is even hotter."

They finally reach their destination. Mikey's Deli in town. They lock their bikes outside. "Can we be quick?" Charles asks. "We're not supposed to be here without signing out."

"Oh yeah," Toby says. "Like they're gonna kick five athletes out of school for buying Doritos. Without us, they'd have to say goodbye to any football or lacrosse victories this year."

"Lowell Night would be a Chandler bloodbath," Bud says.

This whole outing is about Doritos. They were discussing how much it sucks that there are no Doritos in the cafeteria, the school store, or the Tuck Shop when they're the best chips in the world. They enter Mikey's and beeline toward the chips. Each of them grabs multiple bags of Doritos until they've emptied the shelf.

"Hey, Mikey," Bud says. "You don't have more Doritos in the back? Cool Ranch is my fave."

"Hey, Mikey," Toby says. "You wouldn't consider selling us those magazines way up there? The ones in the brown wrapper."

"Don't push your luck, kids. Who's paying?"

Freddy has some money in his pocket, but not enough to pay for this many bags of chips.

"I got this," Charles says, pulling a hundred-dollar bill out of his pocket like it's nothing.

Mikey bags the Doritos in plastic bags, and the boys are on their way out when he calls them back. "Hey, boys."

"What?" Charles says.

"Put the cigarettes back."

Freddy looks at the other boys, confused.

"I said, put them back."

Bud steps forward, haughty and offended. "I'm sorry, are *you* accusing *us* of stealing from *you*?"

Mikey picks up the phone. "I could just call your school. I'm sure some uppity dean would love to know there are some shoplifters at—"

"No, please!" Freddy says. It's the first thing he's said since leaving campus with these guys. If that isn't a sign that he's hanging out with the wrong people, he doesn't know what is. He turns to them. "Guys, if one of you . . . if one of you took something, just give it back." He panics. Sweat starts to form along his brow. He doesn't have the wealth or power to get out of something like this, and he's filled with worry that he'll be kicked out of school. But more importantly, he's thinking he might be kicked out of the Circle.

"Look up at these corners," Mikey says, pointing to covertly hidden video cameras.

"Shit," Toby says, pulling two packs of Camels from his crotch.

Seb pulls three packs of Marlboro Lights out of his jacket pocket and puts them on the counter.

"Did you know about this?" Freddy asks Charles, because he really doesn't want to believe his roommate is a thief.

"I swear I didn't," Charles says.

Toby pulls a wad of cash out of his pocket and tries to hand it to Mikey. "No hard feelings?"

Mikey just shakes his head in disgust. "I don't want your dirty money," he says. And as the boys leave, he screams out, "What I want is your whole fucking school wiped off the map."

The energy is different as they bike back to campus. Less talking. Just the sound of crackling leaves under their tires and crunching Doritos in their mouths. As they get closer to campus, Freddy finally says, "That was really stupid, you know."

Toby shrugs. "Whatever, nothing happened to us. Now we know he has cameras."

They cross the threshold of campus and get off their bikes. They each wave and say hi to their friends. Freddy sees Ramin sitting on a quiet patch of grass, writing in a journal. His hand is moving from right to left, so Freddy assumes he's writing in Farsi. "Hey, Ramin," he says.

"Oh hey," Ramin says quickly before getting back to his writing.

"See you at the next Circle meeting?" Freddy asks.

Ramin doesn't even look at him when he says, "Sure."

"Everything okay?" Freddy asks.

He notices that Ramin's eyes are fixed on Seb and Toby. Freddy remembers telling Ramin these weren't his friends, but he's with them again. Maybe he should've said he *wishes* they weren't his friends, but he doesn't know who else to be friends with. He arrived last year as a new fifth former, and it was easy to fall into hanging out with other athletes.

As the boys walk away, Toby asks, "You know that dweeb?"

"They're in the Circle together," Charles says.

"Douglas's lesbian cult?" Seb asks with a laugh.

"It's just a writing workshop," Freddy says, defensive.

"Well, that blows," Seb says. "Lesbian cult sounds a lot more fun."

86

"I gotta go meet Coach Stade," Freddy says. "Later."

"Lates," Bud says, like he can't even be bothered to say the whole word.

Stade sits outside the Jordan Center waiting for him. "You're late," he says, tapping at his wrist like there's a watch on it.

"Sorry," Freddy says, a Dorito in his mouth.

"And you're eating junk. Come on, Freddy. Keep your eyes on the prize."

He's heard so many coaches say those words to him, the prize being an Olympic medal. There was a time when he wanted that prize more than anything. He's the one who had to convince his parents to let him pole vault in the first place. They rearranged their whole lives for that childhood whim that turned into his identity.

He changes in the empty locker room. Stade has already set up the vault for him on the basketball court, along with hurdles and a pull-up bar. Everything he needs.

"Stretch first," Stade says. "Gotta loosen up those hamstrings."

His hamstrings give him trouble. They cramp easily. He also needs to work on his arm extension when he plants the pole. They'll probably spend an hour just on that today. Run, extend, plant, leap, tumble, repeat. He thinks about Seb and Toby and Charles and Bud as Stade talks him through his routine. "Explode, explode, explode," Stade says. The thing about those other guys is that they all play team sports. Lacrosse, crew, football.

He's considered one of them because he's an athlete, but his sport is solitary. He's usually trained alone, and that didn't change at Chandler, because there are no other pole vaulters on campus. He sometimes does do warm-ups with the track team, also coached by Stade, but most of the time it's just him and the coach.

"Onto the pull-up bars," Stade says. "Let's start with some L-ups and I-ups."

He runs to the bar, raising his legs up to make the shape of an L, then flipping over backward to make the shape of an I.

Up until now, he's used his body to make letters. But maybe now he can use his brain to turn those letters into stories.

"Harder," Stade yells. "Push yourself, Freddy."

Training on his own sucks. He's never felt like he's belonged to a group. But maybe with the Circle, he finally will.

On Sunday morning, they all gather on Professor Douglas's floor in MacMillan for their second Circle meeting.

"Welcome back." She hands their writing back from last week.

He grabs his, hoping for praise. Instead, he finds almost the entire essay crossed out by a black Sharpie pen so thick that the words under it are no longer visible. His stomach sinks. Only one word has been left untouched: *belong*. It's circled each time it appears, five in total. *Belong, belong, belong, belong, belong.* He wrote about how he thinks about quitting pole vaulting, and how afraid he is to do it, because without it, he's not sure where he belongs. He swallows hard when he sees the essay, wondering if he's the only one who disappointed the professor so badly that she needed to cross out the majority of his work.

He glances over at Spence, who holds her handwritten words, also covered in black Sharpie. Only one word remains untouched: *perfect.* Circled each time it appears.

He sees Ramin's work crossed out, except for one word: *fear.*

Brunson's word: *survival.*

Beth's word: *forgiveness.*

"You all did a great job on your first assignment," Douglas says.

Spence laughs. "Is that why you crossed out almost every word? This looks like it was redacted by the CIA!"

Maybe Spence thinks Douglas will laugh, but she doesn't. Instead, she asks, "Did you think your first try would be . . . perfect?"

Spence shrugs, looking down at her paper where that word is circled so many times. "I guess not," she mumbles.

"Your pieces were wonderful. We already know you can all write. But you didn't dig deep *enough*," Douglas says. "You weren't free. You weren't telling the whole truth."

Freddy looks around at his peers. They're all catching each other's gaze.

"But what I found interesting is what was buried underneath each piece of writing. That's what this workshop is about. Finding what is buried underneath and giving voice to it."

"How do you do that?" Brunson asks, her voice shaky.

"Well . . . ," Douglas says, moving from the chair to the floor, so she's on the same level as the students. "For starters, it's my job to help you discover what consumes you. I read each of your assignments many times, and I looked for patterns. In each case, there was a word that appeared more than others. You'll notice I circled that word each time it appears."

Freddy looks at his word again. *Belong.* He thought he was being truthful in his writing. He does think about quitting pole vaulting sometimes. But maybe there's more that he didn't put in there. Like how he doesn't feel he belongs because his parents are from two different cultures, and taught him three different languages growing up. Or how he doesn't feel he belongs because he's into both guys and girls, and who the fuck is he supposed to talk to about that?

"So what do we do with this word?" Spence asks.

"You realize that it's a word that consumes you," Douglas says. "And you dig deeper into *why.*"

"Okay, but you said we weren't free," Spence says. "But I felt free while I was writing. I really did."

Douglas nods. "I believe you did. Maybe it didn't come through on the page. Feeling something and translating those feelings into words are very different things.

And that's what we're going to learn together. How to give voice to those feelings we bury down deep. Feelings so complicated we're not used to giving them a shape."

"Okay, but how do we do that?" Beth asks.

"Practice, for starters," Douglas says. "Like I said, we'll be writing together every Sunday. But I'll also be giving you tools to work with between our sessions."

The professor pulls five packs of lined index cards from her bag. She hands one to each student.

"I'd like you to keep these index cards on you at all times, along with a pen. They're small enough to fit into your back pocket, so there's no excuse." She stands up and waves her hands around as she speaks. "Write every observation that seems interesting to you. Every thought that comes into your head, especially if it relates back to your word. Write the things you don't want anyone to know you're thinking. The fleeting thoughts. The hidden thoughts. Dig until you can't dig any deeper. Do you understand?"

"I think so," Freddy says, but he's not sure he does.

"We all have different ways to feel free. There is no right or wrong way to be creative. Creativity is the only true purpose we have. It's our power, and we have a duty to use that power responsibly."

He hears her words, but he can't help but feel like having his first assignment crossed out is very wrong. It's like the judges deciding not to even score you after you vault for them.

"Any more questions?" Douglas asks.

No one says anything.

"Good, then let's write. Today, I'd like to explore the way we can each take in the same stimuli and yet have vastly different experiences. No two people can tell the same story."

"Then why does every movie feel like it's the same as the last movie I saw?" Spence asks.

Douglas points to Spence. "Aha," she says. "You make a great point. No two people can tell the same story, but people can copy other people's stories. And styles. And voices. When creativity becomes an industry, you'll find countless people copying what was successful before them."

"Is that a bad thing?" Brunson asks. "Wanting to fit in?"

"Not necessarily," Douglas says. "But would you rather be successful for being your authentic self or for copying someone else?"

Freddy thinks of the jocks he hangs out with. The way they learn behavior from each other until they're all making fun of the same things, and lusting after the same girls, and wearing the same fleece sweaters.

"Won't there come a time when every story is told?" Beth asks.

"How many notes are there on a piano?" Douglas asks.

"Eighty-eight," Spence says proudly.

"Correct, and composers have been finding new melodies for centuries. Now tell me how many words there are in the English language."

The students all laugh, realizing they've been tricked.

"You see," Douglas says, "if composers can find new stories to tell with just eighty-eight keys, then we as writers have absolutely no excuse. Now let's write. Today, I'd like a volunteer."

Freddy closes his eyes and prays she won't call on him. He feels like an impostor here.

"Oh fine," Spence says, standing up. "I'll be the guinea pig. What do I need to do?"

Douglas smiles. "You need to close your eyes and pick a book off the shelf."

Spence closes her eyes and stumbles toward one of the bookshelves lining the walls. On the way, she almost trips on one of the books on the floor, but Freddy quickly pulls it out of her way. When she reaches the shelf, she runs her fingers along the spines of the books until she reaches one that feels right to her. "This one," she says, pulling it off the shelf.

"All right," Douglas says. "Now open your eyes and read us the first line of the book."

Spence opens her eyes. She's holding *Anna Karenina* by Tolstoy. She flips to the first page. "Happy families are all alike; every unhappy family is unhappy in its own way."

"Very good." Douglas takes the book from her. "You can take a seat now, Amanda."

Spence sits next to Freddy, so close that he can smell her fruity shampoo.

"Now I'll read the first line of the book again, and I'd like you to write it down as I read it." They all scribble the line as Douglas reads it, then she says, "Spend the hour writing a piece that begins with this line. It can be anything you want it to be. And moving forward, please be prepared to share all your work with the group."

Douglas turns a record on again. This time it's Joni Mitchell's *Court and Spark*. As the album plays, Freddy finds himself writing a story from the perspective of his parents. His dad sacrificed so much for Freddy's training and travel, while his mother works endlessly to pay for it all. The deeper he digs into their points of view, the more he realizes he *can't* ever quit pole vaulting. It would make their sacrifices meaningless.

The hour goes by so fast this time that he can't believe it when Douglas says, "Pens down. Turn in what you've written to me."

They all rip their pages out and hand them to her.

"I'll see you next Sunday," she says. "I'd like you to spend the week filling up those notecards. Take them with you everywhere. You know what I like about the notecards?"

"That they're small?" Beth says.

"Exactly," Douglas says. "There's no pressure to keep going with a notecard. You fill it up, and you're done. It's a great way to practice writing. Think of it as a quick sprint. Not every writing session needs to be a marathon."

She looks at Freddy as she says this, and he wonders if she always compares writing to sports, or if it's her way of easing him into the experience. Of helping him to belong.

The students all get up to leave, but Douglas stops them.

"One more assignment," she says. "I'd like you to spend time together. All five of you."

"Doing what?" Brunson blurts out.

"Whatever you like," Douglas says. "Just bring your notecards. I want each of you to come up with a prompt of your own for each other. It can be anything. You can ask the group to write about their favorite color, their favorite movie. You can ask them to write a story that begins with a certain word, or to write about a season. There's no need to hand those in to me, but commit to the exercise, please. Okay, you may go now."

Outside MacMillan, the five of them linger together.

"We could just do the assignment now?" Freddy suggests. "We could go to the SSC or the Tuck Shop or something."

"I can't," Brunson says. "Brodie Banks is in London for some family wedding this weekend, and I promised I'd fill in for his radio show."

"I hate to pass up curly fries at the Tuck Shop," Spence says. "But winter play auditions are this afternoon, and I have to prepare."

They discuss their schedules and realize next Saturday morning is the only time they'll all be free, which is largely due to Spence's and Brunson's extracurricular schedules.

"We could bike into town," Freddy proposes, thinking he'd much rather go to town with this group than the guys he usually hangs out with.

"I don't have a bike," Ramin says quietly.

"I don't either," Beth says.

"I can borrow at least one," Spence says.

"Yeah, me too," Freddy says.

They make a plan to meet at the Chapel next Saturday morning. Ramin nods and leaves first. Brunson and Beth do the same, which leaves Freddy and Spence alone together.

"Are you heading back to Holmby?" Spence asks. "I'm going there."

He was going to see if anyone was playing ultimate Frisbee on the Main Lawn, but he suddenly decides to change his plans, just to spend a little more time with Spence. "Why are you headed to Holmby?"

"Oh, just to see Sullivan," she says.

Freddy thinks it's really strange that Spence goes and visits Sullivan like he's her friend and not her teacher, but he doesn't point this out. Besides, they all just left Douglas's dorm residence. This is just what Chandler is like.

"I need to decide which role to audition for in *Angels in America*. I mean, Harper's the lead, but some of the theater kids were saying he may have one actor play *both* Hannah *and* the Angel, and that would be a pretty cool challenge. And like, when else am I going to get to play a middle-aged Mormon mother *and* a stuttering angel?"

"I literally didn't understand anything you just said, but it was riveting," he says, his voice laced with irony.

Spence kicks his shin as they approach Holmby. "Were

you born a smartass, or did you become one?"

"I'll give you my mom's number," he says with a smile. "I'm sure she has an opinion."

As they enter Holmby and he sees Sullivan's door at the end of the hall, he remembers something Bud said at the Tuck Shop last year. That maybe the reason Spence broke up with Chip Whitney is because she's secretly *with* Sullivan. The boys they were with all found this very funny, but Freddy told Bud that he shouldn't make accusations like that if he doesn't have proof. Bud told Freddy to get a fucking sense of humor, and then they moved on to some other topic.

But now, walking with Spence through the Holmby hallway, Freddy can't help but wonder.

"Oh wait, you never told me what happened with the rats in the common area," she says.

"Oh," Freddy says, "it wasn't rats. It turned out someone who lived here last year was hiding food above the ceiling panels. And they just left some there to rot."

"That's so disgusting." She grimaces.

"Yeah, I mean, we're lucky we didn't have rats since there were rotten sandwiches up there. And you want to hear the best part?"

"What?"

"The crusts were cut off the sandwiches. Like, could you imagine going to all that effort, and then just leaving them to rot?"

She laughs. "And on that note, bye," she says, disappearing down the hall and knocking on Sullivan's door.

He watches as Sullivan opens the door to greet her. She enters his place, and Sullivan closes the door behind them. He tells himself to get those thoughts out of his mind. Students visit teachers in their classrooms or offices all the time. They meet with deans in private, and college counselors, and coaches. Sullivan is like Spence's coach. How many times has Freddy been alone with Stade?

And yet, there's one detail that he can't get out of his mind. Sullivan was barefoot when he answered the door.

That's quickly followed by another thought. Is he jealous because *he* wants to be alone with her?

Beth Kramer

"Honestly, nobody gets more care packages than Bud Simonsen," Spence says. "Look at this one."

Beth looks over at the package that Spence holds. It's addressed to Bud, with a logo on it that she's never heard of before. Bang & Olufsen. She wants to ask what it is, but she doesn't want to reveal her ignorance.

"Of course Bud Simonsen's parents sent him the most expensive speakers in the world," Spence says, like her own parents couldn't afford to do the same.

Beth places an orange note in Bud's box to let him know he has a package at the main desk. Then she looks back up to Spence and says, "Bang & Olufsen sounds like a Nordic porn studio."

Spence laughs conspiratorially. Moving close to Beth, she says, "We'll have to ask Dean Fletcher about that. Apparently, he has a massive porn collection."

"No!" Beth says, her heart beating fast. She tries to

stay focused on sorting the mail. And on not chewing her hair. She needs to savor this moment. Not only does her mailroom shift overlap with Spence's this morning, but they'll be hanging out after this. All of this would've been unthinkable last year.

Spence gets to the J.Crew catalogs and starts rolling them up so they'll fit. "The only reason I know that is because Whistler babysat his kid one night, and the kid kept begging to watch *101 Dalmatians*, so she went looking for the DVD and, well, you can figure out the rest . . ."

Beth can't stop laughing. "I think the lesson here is *never* look through a faculty member's things, 'cause you just don't know what you'll find."

"I've never watched porn," Spence says. "Have you?"

Beth's face gets hot. This feels like a trick question, like being asked if you're a virgin, which she obviously is. Can't people see on her face that she knows nothing about sex? She's not even sure what constitutes one girl losing her virginity to another. And who is she supposed to ask?

"No," she whispers. "It sounds gross."

"*Thank* you," Spence says. "Honestly, I revere film-making and performers way too much to watch that shit. Like, my porn is watching a Satyajit Ray movie."

"Cool," she says, because she's never heard of that person. It's bad enough she didn't know about those high-end speakers. She's studied this place all her life, and there's still so much to learn.

"Should we go to the Chapel?" Spence asks when she sees it's almost ten. "I borrowed Rooney's bike for you."

"Sure," Beth says.

She notices Jane King arrive for the next mailroom shift, and she makes a point of walking very close to Spence as she hands Jane the stack of mail in her hands.

"Hey, Jane," she says.

"Oh, hey, Beth."

"Do you know Spence?" Beth asks, luxuriating in every word that comes out of her mouth.

"Uh, I don't think we've met," Jane says. "You were so good in *A Chorus Line* last year."

"Jane's in Carlton House with me." Beth can't help but smirk a little. Jane thought she was a day student. Well, she won't forget her now.

"You're so lucky to be living with Beth," Spence says. And then, she puts an arm around Beth, who can't believe it. "Beth is the best."

She's never thought of herself as the best at anything. But all of that might change now. Not only has Douglas chosen her, but Spence seems to like her.

They hop on the bikes and pedal toward the Chapel. Everyone they pass either says hi to Spence or seems distracted by her presence. Beth doesn't feel so invisible anymore.

On the Main Lawn, they run right into Mr. Plain, who's set up a tent outside the Humanitas Building. "What are you doing?" Spence asks.

Mr. Plain raises his chiseled arms toward the top of

the tent. She's heard some kids call Mr. and Mrs. Plain "Professor Ken and Professor Barbie," on account of their youthful California looks. "I want Chandler students to think about their privilege," Mr. Plain says. "So I'm going to be sleeping out here to raise awareness of homelessness."

She's not about to point out how ridiculous that sounds without seeing what Spence thinks about it first. Spence just says, "That's really cool."

They get back on their bikes and head to the Chapel, where she experiences her favorite part of the day so far. The look on Brunson's face when *she* arrives with Spence.

"We're all here," Freddy says. "Where should we go?"

"We may as well head into town, right?" Brunson asks.

"Yeah, we can figure it out once we're there," Spence says.

They bike the half-mile stretch of woods it takes to get to town, and she's never felt more free. But the moment they get to her little town, she instantly loses that feeling. That new person she was becoming by hanging out with Spence is gone. Here in town, she's her mother's daughter, her father's little girl. She's a townie.

"Let's go to Toppings," Spence says as she locks her bike outside the town post office.

"It doesn't open 'til noon," she says. She should know. She opened up the shop all summer, and the summer before that. The last thing she needs is to be reminded of how she used to serve Chandies their ice cream.

"If we could avoid Mikey's Deli, that would be great," Freddy says.

"Okay, there's a story there," Spence says. "And we're gonna get it out of you."

"No story," Freddy says awkwardly. He's a terrible liar. "I just got sick from the cold cuts there once."

There's so much she could say about Mikey and his deli, since Mikey's her dad's poker buddy. But she doesn't say any of it. There's no way to talk about her town without talking about how much they all hate Chandler and everything it stands for.

"Maybe Beth can lead the way," Brunson suggests. "This is her town, right?"

She feels her face heat up. Did Brunson *have* to point out that she's a townie?

"Almost everything is closed," she says, feeling a desperate urge to pull a hair from her scalp. "Maybe we should just go back to campus."

"Campus is so distracting," Spence says.

"Yeah, it's hard to feel free like Douglas wants us to when we're around so many people we know," Freddy says.

The thing is, *she* knows everyone in this town. Most of her former public school classmates have jobs at one of the stores in town, delivering pizzas or scooping ice cream or bagging groceries. They mow grass in the summer, rake leaves in fall, and shovel snow in winter. That's what seasons are for them. Opportunities for work. Seasons for Chandies are about fashion or TV shows or vacationing, which is definitely a verb on campus.

"If we were in Philly," Brunson says, "I'd take you guys to get the best sandwich you've ever had in your life."

"If we were in New York, I'd take you guys to get sushi," Spence says.

"I've never had sushi." It's the first thing Ramin has said. He's so quiet.

"Oh my God, it's the best." Spence smiles. "There's a place downtown where you don't even order. You just eat what the chef gives you. If we're ever in the city together, I'll take you guys. My treat."

And there it is. Money. One of the reasons Beth likes Chandler is that there's no money on campus. Not the physical kind, at least. Just Chandie Codes. But you can't use a Chandie Code in town, and it's a stark reminder that Beth isn't one of them. She can't even imagine how much the bill would be for five people at Spence's favorite sushi restaurant. Probably more than she made all summer scooping ice cream.

"If we were in Miami," Freddy says, "I would treat you to the best Cuban food you've ever had in your life."

"I've never been to a Cuban restaurant either," Ramin says.

"I'm not talking about a restaurant," Freddy responds. "I'm talking about my home. My dad thankfully ditched his machismo and embraced his role as the chef of our home."

"My dad cooks for us too," Brunson says.

"But does he make ropa vieja and prova de amor?" Freddy asks slyly.

"Proof of love?" Ramin asks, blushing.

Freddy laughs. "It's the best Brazilian dessert. My dad learned how to make all my mom's favorite childhood dishes. That's the kind of guys we Bello men are."

"Cool it now," Spence says before turning her attention to Ramin and asking, "So where would you take us if we were in Tehran?"

"Oh." Ramin stammers through his response. "Well, uh, you would *never* be in Tehran, would you?"

Sensing the sadness in Ramin, Beth feels less alone. She's not the only one who doesn't fit in.

Spence surprises them all by saying, "My dad's been to Tehran, actually, and I would love to go. He unsuccessfully tried to convince Kiarostami to direct a movie in Hollywood, and he got a visa to visit the country. He said it was one of the most beautiful and hospitable places he's ever been to."

"It can be," Ramin says. "There's so much beauty there. The food, the music, the ancient sites." It's clear he wants to say more, but he doesn't.

"Guys, can we go somewhere?" Brunson asks, wiping sweat from her forehead. It's almost the end of September, and yet it's still sweltering.

"Let's go to the pizza place," Freddy suggests. "I know they're open, and I could use one of those huge breakfast calzones right about now."

"I never say no to pizza," Spence says as she and Freddy

lead the way to Mamma Mia.

The smell of the restaurant brings Beth right back to her childhood. At least once a week, her mom would take Beth with her to pick up pizza for dinner.

"Ooh, a booth," Brunson says, snagging it. Everyone piles into the booth. Beth goes in last, mostly so that she'll be sitting far from Brunson.

Once in the booth, Freddy asks, "So what do you guys think of the Circle so far?"

"It's a little weird that we spend most of the sessions writing," Spence says. "Like, couldn't she be spending that time *teaching* us?"

"Maybe what she's teaching is how to write," Freddy says playfully.

"Smartass," Spence says before continuing. "I'm also taking Sullivan's student scenes class, and it's so different. He spends most of the class giving us a lecture about different scenes and plays, and why they work. And we do all our writing on our own time."

"Maybe that's the difference between a male writing teacher and a female writing teacher," Brunson says. "He wants to hear what *he* has to say, and she wants to hear what *we* have to say."

Spence laughs. "That's a little harsh, but okay."

"Does he even teach any female playwrights?" Brunson asks.

Spence shakes her head sadly. The silence is interrupted by Bobby Rinaldi, who wears a Mamma Mia apron over a Nirvana T-shirt. "What can I get you guys?" he asks.

They all order and when it's Beth's turn, she pushes the hair off her face, and says, "I'm okay, Bobby. Just a water, maybe."

"Oh wait," Bobby says. "Don't I know you?"

She sinks low into the booth, trying to escape this unbearable proof that she was as anonymous at her old middle school as she is at Chandler.

"Yeah," she says. "Beth Kramer. I went to—"

"I remember now," he says. "You got into Chandler, right?"

She nods shyly, realizing she's as embarrassed about her Chandler friends knowing where she comes from, as she is about her former townie classmates knowing she's a Chandie now.

When he leaves, Brunson turns to Beth. "You're lucky you're so close to home. I wish I could see my parents and my sister more often."

Beth forces a smile. Brunson just won't stop reminding the group that she's a townie, will she?

"It's not Sullivan's fault that there aren't that many female playwrights," Spence says.

"There's a random thought," Freddy teases.

"I'm just answering Brunson's question, asshat," Spence says. "About Sullivan's student scenes class. 'Cause she's right, and I wish she wasn't. But also, there just aren't many female playwrights to choose from, which sucks, but—"

Brunson leans in as she says, "Lorraine Hansberry, Lillian Hellman, Wendy Wasserstein. Um, I'm sure there are more."

"Whoa," Spence says. "I didn't know you were so into theater. Did you audition for *Angels*?"

Beth notices Brunson's lips tighten as she shakes her head.

"Speaking of badass female writers," Freddy says. "Why do you think Douglas only wrote one book, then stopped?"

"I don't know," Spence says.

"Maybe it was a bad experience?" Ramin asks. "Or maybe she just prefers teaching?"

"Do you guys know why the movie never got made?" Spence asks. No one says anything, so she continues. "I asked my dad. He knows the producer who was trying to make it. Apparently, they would only green-light the movie if they made the lead character straight, which is so stupid because the whole story is *about* the lesbian experience."

Beth squirms in her seat when she hears the words *lesbian experience* come out of Spence's mouth.

"Well, it's a brilliant book," Brunson says. "Have you guys read it?"

"No!" Spence says. "It's so hard to get your hands on. It's not in the Chandler Library. It's out of print. How'd you get a copy?"

Glancing over at Beth with a sheepish smile, Brunson says, "My third form roommate had a copy."

"You read my copy?" Beth asks, her muscles tensing.

"What? Is that a big deal?" Brunson asks defensively. "It's not like I read your journal. It's a book."

Bobby arrives with the food and drinks, placing them all in the middle of the table along with an additional whole pepperoni pizza. "I told my dad you were here, Beth, and he insisted on sending out a pizza on the house." Spence reaches over and takes a slice of the pie.

"Thanks," Beth says, touched. "And tell your dad thanks."

"Holy shit, that's hot," Freddy says, having taken his first bite of calzone. Cheese and eggs ooze out onto his plate.

"I've always thought breakfast sandwiches are kind of gross," Spence says. "Like, breakfast should be breakfast, and lunch should be lunch, you know."

"Well, thanks for judging my food as I'm eating it," Freddy says.

Beth takes note of the ease with which Freddy and Spence tease each other. She wishes she could be that light and playful again. But she has too much resentment in her. How could Brunson read one of her books and not even realize how rude that is? Beth underlines her books. She writes notes in the margins. So it *is* like reading her journal, in a way. It's a total violation. Instinctively, her hand goes to her scalp. But she can't pull out a hair in front of them all. They'll notice. They'll think she's a freak.

"Why don't we take our notecards out?" Freddy

suggests. "That's what we're here for, right?"

"Good idea," Spence says. "I have an idea for the first prompt. Why don't we each write about one of our pet peeves?"

"My privacy being invaded," Beth says, sulking. "That's my pet peeve."

"Beth, I'm sorry, okay?" Brunson pleads. "It was a book. I didn't realize it was private. I would never have read it if I thought it was. I swear."

"You know what I hate?" Spence says, trying to lighten the mood. "Songs with a proper name in the title. I don't know why."

Freddy is shocked. "Uh, 'Martha My Dear'? Come on, you can't hate the Beatles."

"I don't hate the Beatles!" Spence argues. "But I do hate that song."

"Okay, 'My Sharona,'" Freddy says.

Now Brunson jumps in. "Have you listened to the lyrics? *I always get it up for the touch of the younger kind?* It's basically a song about pedophilia!"

"Oh," Freddy says apologetically. "I guess I never did listen to the lyrics, actually."

"Do you guys ever listen to music from this decade?" Ramin says with a smile.

"Welcome to boarding school," Spence says. "Old white male rockers are all we agree on here."

"That's funny," Ramin says. "I had a friend in Iran who bought us all the latest CDs on the black market. Lauryn Hill. Ricky Martin. Destiny's Child. The sound quality wouldn't always be great, and the covers were bad photocopies, but I loved all that music."

"That sounds like a great story for the notecards," Spence says. "Should we write?"

Everyone obeys Spence. She's easy to follow. Beth holds on to her pen tight. At the top of the notecard, she writes the words *pet peeve*. There's so much she could write. She certainly has no lack of pet peeves. But her thoughts just won't flow from her brain to her hand. The words are all stuck inside her. Meanwhile, her fellow Circle members are scribbling away.

"Done," Brunson says.

"Me too," Ramin says.

Freddy puts his pen down. So does Spence. All four of them have notecards that are covered in writing. Only Beth left hers blank.

"So do we share what we wrote, or move on to the next notecard?" Freddy asks.

"I don't know if you guys wanna hear me talk about my hatred of mushy foods out loud," Brunson says. "Seriously, just thinking about old bananas makes me feel ill."

"Ew," Spence says.

Beth looks up and notices Bobby's dad is leaving the kitchen and walking toward them. She can't take any more. She can't take this feeling of being stuck between two worlds, belonging in neither. She quickly puts her notecards in her backpack and gets up. "You guys, I don't feel well," she says.

"Oh no, what's wrong?" Spence asks.

"I just—I think I need to go back to my room. I'll return the bike, Spence."

As her classmates express concern, she makes her exit. Sitting at the end of the booth was definitely the right decision. She allowed herself an easy escape.

When she's outside, she gets on the bike Spence borrowed for her and starts to head toward campus. But then, she feels herself turn in the opposite direction. She's already signed out for the day. She has permission to be in town. And home is just a few blocks away.

Her dad works weekends, but her mom is home when she gets there. "Beth!" she says when she sees her. "What a pleasant surprise."

She hops off the bike and into her mother's arms, hugging her close.

"Hey, what's going on?" her mom asks.

But Beth doesn't want to talk about it. What's there to say anyway? That her former roommate, who she barely spoke to last year, has mastered the art of the passive-aggressive insult. That she doesn't fit in, and maybe she never will. That she thought writing was her way out, but now she can't even do that anymore. Because it's not just her sexuality that's in the closet. It's her emotions too.

"Nothing's wrong," Beth lies. "I just forgot some stuff in my room that I need."

"Well, I could've brought it for you. What do you need?"

She heads inside, trailed by her mother.

"What happened, Beth?" her mom asks, her face worried. "I know you."

"Nothing, I swear. Please stop hovering," Beth begs. She's not going to give her mom an opportunity to list everything she hates about Chandler. Her parents hate the very existence of the school. They hate that its students come into their town to look down on them. They hate that the school gets tax breaks when they should be paying *more* taxes.

She's not sure what her next move is. Maybe she should just drop out of the Circle. Or drop out of school. When she gets to her bedroom, she sees all the Chandler memorabilia on the walls. She put it there to inspire herself, back when Chandler was just a distant goal and not her reality. She reaches into her scalp. Each hair she pulls out relaxes her a little more. She closes her eyes, and . . . She has to be imagining it, because she thinks she can hear Spence's voice.

She follows the sound and finds Spence talking to her mom in the hallway, which is covered in embarrassing childhood photos of Beth.

"Hey," Beth says with a shaky smile.

"Hey." Spence waves. "I just—I chased after you, but you were so fast. But then I saw the bike outside this house, so I figured I'd knock and here you are."

"Here I am," Beth says. Her heart beats fast. "This is my house. This is my mom."

"Elizabeth Kramer." Her mom puts her hand out, and Spence shakes it.

"You have a beautiful home," Spence says.

Oh please. Beth knows exactly what Spence's house looks like because it was in *Architectural Digest*. It's stunning, just like her mom.

"Can I fix you girls a snack?" Beth's mom offers.

"We just had pizza," Spence explains kindly.

"Pizza at ten in the morning. You boarding-school gals live on the edge."

"We were actually just heading back to school," Beth says, taking a deep breath. What was she thinking running away from the Circle, from Chandler, from Spence?

"At least let me send you back with some homemade Kramer cookies."

"Mom, you don't have to do that."

"I already made a batch. They're your favorite."

"Thanks, Mom," Beth says, glancing nervously at Spence to make sure she's not boring her.

"I don't know what a Kramer cookie is," Spence says. "But I've never met a cookie I didn't like, so . . ."

Her mom smiles. "A woman after my own heart." Then, turning to Beth, she says, "I had started setting it up for the next time you came home, but I wasn't expecting you back so soon, so . . ." She pulls a piece of paper out of the yellow pages and hands it to Beth. "Here's your first clue. Good luck."

"What is this?" Spence asks.

Beth feels a little embarrassed when she says, "A scavenger hunt. It's this thing we did when I was a kid."

"It started on her seventh birthday. I set up a scavenger

hunt for her to find her present, and she loved it so much."

"Yeah," Beth says, blushing. Spence's mom probably takes her to a movie premiere on her birthday.

Beth's mom vacates the room as she looks at the first clue. *I'm a chip off the old block.* Spence looks over Beth's shoulder. "Chip off the old block?" she asks.

"It's my dad's favorite mug," she says. "It's chipped and we're always telling him he'll cut his lip on it, but he refuses to throw it out."

She leads Spence to the chipped mug, where she finds the next clue. And then the next, until the clues lead them to a huge Ziploc bag of cookies. As Beth hands Spence the bag, she whispers, "You don't have to be nice to my mom, you know."

Spence smiles. "*My* mom taught me manners."

"It's just oatmeal raisin with chocolate chips," Beth says. "And cinnamon. And coconut."

Her mom returns. "You found them," she says, beaming. "Nicely done."

"Thank you, Mrs. Kramer," Spence says. "It was really cool to see where Beth comes from."

Beth smiles in surprise. She's never thought of her home as a place that people come from, more as a place that people leave.

Once they've said their goodbyes and they're back on their bikes, Spence asks, "You okay?"

Beth nods. "Yeah, it's just . . ."

"You can tell me," Spence says. "We're in the Circle together."

"It's just . . ." She's about to tell Spence everything about Brunson. How they barely spoke last year. How it all culminated in that absurd hairnet suggestion. How weird it feels to be reunited with Brunson now. But then she realizes that in order to tell Spence the whole truth, she's going to have to tell her that she pulls her hairs out because she has this anxiety that won't stop. And she's not ready to go there. So she says, "It's just that my stomach felt really bad."

Spence laughs. "Oh God, if I had to go number two in a restaurant, and my home was just a few blocks away, I would *one hundred percent* have done the same thing."

Beth laughs.

As they cross the threshold of campus, she feels herself relax into her new life. She's finally starting to feel like she belongs.

Amanda Spencer

"Want to come to the arts center with me?" Spence asks Beth when they get to campus. "Sullivan is posting the cast list for *Angels* and the anticipation is killing me."

"You're obviously going to get the lead," Beth reassures her.

"I actually asked him *not* to give me the lead. I'd take an interesting part over a big part any day," Spence explains as she bikes to the arts center just as Sullivan posts the cast list on the glass entrance door.

The theater kids swarm the door, making it impossible for her to see who she'll be playing. She hears a few cheers from the crowd. Connor Emerson, who wears a bowling shirt and bell-bottoms, screams, "Holy shit, I'm Prior Walter. He's the lead. Holy shit. Oh my God."

Sloane Zimmerman does not look happy. "It's completely unfair," she says. "The play already has like, three times as many male roles as female roles. Double casting a female role makes no sense."

Dallas Thompson smiles. "Hey, Connor, we're playing lovers." Dallas and Connor find each other. Putting their hands in front of their mouths, they pretend to kiss.

"Oh Prior," Dallas says.

"Oh Louis," Connor groans.

"Grow up," Jennifer Whistler says. Then, getting a peek at the cast list herself, Whistler says, "Holy shit."

Unhappy students stream away in their platform shoes, many of them in tears. Beth turns to Spence. "Is casting the school play always this dramatic?"

"You're dealing with thespians," Spence says, teasing.

"Say hello to Belize," Fuad Sani says. He leaps atop a bench and quotes the play in character. "*The white cracker who wrote the National Anthem knew what he was doing. He set the word* free *to a note so high nobody could reach it.*"

A bunch of students clap for Fuad, including Wrigley Overstreet, who says, "You guys, I'm playing Roy Cohn. My dad knew the real Roy Cohn. That's weird, right?"

Whistler approaches Spence. "Hey," she says. "I just want you to know I fully expected to play one of the supporting parts. You deserved to be Harper."

Spence approaches the cast list, which she can finally see. Next to her name are two roles. Hannah Pitt and the Angel. She got what she wanted.

"Congratulations," she tells Whistler. "You're the female lead." But secretly, she's congratulating herself. She asked Sullivan to cast her in these two roles. She wants to challenge herself.

"I'm your husband, Whistler," Finneas Worthington says.

"Well, how lucky am I?" Whistler jokes.

As they bike away, Spence tells Beth, "I have to go to senior dance lessons now, so I guess this is where we say goodbye. I can walk the bike back to Livingston if you want."

"Oh sure," Beth says, hopping off her bike. "Or I could take it, but if it's easier, you can just take it, or—"

"Beth, I borrowed it. I can return it." Spence hops off her bike as well. She clutches onto each bike. "Thanks for keeping me company," she says.

Beth laughs nervously. "Oh, I mean, thank *you*."

Spence holds up the Ziploc bag of cookies. "You sure you don't want to take some with you? Give them out to the Carlton House girls."

"Honestly," Beth says, "I really do love those cookies. But they remind me of home. And I'm here to, you know . . ."

"Be a new person?" Spence finishes for her.

Beth is stunned. "Exactly."

"Well," Spence says. "Don't change too much, 'cause Beth Kramer is pretty interesting."

"Interesting?" Beth says. "*National Geographic* magazine is *interesting*. Father Close's sermons are *interesting*."

"Okay, okay, you're more than interesting," she says, laughing. "You're . . ."

"Different? Unique? Weird?"

"Stop," Spence says. "You're cool. You just don't know it yet."

"Oh, I don't know about that," Beth says. But she's smiling.

The entire senior class has gathered in the Jordan Center by the time Spence arrives. Whistler beelines to her when she sees her. "Hey, you're not mad, are you?"

Spence could tell Whistler that she asked for the roles she got, but she doesn't want to ruin Whistler's moment of glory. "Whistler, seriously? I'm so happy for you. And I get to play two amazing roles."

"Okay, just making sure. At least we'll get some scenes together."

Spence nods. In the distance, she sees Freddy huddled with a group of jocks. Bud and Toby and Charles and that new PG who looks like Jean-Claude Van Damme. She can't hear what they're talking about, but for some reason, Toby tackles Freddy to the floor.

"Attention, seniors," Sullivan says, tapping on a microphone to make sure it's working.

"SENIORS!" Charles screams, mocking Sullivan before leaping atop Toby and Freddy.

"Okay, I know you're all excited to fox-trot, but let's calm down, sixth form," Sullivan says.

"SIXTH FORM!" Laird Tyson screams, and joins the pileup. Then the whole lacrosse team joins, and the crew team, and the football team, until it looks like the whole male senior class is lying on top of poor Freddy.

Sullivan forces a laugh, then says, "Okay, have you had your fun now?"

"NO," the boys all yell in unison, except Freddy, who looks pretty miserable. "Fine," Sullivan says. "Then I'll choose to ignore you and address the more sophisticated sex."

"SEX," half of the boys yell.

Spence gives Sullivan a supportive nod, like she's apologizing on behalf of all boys her age.

"SUNDAY DETENTION," Sullivan yells, and the boys get the message. They quickly peel off of each other, until they're all sitting on the floor.

"Ah, the sound of silence," Sullivan says. "Okay, as you probably know, it's Chandler tradition for the senior class to take ballroom dancing lessons once a month. At the end of the year, you and your date will dance at the Last Huzzah. A panel of judges, consisting of myself, Dean Fletcher, Mrs. Plain, and Madame Ardant, will tap you on the shoulder if you've been eliminated."

Whistler, who still hovers next to Spence, whispers, "It's just like *Grease*, right? You know, that whole scene with Cha Cha, the best dancer at St. Bernadette's."

At the same time, Spence and Whistler say, "With the *worst* reputation."

"This year, we'll be learning five dances. The foxtrot. The waltz. The swing. The rumba. And the cha-cha."

Spence and Whistler both giggle at the word *cha-cha*.

"We will begin with the foxtrot. I'd like you all to watch as Madame Ardant and I demonstrate." Madame

Ardant, who was hidden in a corner of the room until now, steps up to join Sullivan.

When they finish an effortless foxtrot, Madame Ardant takes the microphone. "Now, the basic steps are easy. What's hard is being in sync with your dance partner."

Sullivan takes the mike back. "Okay, let's start. I want all the girls to line up on one side of the gym. And all the boys on the other side. When we say go, you walk straight across the gym and dance with the first partner you run into. When we say switch, you find the new partner closest to you."

Spence gets up and stands in a line. On the other side of the gym, the boys stand shoulder to shoulder. Seeing a group of them like that makes her head spin. She's spent the last three years completely ruling out dating most of these guys based on some stupid or mean thing they said.

To her left, Amira Khan and Lashawn Alvarez stand next to each other, talking animatedly. "Honestly, I couldn't believe my eyes," Amira says.

"It's some classic Professor Ken Doll behavior," Lashawn says.

"Imagine thinking that sleeping in a tent in the middle of *this* campus is like being homeless."

Ah, they're talking about Mr. Plain.

"No, but seriously, the best part is that I saw Mrs. Plain bringing him food in Tupperware when I was on my way here."

Amira can't stop laughing at this.

"I can't wait 'til winter. I bet he's back in the comfort of Livingston as soon as it's too cold."

Spence knows she shouldn't insert herself into their conversation. She hates when people do that. But she likes Amira and Lashawn. They were all close as third formers, and Amira is one of the only other Indian American kids on campus. So she finds herself saying, "You guys, Mr. Plain means well." Amira and Lashawn look over at her. They say nothing, which makes Spence feel like she has to keep talking to fill the empty space. "I mean, I know, I get it, okay. I really do. But like, if he makes one person think about what it means to be homeless, then maybe he's doing a good thing, right?"

Their exasperated looks say it all.

"You know what I think?" Amira says.

Spence wants the dancing to start, but the boys are taking so long to get organized.

"I think everyone at this school feels intense guilt about who they are," Amira says. "And so much of what they do is just a way to alleviate that guilt. Mr. Plain sleeping out there in that tent isn't to raise awareness. It's to make himself feel better about looking like a Ken doll and teaching in a place like this. Honestly, the whole school needs a perspective shift, and they're not gonna get it watching a teacher camping on school grounds."

"Performative activism," Lashawn says.

Spence has a horrible thought. Was she just being nice to Beth because it made her feel better about herself? She could tell how happy it made Beth to be around her.

But she also genuinely likes Beth. Maybe it's a little bit of both.

"I mean, he means well," Spence says weakly.

"They all mean well. Your friend Sullivan means well with his 'color-blind' casting policy, but for the most part, he casts *one* nonwhite kid per play," Amira says, her words laced with bitterness. Softening a bit, she adds, "I'm not saying you haven't earned those roles."

Spence feels her face get hot. "Look, I hate being the only nonwhite kid in a play. It can feel like a lot of pressure and it's really isolating. I'm glad it won't be the case with *Angels in America*. But I still think we're lucky Sullivan teaches here."

"That's great about *Angels*, but it's just one show. We'd be luckier if Sullivan realized that color-blind casting is more than taking credit for one Indian girl's talent, while somehow continuing to cast white kids in pretty much every other role."

Spence knows she's right. She remembers Amira auditioning for *Romeo and Juliet* freshman year. She was really good, but she didn't get cast. But then again, third formers never get cast. Except for Spence, of course. She never saw Amira audition again after that, and Spence bets Amira would have gotten a role if she kept trying.

"Sorry," Amira says. "I know how much you love the guy."

Spence doesn't like the way that sounds, but she doesn't push back. She knows that will just make her look defensive. She learned that from her mom, who ignores every absurd rumor the tabloids publish about her.

Thankfully, Sullivan and Madame Ardant both yell into the microphone at the same time, "GO."

The girls and the boys beeline toward each other, many of them obviously avoiding the person directly across from them. That PG kid walks straight to Spence. "Guess we're partners," he says flirtatiously.

"Hey, I'm Spence," she says.

"I know who you are," he says. "Seb. I was here for a year as a third former, but that was before your reign."

"My *reign*?" she says.

"You're the queen of Chandler," he says. "Who's gonna be your maharaja?"

He says the word like he's proud of himself for knowing it, when he's actually objectifying and exoticizing her in one swoop. He puts his arms around her waist, and she quickly squirms away from him. "I'm not looking for a boyfriend."

"Maybe just someone to fool around with?"

She doesn't even bother answering that. She just takes his hands, making sure their bodies are far enough away from each other not to be touching and waiting for the moment when Sullivan and Madame Ardant yell, "SWITCH."

Spence ends up with Aiden Cameron, a computer lab kid, this time. He's the opposite of Seb. Instead of trying to pull her close to him, he seems scared to come near her. "Dance, children, dance," Sullivan hollers. Aiden trips over himself for the duration of their dance as she gently guides him through the steps.

A few feet away from them are Freddy and Whistler. She catches his eye as he glides Whistler across the floor. He nods a hello to her. She realizes that of everyone in this room, he's the one she actually *wants* to dance with. And so, when the teachers yell "SWITCH" again, she makes her way to him, even though he's not the closest partner.

He takes her hands in his, expertly leads her through the steps.

"You can *dance*, Mr. Bello," she says.

"Why thank you, Ms. Spencer," he says. "I guess years of pole vaulting has taught me a little coordination."

She smiles. "Do you ever think about how we usually leave off the 'Mr.' and 'Mrs.' when we say teachers' names? Like we say 'Sullivan' and 'Song,' not 'Mr. Sullivan,' not 'Mrs. Song.'"

"Everyone at Chandler says 'Madame Ardant' and 'Señora Reyes,'" Freddy says. "Not 'Ardant' and 'Reyes.'"

"That's just because people love saying words in foreign languages," she says, thinking about Seb asking to be her fucking maharaja. She appreciates how easy it is to talk to Freddy.

"Is Beth okay?" he asks. "That was a really weird morning."

"Yeah, she's going to be fine." Spence finds herself moving a little closer to him. She likes the warmth of his body. She prays Sullivan and Madame Ardant won't tell them to switch anytime soon. "We should probably get the Circle together again before tomorrow, right? We haven't done the assignment."

"Well, Sabrina Lockhart is having a party tonight," Freddy says. "We could all go. Maybe it would be a better way to break the ice."

"Are you suggesting we teach three fourth formers how to sneak off campus after lights out?"

Freddy blushes. "Am I a corrupting influence on the youth of America?"

She laughs. "Is a splendid time guaranteed for all?" she asks in a British accent.

"Seriously, though, should we go to the party?" He gazes into her eyes as he waits for an answer.

Spence's Saturday nights are always in demand. Henny Dover has already invited her to play spades in the dining hall. Marianne Levinson asked her to go to the screening of *Women on the Verge of a Nervous Breakdown* at the Chapel. And the Sandmen are meeting to discuss what carols to sing at the Festival of Carols in December. But Spence already knows she'll skip all of that to go to a party with Freddy.

"Yeah," she says. "Let's do it."

Ramin Golafshar

"Shrimps in the hallway!" Toby screams from the hall-way.

Ramin is sitting up on the bottom bunk reading an American history textbook, the top of his head hitting the coils of Benji's mattress.

"Shrimps in the hallway!"

Benji leaps off the top bunk, catching himself from falling with his hands. "Come on," Benji says. "Shrimps in the hallway."

"What are shrimps?" Ramin asks.

Benji laughs. "*We're* shrimps."

He follows Benji out into the hall, where Seb and Toby ask the boys to line up against the wall. Ramin notices that the dorm room doors have started to develop their own personalities. Hiro has covered his door with a hand-painted sign that reads "NO FARM ANIMALS ALLOWED" in big letters that are surrounded by an expertly painted illustration of boys in Chandler shirts with animal faces. Matt Mix and his roommate have covered their door in photos from the *Sports Illustrated* Swimsuit Issue, except they've replaced the faces of the models with cutouts of sixth-form girls like Spence and Rooney and Whistler. And on the face of an especially suggestive beach photo, they've placed the face of Madame Ardant.

"We have a problem," Toby says. Toby walks by them like he's a drill sergeant, then stops in front of Ramin before continuing. "Seb and I have seen each of you scrawny little fourth formers shower."

"It's a sad sight," Seb says. "Why are you all so puny?" Seb follows this question with a cocky flex of his shirtless torso. He's wearing nothing but sweatpants.

Ramin swallows hard. He doesn't dare say a word. He doubts anyone will speak, until Hiro dares to. "The question is not why are *we* so puny," Hiro says. "It's why are *you* so big?"

"Excuse me?" Seb says, approaching Hiro.

"And the answer is that you had to repeat your senior year because your grades obviously weren't good enough to get into college. Why did you leave Chandler after one year anyway? And for Montgomery, the easiest prep school in the Northeast? I bet you couldn't handle the academics here."

Under his breath, Benji whispers, "Hiro, shut the fuck up."

But Hiro won't stop. "Technically, you're a *seventh*

former, which isn't even a real grade."

"Hiro, please," Benji pleads.

Seb grabs Hiro's pajama top, bunching the material up until he's able to raise Hiro up into the air. "Say it again."

"Which part?" Hiro asks. "The part about how you're *old* or the part about how you're *dumb*?"

"You're dead." Seb throws Hiro so hard against the wall that Ramin feels the pain himself.

To Ramin's surprise, Toby grabs Seb from behind and pulls him away from Hiro. "Cool it. We're here to talk about the showers, remember?"

The rage in Seb's eyes is vicious. "Yeah, the showers," he says, catching his breath.

Toby approaches Ramin again. "Here's the problem," he says. "One of you doesn't shower." He points to Ramin, and some of the boys laugh. "What's your name again?" Toby asks.

He wishes he could answer with Hiro's confidence. But he finds his voice trembling as he says, "Um, Ramin."

"It's so hard to remember," Toby says, like he's disgusted by the name. "Can't we call you something else? Like 'Ram.'"

"Except he's no ram," Seb sneers.

"Yeah, and Hiro's no hero," Toby says, laughing.

Ramin throws a supportive glance to Hiro.

"So, Ramoon, care to tell us why we've never seen you shower?"

"Oh, it's just . . . I shower at night, after lights out." Why won't his voice stop shaking? He hates it for betraying him like that.

"I'm not sure I believe you," Toby says. He gets even closer to Ramin and smells him. "Benji, you're his roommate. Does Ramoon shower?"

"I think so," Benji says. "But I'm a heavy sleeper."

"Does he stink?" Seb asks.

"I . . . I don't think so." Benji looks over at Ramin apologetically. He's obviously not brave enough to stand up for him.

"Say it, Ramoon," Seb orders.

"Say what?" Ramin asks.

"Say you won't stink up our dorm."

He hesitates, then croaks out, "I won't stink up your dorm."

Then Seb smells Ramin's hair and gags like he's going to vomit.

"Okay, boys, back to your rooms," Toby orders, and all the boys disperse, grateful that tonight's brutality has ended.

When they go back to their room, Benji says, "Don't mind Seb and Toby. Prefects giving kids a hard time is a Chandie thing, especially in the Wilton Blue Basement. I'm sure I'll be on the receiving end of it soon enough."

Ramin nods and forces a laugh. "I get it," he says. "It's okay."

As Ramin writes every detail of what happened in his journal in Farsi, he thinks about the visit he received from Freddy and Spence just before lights out. They told him that the Circle was going to some party, that they should meet at the water tower. Ramin said he wasn't sure that was a good idea. He can't risk getting suspended or expelled. And he can't risk attracting the attention of his prefects. But as he writes in his journal, he feels a burst of defiant energy, like the writing is breathing new courage into him. He didn't come to this school to hide. He came to live. And so he quietly tiptoes out of bed, puts his best button-down shirt and jeans on, and opens his door.

Ramin has one leg out the side entrance when he hears Hiro's voice.

"What are you doing?" Hiro whispers.

He freezes in this awkward position. "I, uh, just . . . needed some air."

Hiro laughs. "I'm not going to get you in trouble."

"Okay." He catches his breath. "I'm going to a party. Please don't tell anyone."

"I won't," Hiro says. With a big smile, he adds, "If you take me."

He doesn't have a choice, does he? And anyway, he likes Hiro, who doesn't even change out of his pajamas to go to the party, because they're silk and paisley and look like a party outfit, not like sleepwear.

"So where are we going?" Hiro asks, luxuriating in his first breath of fresh air.

"The water tower. My friends said it's here on Upper Campus, past those big trees and then—"

"I know where the water tower is," Hiro says. "I've been here a year, remember?"

"Right." They walk in silence into the woods. Finally, he can't help but ask, "How did you stand up to them like that?"

Hiro shrugs. "I don't know. I figured if I stay quiet, they'll harass us. And if I speak up, they'll harass us. So may as well speak up, right?"

"Easier said than done," Ramin says.

"You're new. You'll learn how to fight back."

He nods, but he's not sure he agrees. Sure, he survived one set of bullies in Iran, but those bullies didn't have famous dads and action-star bodies. This feels different. And besides, his guess is Hiro was raised to be confident, by parents who encouraged him to speak up instead of hide.

"Hiro?" he says quietly. "Why did you leave Japan to come here?"

Hiro shrugs. "Not my choice, really. My dad wanted me to get the best education and speak the best English, and he decided Chandler was the answer he was looking for."

"What do your parents do?"

"My mom's a journalist, and my dad's a banker." Hiro hesitates briefly before correcting himself. "Well, he runs a bank."

"Oh, so you're rich," Ramin hears himself saying. He's figured out already that he's not supposed to talk about money out loud, so he instantly regrets saying this. Maybe he assumed every foreign kid was just like him, escaping a horrible life with the help of a Chandler scholarship.

Clearly, that's not the case. At the same time, he's not surprised to find out Hiro comes from wealth. Maybe that's why he can stand up to those bullies. Because he knows he's powerful too.

He feels so much more relaxed when they reach the water tower, where a group of kids have gathered. In the dark, he sees the figures of his four fellow Circle members. Freddy waves. "Ramin, hey."

He approaches them with Hiro. "Hey, guys, this is Hiro. I hope it's okay if he joins."

"Are those the limited-edition Comme des Garçons pajamas?" Spence asks.

"Oh yeah," Hiro says.

As Spence and Hiro discuss the fabric of his pajamas, Freddy explains what'll happen next to Ramin, Beth, and Brunson. "So basically, a couple of day students have volunteered to shuttle us from here to Sabrina's house."

"I'm nervous," Brunson says. "I've never snuck out."

Spence turns back to the group. "There's an unofficial rule about parties," she says. "Basically, the school can't kick out a hundred kids at once in the middle of a school year. It would be disastrous for their bottom line. So they tend to leave parties alone."

A car approaches and Ramin squints under the glow of its headlights.

"Jesus, Myers, turn your brights off!" Freddy says, waving his arms to get the driver's attention.

"I don't know how to do that," the driver says, which

doesn't make Ramin feel great about getting into his car. "I just learned how to drive last year."

Freddy hops into the passenger seat and turns the high beams off himself. "Hop in the back, everyone," he says.

They all get in.

"You know, that's gonna be a tight squeeze," Spence says. "I'll just sit in the front with Freddy." She leaps onto Freddy's lap, and Ramin finds himself feeling a pang of envy.

Beth sits on one end of the back seat, next to Hiro. Brunson sits on the other, next to Ramin. Both girls look out the window, and Ramin can't help but wonder what the history between them is.

The driver, who Freddy introduces as Ben Myers, takes off as Spence plays with the radio dial until she gets to a radio host reading a dedication from a listener. "This song was requested by Belinda. She says, 'Hey Joey, my husband, Patrick, is in the hospital right now and he needs a boost. Can you please play "Homeward Bound" by Simon and Garfunkel for him, and tell him that me and the kids know he'll be home soon?'"

"I love these dedications," Spence says before starting to sing along.

By the time the song is over, Myers pulls the car up to a small home in town, and they all pile out of the car and into the house. A perky girl with dirty-blond hair in a high ponytail greets them all at the front door. "Welcome to Chez Sabrina," she says.

Spence introduces the group to their hostess.

"Oh wait, are you guys the Circle this year?" Sabrina asks.

"Not me," Hiro says, raising his hand.

"Well, congrats to the rest of you. I've now applied four years in a row, and been rejected, drumroll please . . . four years in a row."

"Rejection makes you strong," Hiro says.

"Oh, did you apply too?" Sabrina asks.

"No," Hiro says, "I was just trying to make you feel better."

Sabrina laughs flirtatiously, then with a look of utter seriousness, she says, "My parents are gone 'til Monday, so have fun, but the bedrooms are off-limits and I mean that. And if you break something, I'll kill you." Then with a smile, she raises her arms up in the air and says, "Have fun!"

Ramin follows Freddy and Spence, who lead the way toward the kitchen. Kids gather around two bowls of punch, which they scoop into plastic cups. A girl screams, "SPENCE!"

"Hey, Rooney," Spence says before introducing the group.

In the span of a half hour, Ramin drinks a full cup of punch and is introduced to a dozen people, all sixth formers. Each one of them seems so impressed with them for being in the Circle. He wishes they could tell his prefects to be impressed with him too. Maybe then the bullying would stop.

As he lets Freddy pour him another cup of punch, he wonders if it'll help him escape the haunting feeling that he could be attacked when he goes back to his dorm.

Sabrina blasts a song on the stereo and sings, *"Snoop Doggy Do-o-og."*

The kids all pile into the empty floor space of the living room, dancing. Spence and Freddy pull him and Beth and Brunson onto the dance floor.

"Oh, I don't dance," Beth says.

"Everybody dances," Spence says. "Dancing is like breathing and eating."

"And sleeping and pooping," Freddy adds. "Everybody poops."

"You had to ruin my analogy," Spence says, laughing.

The punch must be going to his head because he's dancing to the music. Swaying his body alongside his new friends. He feels so loose that he raises his arms up into the air like Arya used to when he danced. He rolls his shoulders back playfully as he remembers all those innocent and illicit nights with Arya, blasting American music but dancing like Persian aunties.

"Uh, you guys, Ramin is a bomb dancer," Spence says.

They all look at him, clapping and chanting his name as they form a circle around him.

"This is how everyone dances in Iran," he says. "Look, your hands move in circles, your shoulders roll back. But the most important part is the face. You have to constantly make weird ecstatic faces, like this . . ." He opens his mouth and grunts as he demonstrates Persian-dancing face.

"I love it." Freddy laughs.

They all do the Persian dancing to the tune of a hip-hop song.

"You guys," he says loudly over the music. "My name's pronounced *Rah-min*. The *Rah* rhymes with *Shah*, or *awe*, or . . ."

Beth smiles. "*Now* you tell us," she says.

The circle they form around him gets tighter. They chant his name again, but now they pronounce it correctly.

Freddy Bello

"Okay, you guys brought your notecards, right?" he says, pulling a set out from his front left pocket.

"Excuse me," Spence says, pulling her own cards from her purse. "Are those index cards in your pocket or are you just happy to see me?"

He blushes. The five of them are on Sabrina's porch now, having danced long enough to exhaust themselves. Freddy and Spence sit on a white wicker sofa. Brunson sits on a rocking chair. Beth and Ramin are on the floor, leaning against a wooden fence that looks very unsteady. From inside the house comes the sound of blaring music, at least a dozen sixth formers singing every lyric to TLC's "No Scrubs."

"Both," Freddy says with a sly smile.

Spence raises her glass in the air. "Cheers to the Circle."

Beth and Brunson raise their glasses reluctantly. They all toast, and Freddy takes a big sip of punch. The alcohol quickly goes to his head. He's not exactly a drinker. He's way too concerned with taking care of his body. His body has been his whole life. It's what will make his parents' sacrifices worth it. Unless he quits.

"Okay, who's going to pick what we write our next notecard about?" Spence asks. "I picked last time."

As Freddy takes another sip of punch, he can hear Coach Stade and all his past coaches, telling him that alcohol has ruined many an Olympian's path to the gold. "I've got one," Freddy says. "Let's all write about why we came to Chandler."

"Hey, guys, we need money for pizza," Finneas Worthington says as he pokes his head outside. "Five bucks a pop if you're eating."

He reaches into his pocket, grateful he brought some cash. He looks up and notices that Beth, Brunson, and Ramin all look guilty for not having any money on them.

"Here," Spence says, grabbing his five-dollar bill and adding a twenty of her own. "We're sixth formers. It's only right that we treat you." As Finneas disappears with the cash, Spence screams out, "If it's a bunch of Hawaiian pizzas, I'm gonna torture you, Finneas." Looking back to the group, she asks, "Where were we?"

"I had just suggested we write about why we came to Chandler," Freddy says.

"Such a good one," Spence says.

Inside, the song changes from TLC to Elvis Costello's "Lipstick Vogue." He holds his pen tight as he writes about his decision to come to Chandler. Sure, one of the reasons was that the school offered him a scholarship *and* their track coach, Byron Stade, happened to have a pole-vaulting background. But that's not the real reason, which is that he wanted to be somewhere where he could explore *other* parts of himself. Where he could decide if being an Olympian was even the right path for him. He writes in tiny little letters because he has so much to say. One by one, he sees his fellow Circle members put their pens down. Finally, he puts his down too.

"Does anyone want to share what they wrote?" Spence asks.

"I thought we didn't have to," Ramin says nervously.

"We don't," she says. "I just thought . . . I mean, I think Douglas wants us to get to know each other."

"I can't read my own writing," Beth says, staring down at her notecard. "I was writing so fast."

Freddy glances down at Beth's card. "I don't think *anyone* can read your writing."

Spence says, "I didn't even want to come. I loved the city. But Chandler means so much to my dad. He really wanted his only child to go to his alma mater, and I guess I did it to make him happy." She takes a breath.

"I'm an only child too," Beth says, smiling at her.

"Me too," Freddy says.

"I always wanted a sister," Ramin says. "But I don't have one. Or a brother. It's a lot of pressure, isn't it? Being the only one."

"This is crazy, right?" Beth says. "What a weird coincidence."

"I mean, except that I have a sister," Brunson says, feeling left out. Then her face opens up into the warmest smile Freddy's seen from her. "She's nine. She's the best. I really miss her."

Henny Dover peeks her head out of the house. "Hey, bitches, do any of you want a haircut?"

"Beware!" Spence says. "She cut my hair last year and I looked like a Pom."

"A pom-pom?" Ramin asks.

"No, a Pomeranian," Spence says, laughing. "But come to think of it, Pomeranians kind of look like pom-poms."

"Where were we?" Freddy asks when Henny stumbles into the house.

"Spence was telling us about how she was forced to come to Chandler," Beth says.

"Oh God, shut me up," Spence says. "Anyway, I love it here, so it worked out."

Freddy looks at her curiously. "Will you miss it when you're gone?"

"I don't know," she says. "I'll miss the people, for sure. I'll miss being cast in everything. I don't know if I'm ready for the rejection of the real world."

"Like you're not going to get cast in all the school plays at whatever college you go to," Beth says.

To Freddy's surprise, Spence responds, "I may not apply to college. I want to act, so why put off starting my career?"

"I don't know about college either," he says. "I mean,

I could go and still vault, but also I could just focus on training, or . . . I don't know. The truth is you're going to skip college 'cause you know *exactly* who you are. And I'm going to skip it because I'm paralyzed by having to decide who I am."

Spence cocks her head to the side. "Who said I know who I am? I just said I want to act. I think that means I have *no* idea who I am."

"Oh please," he says. He closes his eyes. "What you do onstage . . ." He stumbles over his words. "To be able to make another human being feel the emotion you're feeling. I'd like that skill."

"Thank you," she says quietly. "I guess I'm more comfortable being other people."

"Being other people sounds fun," Ramin says.

"Yeah, it's pretty fucking great."

"Okay, you guys, I have something to say." Brunson leans forward, and the rocking chair she's on tips back as she speaks. "I don't mean to sound like a dean, but you want to know why I came to Chandler? To get into a great college. It's why I do all the activities I do. It's why I work so hard in class. Maybe it's why I applied for the Circle, because a recommendation letter from Douglas probably means a lot to admissions—"

"Good luck with that," Spence says. "I hear she's real stingy with her recommendation letters. Even for Circle members."

"Fine, whatever," Brunson says. "But my point is, like, why would you not go to college? You can act for the rest of your life. You can only go to college *once*. And you guys are too smart not to go to college."

Freddy wants to believe this, but he's not sure he does. He spent so many years focusing on his body instead of his brain. Early mornings. Counting his calories. Traveling from city to city for competitions. Avoiding romance, with one doomed exception, to stay focused. "I don't know if I'm smart," Freddy says. "I only got into this school because of sports. I don't belong here like the rest of you." He can't believe he said that out loud. But it feels good.

"Wasn't that your word?" Ramin asks. "*Belong?*"

Freddy nods. "Yeah, what was yours?"

Ramin blushes when he says, "*Fear.*"

"And, what are you afraid of?" Spence asks before quickly adding, "I'm sorry, you don't have to answer that if you don't want to."

"What are *you* afraid of?" Ramin asks Spence.

She smiles. "Well, my word was *perfect*, so I guess I'm afraid of not being perfect."

"You know people called you and Chip Whitney the perfect couple last year," Beth says.

"Please," she says. Does Freddy imagine it, or is she looking right at him when she says, "I haven't even spoken to him since he got to Princeton. And honestly, I didn't love him."

Freddy's heart is racing.

"More punch?" Spence asks, standing up. "Come with me, Freddy."

It's not until she pulls him upright that he realizes the punch has gone to his head. Maybe it's because he never drinks. But it's not a bad feeling. In fact, it's pretty nice. He feels light-headed and giddy.

In the Lockhart living room, Whistler puts a Little Richard CD in the player. "Jenny, Jenny" blares out of the speakers and she screams, "Jennifer dance number! Dance your ass off, but *only* if your name is Jennifer!"

Spence leads Freddy out of the living room as Whistler, Sumpter, Rooney, and Harrison dance.

"You must be in hell right now," he says.

"Why? I love those girls," she says.

"No, I meant . . . they're playing a song with not one, but *two* proper names in the title."

She laughs. "Well, technically, it's the same name repeated twice, but gold medal for remembering my pet peeve."

"Highest medal I've won yet," he says, loving the ease with which he's flirting.

"So . . . more punch?" Spence asks.

"I think I need *anything* but more punch," he says, still dizzy and warm from what he's already consumed.

"Honestly, I don't drink much either," she says. "My mom says it's bad for the skin and it bloats you. And Sullivan says drugs and alcohol are the enemies of creativity."

He wonders why she always brings Sullivan up. And where is she taking him right now? She opens a door, and suddenly they're in the garage.

"Uh, are we stealing a car?" he says.

"What, you have a problem with my Bonnie and Clyde fantasy?" she asks, turning to face him.

The garage is dark, and it smells like rubber. But none of that matters because they're facing each other, so close he can smell the mint and alcohol on her breath. He knows he should kiss her. That *has* to be why she brought him here.

"You okay?" she asks. "We can go back if—"

"No, I'm okay," he says. "I'm just . . . nervous."

"That's normal," she says. She moves closer to him.

And just like that, they're kissing. It feels like that millisecond when you're pole vaulting and you're at your highest peak. But that high never lasts long. Inevitably, he comes crashing down onto the mat. It's the same with this kiss. Once his brain takes over, he can't even enjoy the sensation anymore. All he feels is anxiety. How can he compare to Chip Whitney? And what if the rumors about Spence and Sullivan are true? And will he ruin all his hard work if he lets himself become distracted by passion? His thoughts won't stop. He remembers the first and only girl he dated. The way his heartbreak led to his worst pole-vaulting performance. The promise he made to his parents, and to himself, not to let himself be derailed by romance until he's made the Olympics. Thoughts swirl around his head until he pushes her away. "I—I'm sorry," he says. "I think we should go check on the others, because they're just fourth formers and—"

"Hey, did I read the signs wrong?" she asks. "Because I'm usually pretty good at that."

Usually? How many guys has she kissed?

"It's not you," he says. "I swear. It's me."

She doesn't look at him. "Well, this is a little embarrassing. Also, this garage is like, the least romantic place in the world. What was I thinking?"

"Spence, I—" He wants to say that she wasn't wrong. That he is developing feelings for her. But it's too late.

"Let's not make this awkward for the rest of them, okay," she says as she leaves the garage. "We'll just be cool."

"Oh sure, I can be cool," he says, feeling mortified.

He follows her back out to the patio, where Ramin, Beth, and Brunson sit quietly.

"What's been going on out here?" he asks.

"Nothing," Brunson says.

"Not entirely true," Beth says. "Binnie Teel ran out crying after Henny puked in her hair while she was cutting it."

"A splendid time is guaranteed for all," Brunson says sarcastically. "Now can we finish these notecards?"

"Oh yeah," Freddy says, glancing over at Spence. "Should we keep going, or is everyone tired?"

He asks this to give Spence the out, in case she just wants to go home, but she betrays no evidence of what happened in the garage. The only thing is that she wouldn't stop looking at him before, and now she won't even give him a passing glance.

"Maybe there's somewhere quieter we can go," Brunson suggests. "Somewhere where it can be just us."

He notices that Brunson's punch glass is still full. She hasn't taken a single sip. He respects her for not feeling pressured to drink, and also feels suddenly guilty for suggesting they come to this party in the first place. Of course the fourth formers were going to feel out of place around all these older kids. But then, he has an idea that will make things right. "I know exactly where we should go," he says.

"Where?" Brunson asks.

"I probably shouldn't leave Hiro," Ramin says.

"I think Hiro's doing fine." Brunson points to the kitchen window. Leaning against the refrigerator are Sabrina and Hiro, making out furiously.

"Oh," Ramin says, standing up so he can see. "Wow."

Myers drops them back off at the edge of campus, and then Freddy leads them into the woods, leaves crackling beneath them, each crunch underlining their silence. He turns when he sees the river, then turns again at the fallen branch. Seeing Spence walk ahead, he catches up to her and whispers, "Hey, can we talk?"

"Seriously, it's fine," she says. "I swear. You don't make it weird. I don't make it weird. Everyone's happy."

"Okay," he says.

He's not sure everyone's happy, but he does feel a surge of excitement when he hears the gentle rustling of the creek. He loves this place, and for the first time he's excited to share it with friends.

One more turn and they arrive at the lake. "Ta-dah," he says with a smile.

They all look at the dark water, not exactly impressed.

"I know it's not much," he says. "But it's my place." He suddenly starts to question if he should have brought them here.

"You swim in this?" Ramin asks.

"No way," he says. "It's full of algae."

"So you just come here and . . ." Beth doesn't finish the question.

"I don't know," he says. How does he explain this to them? Do they even see the beauty here? Or do they just smell the stink of algae? "I guess that when I found this place, it made me feel less alone."

"I get that," Beth says.

"Maybe this lake reminds me of myself," he says. Then, looking right at Spence, he adds, "Because it may not seem so inviting the first time, but on second glance, it's much more welcoming. Does that make sense?"

She finally looks at him again. "It does," she says with a smile.

"Good," he says. Then he sits down. And they all follow his lead, one by one, forming a circle.

Sarah Brunson

"Okay, I've got one," Ramin says, notecards on his lap. "What's your favorite thing about Chandler?"

They all scribble on their index cards. But not her, not yet. She takes a deep breath of the lake air. It would be so easy to write about her *least* favorite thing about Chandler, but that wasn't the question. And she's not ready to share any of that with them. She promised herself she would put all that out of her memory anyway. Pack her schedule so tight that she doesn't have time to think about it. She knows the purpose of the Circle is to be truthful and free, but some things aren't meant to be shared. So she writes from her head, not her heart.

"Anyone want to share?" Spence asks when they're all done.

"I mean, I don't know if this is really my *favorite* thing," Freddy says. "But it's what came to me. The names. I love the names here. I love that half the students have last names that sound like a museum. Whitney. Guggenheim. Frick. I mean, come on."

"Hey, you forgot the Kramer museum," Beth says, joking.

Brunson laughs, wishing she could turn back the clock and have *this* Beth as her roommate last year.

"The opportunities are my favorite thing," Brunson says. "There's just so much for us to try here. So many activities and student clubs. Like, there's a club for every interest, for every kind of person."

"Is there a club for gay people?" Ramin almost whispers.

"Oh, I don't think so," Brunson says, her heart beating fast.

"Because I'm gay," Ramin blurts out. Realizing what he just said, he adds, "And maybe drunk."

Brunson looks at him, impressed.

"That's great," Spence says. It's a strange response to someone saying they're gay, but at least Spence said something.

Brunson could say a lot more than that. She could say, "I am too." But she doesn't.

"That's why I came here," Ramin continues. "I needed to come to a place where it was safe to, I don't know, be me."

She wants to tell him he's in the wrong place. He should be in Greenwich Village or San Francisco or something. A New England prep school isn't exactly a place where people are going to be kind with information like this.

That's why she hasn't told a soul that she likes girls.

"Anyway," he continues, "I can't tell the boys in my dorm because well, I just can't. So I told you."

"I'm glad you did," Freddy says.

"Me too," Beth says. And then, she hesitantly asks, "How did you know?"

"That I was gay?" Ramin asks.

"Well, yeah," Beth says. "Like, is it enough to just think about it, or do you actually have to, you know, do *it* with someone to know for sure?"

Brunson looks at Beth curiously. Does Beth like girls too? And if that's the case, how did Brunson never sense that last year?

"Who says Ramin hasn't been with a guy?" Freddy says. "I bet lots of guys have been into him."

Ramin doesn't confirm or deny that. "I'm just happy to be in a place where I can say I'm gay without being afraid," he says.

"What happens to gay people in Iran?" Beth asks gently.

"Usually nothing, because very few people get caught." Ramin sighs, like there's more he could say. But he shifts the conversation away from himself. "You know what's interesting? Homosexuality is illegal in Iran, but the government recognizes trans people and even pays for their surgeries."

"Wow," Brunson says. "That's kind of amazing."

"Not that the country treats them very well after the surgery," Ramin says. "But still, it's something."

"India's kind of similar," Spence says. "Homosexuality was criminalized there during the British occupation, but there's some acceptance of gender fluidity, which probably comes from Hindu mythology. But the truth is that most hijras are outcasts. They often have to become sex workers to survive."

"Meanwhile, right here in America, Matthew Shepard was beaten and left to die," Beth says, her voice choking up. "It's fucked-up everywhere, isn't it?"

They sit in silence for a moment, and then Brunson says, "Okay, who didn't share their favorite thing about Chandler?"

Spence pulls her hair back tighter as she says, "It has to be the Theater Department for me. Sullivan's really pushed me to challenge myself. I guess that's what I love about Chandler, being able to have that kind of relationship with teachers."

Wait, did she just admit to having a *relationship* with him? Of course Brunson's heard the rumors, but she wasn't sure what to make of them. She feels her pulse race. There's so much she could say, so much she swallows down. Instead, she just says, "But it's weird too, isn't it?"

"What?" Spence says.

"Just being so close to adults," she says. "Like, we *live* with them. We know their children and see their homes and we call them dorm *parents*."

"I don't know," Spence says. "I mean, our parents aren't with us. We need grown-ups to guide us, don't we?"

Brunson suddenly feels the absence of her parents in

her bones. She thinks of the years she spent caring for her mom, helping her dad, and has a strong urge to write about her family. She wants to get it all out, all the love, but also the feelings she hasn't really acknowledged yet. Like resentment. So she says, "Let's all write about our parents."

They all start writing. She finds herself reliving all the emotions as she writes. When she's done, there are tears in her eyes.

"Does anyone want to share?" Spence asks.

To Brunson's surprise, Beth speaks first. Beth, who didn't say a word about her family in an entire year of being her roommate. Beth looks around at them and says, "My parents didn't want me to be here. They hate this place. They told me that if I come here, all my classmates will see me as a townie."

"I personally hate that word," Spence says. "And I never use it."

"Yeah," Beth says. "But people do. And I guess my parents just thought I wouldn't belong here, you know."

"You do," Spence says. "We all do. We all belong wherever we are."

"Okay, Deepak Chopra," Freddy quips.

"Don't be mocking Deepak Ji." Spence laughs before saying, "Go on, Beth."

"When I got in and got a scholarship, they couldn't stop me from attending," Beth continues. "But they begged me to be a day student and keep living at home. I think they were afraid this place would turn me into some kind of, like, snob or something. Like I'd look down on them."

"And?" Spence asks.

"I *don't* look down on them," Beth says. "I just wish they understood that I don't need to be exactly like them to love them. And I wish they wouldn't keep judging the *school* and what it stands for. If I go home for a meal, all they talk about is why does Chandler keep buying land, and why can't our local public school get a single instrument when Chandler has the New York Philharmonic working with their student orchestra."

"It's hard," Freddy says. "When your parents live in one world and you live in another. It's been like that for me my whole life. My parents always supported me, but they had no idea what to make of my pole vaulting."

"I always figured they pushed you into it," Spence says.

"Yeah, no," Freddy says. "It was all me. I mean, they rearranged their whole lives once it was clear how good I was. But they didn't get it."

"Families are fucking complicated," Spence says.

"What about you, Brunson?" Freddy asks.

"What about me?" God, why does she sound defensive?

"Just—did you want to share anything you wrote?"

She takes a deep breath.

"You can trust us," Spence says.

She wants to trust them, but she can't. Not yet.

Desperate to escape this moment, she says, "It's getting late, guys. Should we head back?"

"I don't want this night to end," Beth says.

As usual, Brunson and Beth are on opposite sides, because she now wants nothing more than this night to end.

"What if we jump in that lake?" Beth asks. "Is that crazy?"

"Didn't Freddy say it's full of algae?" Spence asks.

"I did," Freddy says. "But it also sounds fun." He whips his shirt off in one swoop, like a kid transforming into a superhero.

"Honestly, no," Spence says.

"Is it cold?" Ramin asks.

"Of course it's cold," Brunson says. "It's Connecticut. *Everything* from Connecticut is cold." She flashes a forced smile at Beth, realizing Beth is from Connecticut.

"Whatever," Beth says, peeling her dress off.

"Fuck it, maybe algae's good for the skin." And with that, Spence joins them. And then Ramin, who jumps, yanking Beth's hand in the process. Freddy screams in a combination of disgust and delight when he leaps out of the water for a breath of air. He pulls some algae off his face and flings it in front of him.

Spence jumps in at that moment, and the algae Freddy throws hits her right in the face. "Asshole," Spence says as she flings the algae right back at Freddy.

"Technically," Freddy says, "I'm a sea monster." And he flings more algae at Spence. But she avoids the hit by submerging herself in the water again. And he follows her down.

Brunson watches it all from outside the lake. The water has made them giddy, or is it the rule breaking, or maybe the truth telling? Whatever it is, it's had the opposite effect on her. She feels more alone than ever.

When Freddy comes up for air again, he yells, "Brunson, join us. United we swim!"

"I'm okay," Brunson says, even though she's obviously not.

They're all swimming and laughing together.

Spence joins Freddy above water. "Come on, Brunson!" she says brightly.

Ramin is quieter, but he also urges Brunson in. "Please, Brunson. It's not the same if we're not all together."

"Brunson! Brunson! Brunson!" Spence chants. Freddy joins the chant. Then Ramin.

She has a choice. She can choose to stand alone. Or she can be one of them.

"Come on, Brunson!" Beth says, acting like they're friends now. But they're not. Their relationship is weighed down by a betrayal Beth probably doesn't even know about.

Once again, Spence begins a chant of "Brunson, Brunson, Brunson!"

Fine. She'll play along. She jumps into the water. Feels the algae cloak her. She remembers bathing her mom when she was at her sickest, the humiliation in her mother's eyes. All those baths she gave her sister, teaching her how to wash herself. Brunson wonders what the number would be if she added up all the minutes she spent washing other people clean.

"This is disgusting," she says as she comes up for air.

They all laugh.

Everything feels changed at the third meeting of the Circle. The air is palpably different between them now.

"So," Douglas says. "How did you fare with your index cards?"

"Good," Freddy says. "It was really interesting."

"And you spent time together, as a group?" Douglas asks.

"Oh yeah," Spence says with a conspiratorial smile. "A lot of time, actually."

"Good." Douglas paces the room. "Remember that you're *always* writing. Writing is observing. Listening. If you're a writer, you're not only writing when you're sitting with a pen in your hand, or a typewriter or computer in front of you. You're doing it all the time."

"What about you?" Spence asks.

"Me?" Douglas asks.

"Sorry, I shouldn't have said that." But Spence doesn't stop. "It's just that you wrote one book. And if you're writing *all the time*, like you say, then why just one?"

Douglas doesn't look very pleased when she says, "This workshop isn't about my writing, it's about yours."

"Okay, I'm sorry," Spence says, a little embarrassed.

Douglas closes her eyes and takes a deep breath.

Freddy glares at Spence, who mouths "What?" to him.

When Douglas opens her eyes again, she says, "Knowing *how* to write and *choosing* to share that writing with the world are very different things. I suppose I prefer facilitating other people's stories rather than telling my own."

"So you do write, but you just don't share your writing anymore?" Spence asks, unwilling to let it go.

Douglas smiles. "Why don't we take out our notebooks and pens," she says. "Today, I'd like you to write a story inspired by one of the notecards you wrote this week. I want you to build on the themes and emotions you started to explore, and dig deeper. For this to work, you have to push yourselves to be vulnerable and fully honest."

Brunson starts to write first. She writes about her mom's illness, and about her mom's loss of hair, and about Beth's hair in their dorm room last year. But when she gets to the night she finally snapped and said something to Beth, she stops herself. This is exactly where she should be digging deeper, but she can't. Or she doesn't want to. Just thinking about that night makes her nauseous.

When they're done writing, Douglas says, "For your next assignment, I'd like you to use your word as a launching point for a short story. You have two weeks to turn it in. I want the real *you* in that fictional piece. Does that make sense?"

"Not really," Freddy says. "You want us to write about ourselves, but also *not* write about ourselves?"

"What is the difference between nonfiction and fiction?" Douglas asks.

"Well," Freddy says, "one is based in fact and the other is based in . . . well, fiction."

Douglas laughs. "So fiction is fictional," she says. "That's a start." There's no mockery in Douglas's reaction as she adds, "Nonfiction is about telling the truth. Fiction is about telling *your* truth. Fiction is a mystery only its author can solve. You."

Ramin Golafshar

"Rabbit, rabbit," Ramin says out loud on the first day of October.

He can feel Benji stir above him. "Rabbit, rabbit," Benji says. Leaping down from the top bunk, Benji asks, "So you do believe in superstition?"

"I don't know," Ramin says. "But it doesn't hurt to say it, right?"

Benji, wearing nothing but plaid boxer shorts, smiles. "I'm telling you, it's never failed. If the first thing I say on the first day of the month is *rabbit, rabbit* out loud, then I have the best month."

Ramin thinks to himself that *every* month is the best month for the Benjis of the world, so maybe superstition has nothing to do with it.

"TGIF," Benji says. He throws a striped pink button-down shirt and a pair of khakis on.

"Yeah." Ramin is happy it's Friday. But not because

he wants to go to another party or because he hates class. He longs for the weekends, because Sundays are his days with the Circle. And he's come to cherish those hours he spends sitting on Douglas's floor, feeling safe. It's such a contrast to the Wilton Blue Basement, where brutality is always just around the corner.

That night, he tiptoes out of bed, desperate not to wake Benji, who looks so peaceful when he sleeps. He wishes he knew what that felt like.

He exits the room, leaving the door just slightly ajar so he doesn't have to touch the doorknob to get in, just in case something's on it. He can't believe this is a thought that has to cross his mind.

He still can't bring himself to shower with the other boys. Their ritual of mockery is too much for him. Not to mention the cruel torture of being around that many bodies when the only one he wants is Arya. So he doesn't shower during the day, but if he doesn't shower at all, he'll be told he smells, and that horrible "Dirty Ramoon" nickname will return.

He gets in the shower, turns the knob so the water goes from warm to scalding. That's how he likes it, just shy of burning him. For a moment, he imagines the water will peel his skin off and reveal new skin underneath. He lets the water pour over him for what feels like an hour, imagining this new person it will transform him into.

Then, he hears someone scream from the hallway. It's piercing. He has a brief, panicky thought that Seb and Toby will in fact kill him.

He turns the water off so he can hear what's happening out in the hallway. He makes out voices, but he can't tell who is who. Just a cacophony of panic.

"How the fuck was I supposed to know he's allergic?" someone says.

"You're a fucking doofus, you know that?" someone else says.

He wraps the towel around his waist. He wishes he had a second towel to cover the top half of his body. He hesitates in the bathroom, wondering if he should just hide out there. Will anyone even notice he's gone?

Then he hears Seb's unmistakable action-star voice. "Where's Dirty Ramoon?" he asks, that fucking nickname that manages to insult Ramin twice by butchering his name *and* adding an insulting adjective to it.

"I don't know," Benji says. "He wasn't in the room."

He pushes the bathroom door open and enters the hallway. He's probably half Seb's size, in height and width and weight. Being half-naked in front of Seb is already a humiliation, and he knows there'll be more.

"Hey, everyone," he manages to croak out. "I'm here."

Seb laughs. "Dirty Ramoon! Showering in secret, huh?"

"No, I was just . . ." But he can't finish the sentence.

"What's the matter? Do you get *hard* when you shower around other dudes?" Seb gets menacingly close to him. Ramin closes his eyes, wishing he was with the Circle. It was so easy to be honest with them about who he is. "I bet you'd get turned on by some dude's cum on your doorknob." And there it is. Confirmation that his own prefect, tasked with *protecting* him, is behind that vile attack.

He doesn't know what to say. He's never showered around other boys, plural. Just one, singular. And yes, it made him hard. But Arya was worthy of his hardness, these boys are not. Nobody but Arya ever will be. Except maybe Freddy, who is so beautiful and so sweet. But just thinking this feels like a betrayal of Arya, even if he broke his heart.

Toby approaches Seb and puts a hand on his shoulder. "Lay off, Seb," he says. "We just put a kid in the hospital."

"*We* didn't put a kid in the hospital," Seb says. "That idiot did."

Seb points to Mix, who stands defiant in a rust-and-gold Chandler Lacrosse shirt and a pair of torn Bart Simpson boxer shorts. "I didn't know he'd be allergic," Mix says. "There's always peanut sauce in Japanese restaurants."

This makes Toby cackle. "Wait, dude, seriously? So just because Americans eat peanut butter and jelly sandwiches, you think that means none of us have nut allergies?"

"No, of course not," Mix says, maintaining his swagger.

Toby gets menacingly close to Mix now. Mix may be a lacrosse player with a square jaw and an air of superiority, but he's nothing compared to Toby King with his football build and famous dad. "*I'm* allergic to nuts," Toby says.

"Okay," Mix says. "I'm sorry. Really, seriously, deeply sorry."

"If you had smeared peanut butter on *my* face as a joke, I would've killed you with my bare hands." Toby holds his hands up for dramatic effect. Then he puts one of them down. "Your neck is so small and my hands are so big. I think I'd only need one hand to strangle you."

Ramin feels so awkward in his towel. He takes refuge next to Benji. "What happened?" he whispers to Benji.

"Mix thought it'd be funny to smear peanut butter and jelly on Hiro's face when he was sleeping and take pictures of him. A dick move to begin with, but turns out it's a potentially lethal one 'cause Hiro's allergic."

"I know," Ramin says. "He told us all when we did our introductions."

"Apparently, you were the only one listening," Benji says. "Anyway, they're torturing Mix now. You should've seen the brutal wedgie they gave him." Ramin looks at Mix's torn boxers again. It must have been him screaming when Ramin was in the shower.

"Is Hiro going to be okay?" he asks, his blood running cold.

Optimistically, Benji says, "I think so. He went to the nurse right away."

As Benji reassures him that murder was not indeed committed in the darkness of the Wilton Blue Basement tonight, the conflict between Toby and Mix escalates.

"Get down on the floor," Toby says.

"Why?"

"Are you questioning your prefect?" Toby asks.

"No," Mix says.

"No what?" Toby asks.

"No sir," Mix says.

"Then. Get. Down. On. The. Floor."

Ramin can't stand being half-naked anymore. He slips into the room and throws on a T-shirt and shorts.

When he comes back out into the hallway, Mix is lying down on the floor. His confidence finally appears to be pierced by panic. "What are you gonna do, Toby?"

Toby unzips his pants. "You obviously think putting nuts on someone's face is funny," Toby says. "So let's put some nuts on yours."

Seb claps his hands with delight. "Oh fuck yeah," he says. "This is about to be a legendary move."

"Toby, please," Mix begs.

"SHUT UP," Toby screams as he pulls his pants and underwear down to his ankles.

"Toby, what do you want? My dad can hook you up with tickets to any concert you want to see. Seriously. What's your jam? Jay-Z, Aerosmith, Backstreet Boys."

"You think I like the Backstreet Boys? You calling me a *fairy*?"

Ramin gulps down hard. Just the word *fairy* out in the thick basement air makes him feel vulnerable. He looks around, wondering if anyone felt him flinch at the word.

Can they hear his stomach churning?

"No, I just mean, anyone. I mean—"

"You think my own dad can't get me concert tickets?"

"No, I—Toby, come on."

"Better keep that mouth closed now," Toby says.

Mix stops talking as Toby squats down, placing his balls right on Mix's face. Ramin feels his whole body tighten. His heart races, like he's the one being violated. He wishes he could wipe this image from his mind. He knows how beautiful the intimacy of two bodies touching can be, and he hates the knowledge that this very same touch can be full of violence and hate.

"Oh fuck," Seb squeals, clapping again. "Well played, King."

"Tell me now," Toby says. "You still think putting nuts on someone's face is funny."

Seb unzips and pushes Toby aside, putting his own balls on Mix's mouth now as Toby cheers. "Nuts for dinner," Seb says, laughing.

Mix tries to speak, but what comes out is a jumble of sounds.

"We can't hear you," Seb says. "Louder."

"Mmmhhhhaaaaaooo," Mix mumbles.

"What do you think?" Toby asks Seb. "Has he learned his lesson?"

Seb shrugs. "If he hasn't, there's always tomorrow night."

Toby looks around at the fourth formers, who stare

in horror. "What do you guys think? Has he learned his lesson?"

Ramin can't take it anymore. He needs this nightmare to end. "Yes!" he blurts out. "Please stop." Then he looks around at his fellow fourth formers, so quiet. They're smart enough not to draw attention to themselves.

Seb laughs, then gets up. He doesn't pull his pants back up when he says, "Okay, I'll stop. But only because it's turning Dirty Ramoon on too much."

Toby, his own pants still around his ankles, adds, "What are you morons looking at? I know I'm beautiful, but it's lights out. Get in your rooms."

"And remember that this basement is sacred ground," Seb says. "You tell anyone else what happens here, and there will be consequences. You understand?"

Everyone scurries as Toby and Seb finally pull their pants up. But Ramin can't move. He feels paralyzed by what he's just seen.

It's not until most of the boys are back in their rooms that Mr. Court emerges. He wears a burgundy sleep robe and doesn't have his hearing aid in. "What's going on here?" Mr. Court yells.

Seb and Toby approach Mr. Court. "Nothing to worry about, Mr. Court," Seb says loudly into Mr. Court's left ear, the one he hears better in. "A student had an allergic reaction, but we got him to the school nurse."

"Is Margaret still the nurse?" Mr. Court yells.

"Yup," Seb says.

"When I went here, we used to *avoid* the nurse. But if

Margaret was the nurse, I would've been sick a lot more."

Seb and Toby laugh. "You're a dog, Mr. Court," Seb says.

The two prefects escort Mr. Court to his room, which is at the end of the hallway, removed from the boys both by architecture and by Mr. Court's hearing problems.

When Seb and Toby are gone, Ramin can finally breathe again. He bolts to his room, and finds Benji peacefully reading *1984* on the top bunk. He's leaning against the wall so his feet dangle in the air.

Ramin wants so much to talk to Benji about what happened. But when Benji says, "Don't let it get to you, it's just the Wilton Blue Basement," he knows Benji isn't the right person to process this with. Because Benji doesn't seem at all threatened in any way by what just happened. It was just another Friday night to him. TGIF.

He pulls out his index cards when Benji falls asleep. He considers writing down what happened, then realizes it would never fit on a card, or two, or even three. So he grabs his journal. He thinks about the word Douglas asked him to explore. *Fear.* Maybe what she really wanted him to explore is overcoming fear. Maybe writing is one way to do that.

When the sun comes up, he's still writing. He hears Benji shift above him, the coils of the bed squeaking. He quickly hides the journal.

Ramin wonders what his mom would say if she read this. She would probably see it as the beginning of the end of the world. The last time boys bullied him, he was forced to leave their country.

He stands up. Stares at Benji's peaceful face. How does someone sleep so soundly after seeing one kid go to the hospital and another kid get publicly humiliated? Ramin shakes his head at the irony of George Orwell's *1984*, of all things, resting next to Benji's head. He wishes he knew the secret to shrugging things off like this. But maybe he can never know this particular secret because it comes from a lifetime of having problems handled for you. That's the thing about so many of these Chandies. They've all had families who just shovel all their problems away for them, so they see life as one big open road with no obstacles.

But maybe Ramin is heading toward his own open road. That's how each meeting of the Circle makes him feel, like the world is full of possibility.

At their next Circle meeting, they spend an hour listening to Billie Holiday's *Lady in Satin* record and writing a story inspired by their favorite season.

"Professor Douglas?" he says when they're all done.

"Yes, Ramin?"

He hesitates before saying, "I know we have another week before we need to turn in our short story, but I wrote something this weekend. I—I couldn't stop. It all flowed out of me like it never has before. The only thing is . . ."

"Yes?" It's like she knows exactly what he's thinking.

"Is it that you're not ready to share with the group?"

"I don't know," he says. "I was thinking maybe you could read it first."

Douglas sits next to him on the floor. Crosses her legs like she's doing yoga. "Anything good that we write is deeply private. But if we want to develop as a writer, we must share it. We can't hold our creativity hostage."

He cringes a little at her use of the word *hostage*, a loaded word for him and his people.

Douglas looks right at him as she continues. "Ideas need light to grow, to develop."

Ramin wants to tell the group everything, and at the same time, wants to tell them nothing.

"You know what I think about writing?" Douglas asks. "I think writing is by definition an act of optimism. Even when what you're writing about is painful or tragic."

"Maybe especially when what you're writing about is painful or tragic," Spence says, inserting herself into what felt like a private moment between him and Douglas.

"Why do you say that, Amanda?" Douglas asks.

"I guess, I don't know, by writing about the things that make life more difficult, we release them, and . . ."

When Spence pauses, Douglas completes her thought. "Yes, and when we release secrets, we give them less power, right?"

He notices Brunson bite her lip when Douglas poses this question. Quietly, she whispers, "Right."

Ramin pulls his journal out of his backpack. "It's all in here," he says.

"What's it about?" Douglas asks. "And I don't mean the subject matter. I mean, thematically. What are you exploring?"

"I don't know," he says, nervous. "It's just a story."

"You kids love that word," Douglas says. "To me, that word means what is morally right. I'd like to live in a *just* world, for example."

"So can we read it?" Freddy asks.

Ramin feels a sudden panic at the thought of Freddy reading the story. What will Freddy think of him if he knows his own friends call him "Dirty Ramoon" and harass the kids in his dorm? Will Freddy defend his buddies? Or worse, will he pity Ramin?

He wishes someone would send him a sign of what to do. Or maybe he doesn't need a sign because superstition takes all the control and agency away from him.

He hands the journal to Douglas, enjoying the look of pride on her face.

"I only have this copy," he says.

"Would you be willing to read it out loud for us?" Douglas asks.

He suddenly feels light-headed. Just the thought of saying these words versus writing them is dizzying.

He takes a breath. He's gotten this far, hasn't he? Applying to this school. Getting in. Writing this story. Turning it in. Why would he stop now?

"Okay," he says.

His voice is muted when he begins. "*I say* rabbit, rabbit *out loud on the first day of October.*"

He glances at them, still speaking in a hushed and confidential tone. He feels his voice rise in both volume and urgency as he continues.

Each time he looks up, they're leaning closer to him. Finally, he says the last line of his story. "*I know how beautiful the intimacy of two bodies touching can be. But now I'll always know the very same touch can be full of violence and hate.*"

Beth Kramer

There are tears in Beth's eyes when Ramin finishes reading his story. Tears of empathy, sure, but also of anger. She knows what it's like to feel scared and singled out. She quickly wipes them away when she catches Brunson watching her. She glances at Spence, then at Freddy. They're both quiet. No one dares speak before the professor.

"I think the group is speechless," Douglas says, stating the obvious. "And so am I."

Ramin says nothing.

"I'm not speechless," Brunson says urgently.

"Oh good." Douglas nods, giving Brunson permission to speak.

"I think this story is incredible." Brunson stands up. She cracks her knuckles. "I think it's powerful. And brave."

"I don't know about that," Ramin says. "It's just—"

"Just?" Douglas says the word like a warning.

"It's not *just* anything," Brunson says, pacing the room now. "This kind of thing has probably been happening at schools like this forever. Boys being subjected to disgusting behavior in the name of what, some backward tradition and social order that believes people should be broken down in order to make them tough or something."

Watching Brunson rail against the inhumanity of hazing makes Beth want to stand up and rail against Brunson's hypocrisy. Who is Brunson to say any of this when she's the one who robbed Beth of her freshman year by constantly shutting her out, and then by cutting her down so mercilessly with that hairnet? Brunson doesn't get to be all high and mighty when she's just the girl version of the same thing.

"Thanks, Brunson," Ramin says shyly. He seemed so empowered by the end of his story. But now he's suddenly self-conscious again.

"Ramin," Freddy says. "I—I didn't recognize any of the names in your story, but, well, the characters sounded a whole lot like—well, did this happen to you? Did my friends do this to you?"

At this, Ramin looks up and says, "I thought they weren't your friends."

And Freddy says, "Fuck."

Beth knew it had to be real. It was written like a fictional short story, but she could tell from the details that even though he changed the name of the school, he was writing about Chandler. He may have changed the name of the dorm, but it was the Wilton Blue Basement.

"I'm so sorry," Freddy says.

"You didn't do it," Ramin says.

"I know, but . . ." Freddy doesn't continue.

Beth feels her throat tighten with rage as she replays all the cruelty in Ramin's story. Physical aggression. Sexual aggression. A kid almost killed. "That was Hiro, right?" she asks. "Is he okay?"

"Yeah," Ramin says. "He was rushed to the nurse and they injected him with one of those pens. He's fine. Well, physically. I hope he's fine emotionally. He seems unaffected, but no one could be, right?"

Douglas speaks deliberately. "Everyone responds to trauma differently."

"I've always wondered what goes on in boys' dorms," Spence says. "It's worse than I thought."

"It's not just boys." There's a sad resignation in Douglas's voice. "This kind of behavior can and does happen everywhere. And I'm so sorry it happened to you, Ramin. Is there anything I can do? If you want to report what happened, I could help you with that."

"No," Ramin says, too loudly.

"Are you sure?" Douglas asks.

Ramin shakes his head. "You've already helped so much. And I appreciate it. But . . . well, reporting it will just make it worse. I just need to be like the other guys and get over it."

"I understand and I'll respect your decision," Douglas

says carefully. "But please don't ever feel like you have to be like the 'other guys.' If you change your mind, I'm here."

That's when Beth has a revelation. She knows exactly what she needs to do. Because Douglas is right. It's not just boys' dorms. Maybe boys are more physical, more obviously aggressive. But girls are no different. And aggression is aggression whether it's overt or covert. And maybe the covert kind is more insidious because it's harder to recognize.

That night, just before lights-out, Beth goes where no girl ever goes, to the Wilton Blue Basement. She finds Ramin in his room, reading Persian poetry. Benji Pasternak whistles when Beth enters. "Well, well, well, you've got a female visitor, Ramin." Beth and Ramin both look at each other with a subtle eye roll.

"Hey, Ramin, can I talk to you outside for a second?" she asks. "Well, maybe for more than a second, actually."

"Of course," Ramin says as he follows her out.

As they leave, Benji says, "Have fun, lovebirds."

Outside, she finds a stoop and sits. "I can't stop thinking about your story," she says.

"Oh," he says. "Well, I'm sorry." He sits next to her.

"Why are you sorry?"

"Because nothing in the story is pleasant to think about."

"And what about me makes you think I'm looking for pleasantries?"

Ramin laughs at this. She looks around. Clusters of boys are making the most of these last minutes of freedom. Telling jokes. Kicking hacky sacks. A few of them look at her and Ramin, whispering to each other. They must think she and Ramin are having a romantic moment. If only they knew.

"Look," she says. "Before I tell you why I'm really here, I want to say something I haven't said out loud to anyone." She takes a deep breath, then says, "I like girls." The clarity of the statement shocks her.

"Oh," Ramin says. "That's great. Well, unless it's not great for you. It's hard, right?"

"I don't know," Beth says. "I guess sometimes it's hard. Like living in a world with so few examples of what the future could look like for me. But there's no one I admire more than Professor Douglas and she's gay. But then again, she's the only gay teacher on campus. And that must suck, being the only one of anything."

"I'm the only Iranian here," he says.

"I'm the only townie who isn't a day student."

He smiles. "See, we're not as alone as we think we are."

"Or maybe," she says, "we're alone together."

"So what did you want to talk to me about?" he asks.

"Oh right." And then she pitches Ramin her idea. "Could I, if it's okay with you, obviously, add to your story?"

He squints, confused. "Add what?"

"I'm not explaining myself very well." There's sweat on her brow. "I wouldn't touch your words. I would

basically write my own story about the cruelty that happens in girls' dorms. Because your story really inspired
me to think about some of the stuff I've been through."
She pauses to check his reaction. "Then I would splice
the stories together, so it would be a contrast between the
brute physical cruelty of boys and the subtle emotional
cruelty of girls."

The distant sound of the Chapel bell rings. It's
lights-out, but she needs his response. This can't be a
conversation left dangling.

"So what do you think?" She leans in closer to him.

"Sure," he says, nodding slowly. "I think that's a cool
idea. I just—I don't want to show it to anyone outside the
Circle. The last thing I need is those guys knowing—"

"Ramin," she says, "I would never do that."

Ramin gives her a hug before he leaves. She doesn't
want to let go of him, even though she can hear a few
boys make gross comments about them.

She runs back to her dorm, knowing she'll be late for
lights-out. She's already writing the story in her head
as she runs. She'll change the names, but Brunson will
know. She'll know just how badly she hurt Beth.

At the fifth meeting of the Circle, they spend a half hour
discussing character development, then an hour writing
something inspired by the color red.

When that's done, Douglas asks the group to turn in
their short stories. Spence, Freddy, and Brunson hand her
typed and stapled pages.

"Professor Douglas," Beth says, "I made copies of the story for everyone, in case they want to read along."

"You want to read yours out loud today?" Douglas asks.

"Well, maybe I'll read my part. It's just that the story is half mine, and half Ramin's. It's a collaboration, I guess."

"Then read your part," Douglas suggests.

"Just be warned, I'm not much of a public speaker."

She starts handing out the copies, starting with Douglas, then Spence, Freddy, and Ramin. She hesitates before giving one to Brunson. This is the moment of no return. After this, Brunson will know exactly how she feels about her. She must hesitate a long time, because eventually Brunson takes the story from her hands.

Beth doesn't stand up when she reads. She's not sure she could hold herself steady that long. Not as she reads a story about a roommate who treated her like she was invisible, until she finally acknowledged her by asking her to wear a hairnet. She changed the roommate's name, of course, but but the group will know and so will Brunson. And she'll also know why those hairs were all over the room. Because of Beth's anxiety, something she couldn't control. She wants Brunson to know she was kicking her when she was already down.

She feels relieved as she gets to the last paragraph. She puts her notebook down, her eyes on Brunson, who shifts uncomfortably. "That's it."

Douglas nods, taking the story in. "It's very powerful, Beth. I assume some of this happened to you. And if I'm right, I hope you found some catharsis in writing about it."

Then, to her surprise, Brunson blurts out, "This story is about me."

"What do you mean?" Douglas asks.

"I mean, I was Beth's roommate last year. And I did exactly what she writes about. I did hang out with other girls in our room, but she was always on her headphones. That's why we never included her. It felt like, well . . . like she didn't want to be included."

Beth feels her eyes blinking too fast. She didn't expect Brunson to say anything.

Brunson takes a short breath before saying, "I asked her to wear a hairnet. But I had no idea she pulled her hair out like that, and I didn't know how much it humiliated her." Brunson turns to Beth now. "I didn't know any of that. I swear, Beth."

Beth feels her heart pounding in her chest. If Brunson is expecting forgiveness, she's not going to give it to her.

"This makes me very uncomfortable," Douglas says.

"Me too," Ramin says. He turns to Beth. "You didn't tell me you were going to write about Brunson."

Douglas speaks again. "I want you all to feel free to express yourselves, but writing about each other like this. It can be hurtful."

"I was just telling the truth," Beth says. "Isn't that what you've been teaching us to do?"

Douglas sighs. "I suppose I have. But truth telling is complicated, and we can't weaponize the truth to hurt others. That's why I asked you to sign the Circle Honor Code. You remember what it said, Beth?"

In a small voice, she says, "Yeah, that we would commit to respecting each other."

"And what was the word you were meant to explore?" Douglas asks.

"*Forgiveness*," she says, mortified at how she completely missed the whole point of the assignment.

"The thing about writing stories is that we're forced to see the world from different perspectives," Douglas says. "My guess is that there's a whole other side of this story from Sarah's perspective."

"Yeah, there is," Brunson says, her voice tinged with sadness.

"It defeats the mission we set at the very beginning of the year, remember? To create a safe space." Douglas draws an imaginary circle with her index finger. "This circle is safe. This is a place where no one will be made to feel less than. I need this to be the last story one of you writes about the other. We are not each other's subjects. Do you understand?"

They all nod.

"All right, why don't we stop now?" Douglas suggests.

She breathes a sigh of relief. All she wants to do is escape. This was a terrible idea. Then Douglas says, "Beth, I'd like you to stay behind."

She feels a desperate urge to pull a hair out of her head. Douglas is probably going to kick her out of the Circle for what she did.

Once the other kids are out of sight, she begs Douglas, "Please don't kick me out."

"Beth, I'm not asking you to leave," Douglas says.

Beth takes a deep breath. It's so different being alone with Douglas. Her presence feels so much bigger and more intimidating when it's just the two of them.

"Beth—" Douglas begins.

"I'm really sorry," Beth says. "It's just—Ramin wrote that story, and it was obviously about what happens in his dorm, and I thought, well, what if I show what happens in girls' dorms. It seemed like such a good idea. I didn't think."

"Beth." Douglas leans toward her. "I believe you're sorry. I understand why you did what you did. And you're a very talented writer."

"I am?"

"You are. But—"

"But?" she repeats.

"But I'm concerned about you. Pulling your hair out ritually like that, it's a sign of a deep anxiety. Are you seeing someone?"

Her face gets hot. "Oh God, no."

"I meant a therapist," Douglas says. "I think a visit to the school counselor could help you to—"

"Oh wow," she says, crossing her arms. "You're just like my mom."

"She's asked you to see a therapist?"

"Yeah." Beth feels shaky as she says, "I just—I don't think it's that bad."

"I didn't say it's *that* bad," Douglas says. "And if it makes you feel better, I think we *all* need help."

"So you've seen a therapist?" Beth asks.

"The question is, how many therapists have I seen?" Douglas says with a laugh. "There's no shame in it."

"I'm—I'm afraid," she says.

"What are you afraid of?" Douglas asks.

She can't quite put her fears into words, so she asks, "Can't I just talk to you?"

Douglas smiles warmly. "Of course you can. Anytime. But I'm not a therapist. I'm a teacher. It's different."

"It's just . . ." Her throat feels so dry. She pushes through. She has to get the next part out. "It's just that I know you won't judge me, and maybe the school counselor will. We're the same."

"Is it because he's a man?" Douglas asks. "Because I can assure you that Dr. Geller has helped many young women."

"Not just that." Beth looks at her meaningfully.

"Oh." Douglas glances at her. "I think I understand. Beth, I know how hard it is to feel different. To keep secrets. If you're telling me what I think you're telling me, then just imagine how hard it was for me in Texas, decades ago."

"I know, but—"

"Not that I'm trying to downplay how hard it still is, especially in a hermetically sealed environment like Chandler." Douglas sighs. "But trust me when I say that hiding from yourself is never the answer. We need light

184

to grow. Just like our stories do."

"I'm scared," Beth says, tears forming in her eyes.

"We're all scared," Douglas says. "I'm scared."

"You are?" Beth asks. "What are you scared of?"

For a moment, it looks like Douglas herself might cry. But she steels herself. "We're all babies, Beth. Crawling before we walk. Every new step is a challenge. But if we don't take those baby steps, those risks, then we never grow. Does that make sense?"

Instead of responding, she says, "I told Ramin too. About liking girls. And now you."

"And you don't have to tell anyone else until you're ready. Just don't lie to *yourself*. That's where the real trouble is."

She nods. "Okay," she says. "I'll go see Dr. Geller." She wonders what her mom will think.

Douglas stands up. She pulls two books from her shelves and one from the floor. Rita Mae Brown and Alice Walker and Fannie Flagg. "Read these," she says. "Maybe they'll help. Seeing yourself in the pages of a book is an empowering feeling."

Beth walks out of MacMillan, the books weighing down her backpack. But she feels lighter than she's ever felt. She went into the Circle with a mission to expose Brunson. Instead, she revealed herself.

Freddy Bello

"Faster, Freddy. Faster," Coach Stade yells.

Sweat pours down Freddy's face as he runs over hurdles that Stade has placed across the Jordan Center. He collapses against the wall when he gets to the end of the gym, catching his breath.

"Again," Stade says.

"I need a minute."

"You think the Olympic judges are going to give you a minute when you need it?"

Freddy pulls his hair off his face. Runs back to the other end of the gym, over the hurdles as he goes.

"Knees higher," Stade says. "Shoulders square. Stand tall, Freddy. What's going on this morning?"

It's the same kind of coaching he's always gotten from Stade. Every coach he's ever had has been the same. Tough, cold, focused. And he's always appreciated it. He wanted to be the best, and they were getting him there.

But something feels different as Stade screams, "You're slow, Freddy. You're lagging." He doesn't hear Stade anymore. He hears Toby and Seb, torturing Ramin and those boys in the basement.

He stops when he gets to the end of the hurdles. He knows he hasn't been *on* this morning. "I'm sorry," he says. "I'll do it again."

"What's going on?" Stade asks. "You seem distracted."

"I don't know," he says. But he does know. He knows that he's been writing in the morning and writing at night, filling up notecards with words and thoughts. And yet nothing seems to become clear for him. He can't stop thinking about kissing Spence in that garage. He's still unsure whether he wants to keep pole vaulting. And most importantly, he has no idea how to stop being friends with Toby. Seb, too, but he just met Seb this year. He's carefully avoided them all week.

"Did you sneak out last night?" Stade asks.

"What? No," Freddy says.

"It was Friday night. Kids will be kids." Stade puts a hand on Freddy's shoulder. "But you're not an ordinary kid."

"Yeah," he says, wondering why he wanted to be extraordinary in the first place.

"Is it the Circle?" Stade asks. "If it's distracting you from your training . . ."

"No," he says. He doesn't elaborate.

"You know what separates you from other kids?" Stade asks.

Freddy shakes his head.

"It's not your strength or your form. It's up here." Stade taps at Freddy's head. "You have the ability to stay in the moment. That's what separates champions from regular athletes. You can't let anything distract you when you're training or vaulting. And you don't. Usually."

He feels his whole body tighten. Stade is right. And that's exactly why he promised his parents he wouldn't date anyone until he made it to the Olympics. Because, like his last coach told him and his parents, he can only be consumed by one passion at a time. And right now, he's consumed by Spence and the Circle instead of his training.

"Let's call it," Stade says. "Get some rest. Tomorrow's Sunday, so I'll see you in two days. You going to Lowell Night?"

"Oh yeah, of course," he says. "I mean, the whole school's going."

"See you there."

Freddy doesn't shower after training. And he doesn't go back to Holmby House. He finds himself heading up the hill to Wilton Blue. He needs to deal with what's eating away at him, and that means he needs to confront Toby and Seb.

He plans exactly what he'll say to them as he heads down the steps to the basement and into the dorm. He enters the common area first, where he finds Ramin and Hiro playing cards.

"Freddy!" Ramin says.

"Oh, hey, guys," he says. "How's it going?"

"Great," Hiro says, a big smile on his face.

"Yeah? You sure you're okay?" Freddy gets what Ramin was saying about Hiro seeming unaffected.

"Well, Ramin owes me thirty thousand dollars, so that's made things a lot better."

"We're playing with imaginary money," Ramin clarifies.

"Yeah, I got that," Freddy says, laughing.

"What are you doing here?" Ramin asks. "We're not getting together 'til later, right?"

He nods. Lowell Night is the night of Chandler's lacrosse game against its rival school, Lowell Prep. The biggest athletic event of the year, and this year it's on home turf. The Circle is meeting at Livingston in the afternoon to go together.

"You guys going to the game?" Hiro asks.

"Yeah, aren't you?" Ramin asks.

"To see those assholes play? No thanks." Hiro bites the last part out before smiling again and saying, "Besides, the whole school's going to be at the game. It's the *perfect* time to sneak Sabrina into my room without getting caught."

Freddy smiles. "Nice. Glad to hear you two are going strong."

"She's the best," Hiro says. "Ten of diamonds is mine, sucker." Hiro snatches two cards, adding them to the pile in front of him. "And I have this kid to thank for it all. If he hadn't taken me to that party, I never would've met her."

"The least you could do to thank me is let me win one game," Ramin teases.

"What are you guys playing anyway?" Freddy asks.

"Pasur," Ramin says. "It's an Iranian game I taught him."

"Wait," Freddy says, laughing. "He's beating you at an Iranian game he just learned?"

Ramin blushes. "So why did you come up here anyway?"

"Oh, just to see . . . to talk to, you know . . ." He drifts off. "I'll see you this afternoon, Ramin. Later, Hiro."

He's halfway down the hallway when Ramin rushes after him and pulls him into his bedroom. "What are you doing?" Ramin asks, panicked.

"I was just gonna—Ramin, I can't just let them treat you guys like that. I can make them stop."

"Yeah, but if you do that, then they're going to know I told you what happened." Ramin's eyes dart wildly around the room. There's sweat on his brow.

"I won't say it was you," Freddy says gently.

"Who *else* would it be? They know I'm in the Circle with you. Don't you see that it'll only make things worse? They'll come up with some horrible way to punish me. I appreciate you wanting to do something. Just like I appreciate Douglas wanting to help me turn them in. But I'd rather not rock the boat. Please."

"Hey," he says. He puts a hand on each of Ramin's shoulders, trying to steady him. "You sound terrified."

"I am," Ramin says, letting out a heavy breath.

"Which is why you can't say anything. Okay?"

He thinks for a moment. He wanted so badly to sweep into this basement and be the savior. But Ramin is right. What good will it do? It won't change Toby and Seb. And if they retaliated against Ramin, then Freddy would be to blame.

"Why's it so cold in here?" Freddy asks.

"The basement doesn't get heat," Ramin explains. Then Ramin hands Freddy a sweater. "Here, you can wear this."

He throws the sweater on. It fits him perfectly. "Isn't this sweater too big for you?"

"It's not mine," Ramin says. He turns away from Freddy. It sounds like he's about to cry.

"Hey, it's going to be okay," Freddy says. "If this is about Toby and Seb, we'll figure something out. There has to be a way to stop them."

"It's not that, it's just . . ." Ramin turns to him. There are tears in his eyes. "This was my boyfriend's sweater. Ex-boyfriend. It's just strange to see someone else in it."

"Oh," Freddy says, understanding dawning. "The friend who would buy those black-market CDs?"

"Yeah," Ramin says, a sad smile on his face. "You look a bit like him."

Freddy sits down on the bottom bunk. "What was he like?" he asks.

Ramin lets out a sad sigh, then sits next to him. "He'd make me laugh all the time. He did impressions of every-one. His dad. My mom. He always left me little hidden notes everywhere. I don't know, I couldn't believe he chose me. He had a big personality, you know. So I guess he brought me out of my shell. We were so good together. For a while."

"So what happened?" Freddy asks.

"What do you mean?"

"Well, why'd you break up?"

He can feel Ramin struggling to answer. "It's just—well, you know you can't be gay in Iran. I mean, you *can* be gay, people just can't *know* about it. And, well . . . people found out about us."

"I'm so sorry," Freddy says.

"Yeah, thanks." Ramin looks right at him as he continues. "It was boys at our school. They caught us together at this lake. They probably followed us. And once they knew we were together, they bullied us constantly." He looks down at the floor now. "It was mostly verbal. So much name calling. We don't have a real word for gay people in Iran, but we definitely have insults. Once or twice it was physical. They gave him a black eye and no one cared. But the worst part was that they threatened to tell the school about us. Which in Iran would mean . . ." Ramin drifts off.

"Yeah, I think I get what it would mean there," Freddy says softly.

"That's when he broke up with me. He just couldn't risk it anymore. And his family moved to Turkey." Tears form in Ramin's eyes.

"That's horrible," Freddy says, taking Ramin's hand.

"Yeah, well, I'm here now. I got away. He got away. And my parents never even met him. That part really bothers me."

"I'm sorry."

"It's my fault. I should've told my parents about him sooner. They only found out once I was heartbroken. They never got to see how happy he made me."

"It's not fair that you came here to escape bullying and found more bullies," Freddy says sadly. "That's not how it should be."

Ramin moves closer to him as he says, "Not all boys are like that, though. Some are sweet."

Their faces get closer and closer to each other. Ramin is beautiful, and he wants to comfort him. But in that moment, he realizes he definitely has feelings for Spence because this feels very wrong.

"Ramin, wait," he whispers.

Ramin quickly pulls away. "I'm sorry. I don't know what I was doing."

"No, don't be sorry," he says. "I think you're amazing, and strong, but, well, I'm into Spence."

"Oh, of course," Ramin says. "You're not gay."

"No," Freddy says. He feels his heart flutter as he admits, "I am into guys too."

"Oh," Ramin says, his eyes locked on Freddy.

"And if I wasn't into Spence, then . . ."

Ramin stands up abruptly. "It's okay, you don't need to say any more." With a smile, he says, "I'll see you tonight."

"Make sure to wear rust and gold," Freddy tells him. "People get really upset if you don't show school pride on Lowell Night."

When Freddy gets back to his room, he writes on a notecard. And then another. His words find a clarity as he writes. It's like every word Freddy writes reveals something. And he finally has clarity about at least one thing. He needs to try with Spence, whatever that looks like. He's been so focused on his body his whole life. And now he's finally paying attention to his brain. But what about his heart? He's been ignoring it way too long.

"Lowell Night!" Charles says when he comes back to the room to grab his lacrosse stick.

"Go kick ass," he says. "You're gonna crush them."

"We're gonna be purple people eaters tonight." Lowell Prep's school color is purple, and on Lowell Night, this is what Chandies call themselves.

"I'll be cheering you on," Freddy says.

Later that afternoon, he showers and puts on a rust-and-gold long-sleeved T-shirt and a pair of jeans. That seems patriotic enough. But when he arrives outside Livingston, Spence shares a very different idea with the Circle.

"You guys," she says. "I have barrister costumes for us. Should we do it?"

"What costumes?" Ramin asks.

"Barristers are the official Chandler mascot," Brunson explains.

"Like, British lawyers?" Ramin asks.

"Yeah, exactly," Brunson continues. "It's because the first headmaster, Headmaster Cook, was British."

"The Brits even colonized Chandler," Spence says with a roll of her eyes.

"Cook's dad was a barrister," Beth adds. "Which is kind of funny. Like, he turned his dad into a mascot."

"Oh, I didn't know that," Brunson says, sounding both annoyed and impressed. Freddy wonders if Beth and Brunson have spoken since Beth read her story to the group.

Sixth-form girls stream out of Livingston in their rust and gold as the Circle enters. Some of the girls have found inventive ways to wear the school colors. They've turned Chandler T-shirts into tube tops. They've drawn the school's insignia on their cheeks. They've matted their hair down with gold paste.

Spence orders them to hang out in the common room until she returns with five barrister robes and a Ferragamo bag full of white wigs. She throws the robes and wigs to the group, starting with Freddy.

When they get to the lacrosse field in their costumes, the game has already begun. On one side sit the visiting Lowell students and faculty, a sea of purple. On the other side sit the Chandler community, in their rust and gold.

When Charles Cox scores, he lifts his stick up into the air and screams, *"Oh Chandler."*

And the crowd responds with a melodic *"My Chandler."*

"Good on your roommate," Spence says.

Chandler has an early lead in the game, and the mood on campus is light and celebratory. The crowd bellows out lots of Chandler cheers, endless renditions of the school song, and a few bars of that "Purple People Eater" song to taunt the Lowell Preppies.

The next person to score is Toby King, and once again the crowd goes wild. When Toby raises his stick up and screams, *"Oh Chandler,"* Freddy looks at Ramin, who cringes as the whole school responds to Toby's call like he's a hero.

"Hey, guys," Freddy says. "Should we ditch the game and go to the lake?"

One by one, they all nod. Freddy leads them back to the lake. He feels so light as they walk. They must all remember the way because they're not even following him this time. Brunson speeds up until she is ahead of the rest, Ramin and Beth a few feet behind her.

"Hey," Freddy says to Spence, the two of them lingering behind the others.

"Hey," she says.

"Can we talk?" he asks.

"We're talking," she says.

"No, I mean . . . you know, like, just us," he says.

"It is just us, Freddy. They can't hear us from up there."

"Yeah, you're right," he says. He realizes he's just stalling, avoiding what he wants to say.

A moment passes between them. The far-off sounds of celebration can be heard from the lacrosse field, and leaves crackle under their feet. But it feels so quiet in his head. Like he finally has clarity.

"I've been meaning to talk to you about that kiss in the garage," he finally says.

"So why haven't you?" she asks softly.

He takes a breath, but says nothing.

"Are you gay?" she asks. "Because if you are, I'd be your biggest cheerleader. Honestly."

"No," he says. "But . . . I think I'm bisexual."

"Oh," she says. "Okay. Well, *still* your biggest cheerleader."

"Am I making you uncomfortable?" he asks.

"Who the fuck cares about my comfort right now?"

"The thing is, I really like you, but—"

"Uh-oh," she says quietly.

"Just listen," he says, taking a breath before continuing. "I only dated one other girl. She was, well, from a pretty wealthy conservative family. And they didn't approve of me or whatever. I don't think they liked that my parents were immigrants."

Spence cringes. "My family's not like that, if that's what you're worried about."

"No, I know that," he says. "The thing is, she broke up with me days after introducing me to her parents. And it threw me into a bit of a tailspin. Made me totally fuck up an important competition. And I promised my parents, and myself, I guess, not to let that happen again."

"Are you done?" Spence asks, gazing at him.

"Yeah," he says.

"I also told myself I wouldn't date anyone my senior year," she says.

"Oh, why?" he asks, genuinely curious.

She sighs. "For starters, most guys are sex-obsessed jerks."

Freddy laughs uncomfortably.

"But also," she continues, "no one here really gets me. But with you . . . I don't know, I think maybe you do get me."

"I think I do too," he says.

They've reached the lake. Brunson turns to them and says, "You guys, no swimming this time. Please. That water is vile."

"To be continued?" Freddy asks Spence. "Because I really want to continue . . . whatever this is."

"Definitely to be continued," she says, her smile brighter than the moon.

Freddy can't remember when he last felt this happy. He sits at the edge of the lake next to his friends.

"Hey, guys, there's something I wanted to talk to you all about," Brunson says as they all stare out at the water.

"Is it about my story?" Beth asks, her lips tight. "Because if it is, please let me say first that I'm sorry. I was hurt because of how you treated me last year, but that doesn't give me the right to hurt you back like that."

"Maybe you were right to do it," Brunson says. "I couldn't sleep all night thinking of how I treated you.

I deserve to feel guilty. I really fucked up. I'm so sorry, Beth."

"Thanks," Beth says. "But I still shouldn't have written that story. Douglas made that pretty clear."

"Okay, I get that, but please think about what I'm going to say, and don't reject it right away, because I've given it a lot of thought."

"What is it?" Ramin asks.

"You guys know I'm a peer counselor, right?" Brunson asks.

"Yeah," Spence says. "I did that when I was a fourth former. No one ever shows up."

"I know," Brunson says. "Except yesterday I had an afternoon shift. And for the very first time, a girl showed up. A third former."

They all wait for her to continue.

"She said she needed someone to talk to about what was happening in her dorm. She said a group of girls mock her because she's so tall. They call her the Jolly Green Giant and shit like that. They've even started leaving those Green Giant bags around to taunt her."

"What the hell is wrong with people?" Freddy asks.

"What's wrong is that no one suffers any consequences," Brunson says. "That's what I realized as this girl was opening up to me. Toby and Seb haven't faced any consequences for how they treat the fourth formers. Same with this girl's bullies. And same with me, by the way. I made Beth feel like shit, and I deserve some kind of penance."

"I mean, what you did is different than what Toby and Seb did," Beth says.

"That's not the point," Brunson says.

"Okay, so what's the point?" Spence asks, impatient.

"I think we should publish Ramin and Beth's story in the *Chandler Legacy*," Brunson says, taking the ridiculous white wig off to indicate how serious she is.

"Sorry, what?" Beth says. "No, it's a crazy idea. And why would you even want that story out there, when it makes you look like shit? You're the bully in my story."

"Yeah, and people should know what I did," Brunson says.

"Douglas wouldn't want us to do this," Ramin says firmly.

"Maybe she would if she knew how fucked it is here. About what really happens and how common it is. And the *Legacy* is our newspaper. And we publish the stupidest articles when we should be reporting about what actually matters."

Beth takes a deep breath. "But it's not your story to tell. It's mine, and Ramin's, and—"

"If that story is published," Freddy says, looking at Ramin, "then Seb and Toby will make Ramin's life hell."

Ramin gives him a grateful nod, then says, "Exactly. Not to mention that it would violate our Circle Honor Code."

"I know all that," Brunson says. "But *veritas vos liberabit.*"

"What?" Ramin asks.

"It's the school motto," Beth explains. "The truth will liberate us all."

"And it's about time we started living by it." Brunson speaks with a force that scares Freddy. He doesn't know where it comes from, but he knows it can't be directed only at Ramin's tormentors. "Bullies should feel the same pain they inflict." Brunson looks at Ramin when she says, "Every bully should. And that includes me."

"Okay," Beth says. "I get that you're sorry, but that doesn't change the fact that we can't publish that story."

"They'd never let us publish it anyway," Spence says. "I know Barman. She's not gonna put that in her paper."

"Who said we need to ask?" Brunson says. "I have the keys. I can sneak us in before it goes to print, and we could change the layout."

"Will it even make a difference?" Freddy asks. "In pole vaulting, there's so much fucked-up stuff behind the scenes. But it just happens, year after year. It never changes."

"And that's a reason not to speak up?" Brunson asks. "You guys, actions *must* have consequences."

Beth quietly says, "Look, if this is about your guilt or whatever, then let me make it clear that what you did is not the same as what those prefects did. There are levels of wrongness. I just want you to know that, okay?"

"I need to feel safe," Ramin says. "That's why I came here. To be safe. Not to be a hero."

"Did you write this story so it could stay in a vacuum?" Brunson asks. "So the same thing could happen to more kids?"

"I live in a country where being myself is punishable by death," Ramin says, a sudden anger in his voice. "You can make all your idealistic speeches about the truth liberating you, but if the truth gets you killed, then maybe a secret is safer."

"Tell them, Ramin," Freddy says. "About what happened back home."

Ramin tells the group everything. He tells them about the classmates who caught him and Arya, who then bullied and blackmailed them until Arya and his family escaped the country and Ramin found his own way out.

"Shit," Brunson says, her whole body seemingly deflating. "I didn't know."

"Now you do," Ramin says. "So can you—can we just . . . drop it?"

"Yeah," Brunson says. "I'm sorry. I get it. I'm so sorry."

They all stare out at the lake together. Freddy's thoughts feel as thick and muddy as that dark water. He looks over at Spence. They're sitting next to each other. Their hands are so close to each other that he can feel her pulse racing.

"Hey," Freddy says, suddenly filled with a desire to commemorate this moment. "Let's carve our names in that tree." He pulls a Swiss Army knife from his pocket.

"Um, against the rules," Brunson says when she sees the knife.

"We're at a lake after hours," Freddy says. "We've snuck out to a party. We left the rules behind a long time ago."

Freddy leaps up and carves his initials into the trunk of the tree. *FB*.

Beth gets up next. *BK*.

Then Brunson. *SB*.

Spence goes next. *AS*.

Then she hands the knife to Ramin, who stares at their initials for a beat, then carves his slowly into the trunk. *RG*.

Amanda Spencer

She knocks hard on Freddy's window early on Sunday morning, already looking forward to seeing what he looks like when he wakes up. But it's Charles who opens the window. "Uh, hi Spence," Charles says. Then, louder, he says, "Freddy, visitor!"

Freddy rubs his eyes. "What, who?" he mutters.

"Me!" Spence bellows through the window.

"Can't have girls in the dorm 'til visiting hours," Charles says jokingly. "But come on in, Miss Spencer."

"How about you tell Freddy to come on out?" she asks.

"Freddy, she wants you outside."

She watches as Freddy, wearing nothing but navy blue boxers, jumps off the top bunk and onto the floor. She can't help but notice every beautiful muscle in his body as he lands like an Olympian. Catching the perfect form, Spence laughs and says, "A ten from the New York City judge."

"Ha ha," Freddy says, throwing on shorts and a T-shirt. "I deduce from your outfit that we're going for a run?"

"If you can keep up," she says.

They start a brisk jog around campus. It's early, and very few people are out. In front of the Humanitas Building, Mr. Plain sleeps in his tent. Outside the Harbor Arts Center, the dance club practices a routine.

"So," she says, "I thought we could pick up where we left off last night."

"Where did we leave off again?" he asks.

"Neither of us planned on dating anyone this year," she says with a smile.

"Right," he says. "But plans change."

She laughs, then stops jogging. She leans against a birch tree. "The thing is," she says, "I've had three boyfriends, but I didn't really care about them."

"You just dated them to be nice?" he jokes.

But it doesn't sound like a joke to her. It sounds like a sliver of truth. "Honestly, kind of. I mean, yeah, I can be a people pleaser. I guess I stayed with each of them way too long because breaking up with them would've made me the bad guy."

"That doesn't sound fun," he says.

"It really wasn't. It was like I was waiting for each relationship to run its course, like a bad cold or something."

He laughs. "So the guys you dated were like viruses."

"Basically." She stares into his eyes when she says, "But you feel different."

He's looking into her eyes. She waits a beat before saying anything more, hoping he'll kiss her. But he doesn't.

"I'm glad you're here. You could've just like, been an Olympian. But you chose to come here."

"Yeah," he says. "I guess I wanted to learn more than how to throw myself into the air."

"Don't downplay it, though," she says. "You're exceptional. And you have a total lack of attitude about it. Most exceptional people remind you of how talented they are all the time."

"Maybe it's because I think about quitting," he says, his body tensing.

"Quit pole vaulting?" she asks.

"Yeah, maybe, I don't know," he says. He seems to deflate under the weight of this indecision.

"Does it make you happy?" she asks softly.

"It did," he says. "But then it didn't. I'm figuring it out."

"We can figure it out together," she says, unsure if they're talking about pole vaulting anymore.

She waits another few breaths. He raises an arm and leans on the trunk of the tree. And then he kisses her. They're not in a smelly garage this time. It's a perfect October day. The sun shines just for them. She can feel a gentle breeze.

When they finally pull away from each other, she says, "I think I know what a first kiss is supposed to feel like now."

"Ten from the New York City judge?" he asks with a smile.

She kisses him again. They stand against that birch tree, making out for at least a half hour, until kids start emerging from their dorms and the two of them become a public spectacle.

"Want to get breakfast before the Circle?" she asks.

They head to the dining hall together, holding hands. Spence leads the way to the muffin station. "Bud Simonsen always empties out the blueberry muffins when he gets here," she says, grabbing a whole tray of them. He tries to keep up with her as she fills her tray with multiple glasses of milk, a big plate of pineapple, and five bagels. He can already see their dynamic forming. Spence leading the way. Him close behind. He's okay with it. Loves it, in fact.

They sit in the senior section, where they're eventually joined by Henny Dover, Marianne Levinson, and Jennifer Rooney. "Thank God you got to the muffins before those beasts," Henny says, eyeing the table where Bud, Toby, Seb, and Charles have gathered.

Rooney pulls out a deck of cards with photos of Old Hollywood movie stars on them and shuffles them expertly.

"So," Marianne says, "you're joining us today, Freddy?"

"Yes, he is," Spence says before he can answer.

The girls play spades, Spence talking Freddy through the rules as they play. "So basically, your partner sits across from you, so me and Henny are partners," she says. "You have to play the suit that's led, but if you're out of it, then you can spade it and you win." She takes a bite of muffin, and she must have crumbs on her face because Freddy wipes off the left side of her mouth with a napkin.

"Aw," Henny says. "What a gentleman."

"I bid seven," Spence says.

"Seven alone?!" Marianne cries out. "I give up." Then, looking over at Freddy, she adds, "You've hitched your wagon to the luckiest girl I've ever met."

"I know I'm lucky," Spence whispers, looking at Freddy as she says it.

He smiles. "So am I."

"You two are disgusting," Henny says.

After she and Henny have completely humiliated Marianne and Rooney, Spence looks at the time on the ancient dining hall clock. "We need to go. Circle time. Here, you take over." She hands her cards to Whistler, who has joined their table.

"Bye, girls," Freddy says as Spence leads him away.

Before they're out of earshot, she can already hear the girls gossiping about them.

They head to MacMillan and find Beth, Brunson, and Ramin waiting outside Douglas's door when they get there. "What's going on?" Spence asks.

"She's not answering," Brunson says.

Finally, Douglas opens the door. She wears her leather jacket and holds a thermos. "Good morning," she says.

"Good morning," they all say in unison.

"I thought we could do something different today," Douglas says. "A change of scenery can be very inspiring for your writing. So, let's go for a walk."

Douglas leads the way out of MacMillan back into the fresh air.

"Observation is crucial for writers," Douglas says. "Knowing just the right details to share to take the reader into the world you're depicting is so important. That's another reason why I encourage you to keep those note-cards on you at all times. If you ever observe something you need to write about, jot it down so you don't forget it." She keeps walking as she talks. She stops outside the Humanitas Building. "Okay, each of you, tell me some-thing you observe."

"The autumn leaves are the school colors," Beth says.

"Oh wow, they are," Spence says. "Rust and gold. Nature has school spirit."

"Very good, Beth," Douglas says. "Anyone else?"

"Mr. Plain has a new pair of boots," Freddy says.

They all look over at the tent. Mr. Plain sits outside it, reading a hardcover copy of an FDR biography.

"Last week, he was wearing tan boots," Freddy says.

"The windows of the Humanitas need to be cleaned," Spence says.

"There's not a single cloud in the sky," Ramin says.

Brunson looks around for a moment before saying, "I can smell tonight's dinner coming from the dining hall. Chicken patties."

"We know what we'll be cleaning in the kitchen," Freddy says to Ramin, and they high-five.

"Very good," Douglas says. "Now imagine all those

observations in the opening paragraph of a story. They would give the reader an immediate sense of place, wouldn't they? Follow me."

Douglas leads them to the huge field outside the Beckett Science Center.

"I want each of you to find a spot that inspires you. Once you've found it, take your notebook out and write something about it. Make sure to include at least five specific observations to establish a sense of place. Beyond that, you can let your imagination run wild. I'll stop you in an hour."

They all disperse to different spots. Brunson sits on the bridge between the two wings of the science center. Freddy climbs a tree and dangles his feet from a heavy branch. Ramin lies down by the tiny creek under the bridge. And Beth walks farther away, to the outdoor statue of Galileo.

Spence can't decide where to sit or what to observe. "How's it going?" Douglas asks her.

"Oh, I don't know," Spence says. "It's just—I guess I'm mostly interested in writing about people. Like, dialogue. Descriptions and observation don't come naturally to me."

"Well, that's why you're here, isn't it? To learn the things that don't come easy."

"Yeah, you're right," she says. She's struck by an emotion she doesn't feel too often. Insecurity. "Professor Douglas?" she asks.

"Yes, Amanda?"

"I belong in this group, right? You didn't just let me in because Sullivan asked you to."

Douglas squints her eyes as she says, "Mr. Sullivan did what?"

"Asked you to let me in," Spence repeats. "Didn't he, um, put in a word for me?"

"He did no such thing," she says. "And he knows better than to try to influence my decisions."

She feels her heart beat fast. A big part of her feels proud of herself, for getting in without his recommendation. But an even bigger part feels betrayed by Sullivan, who promised he would help her. Why didn't he? Does he not believe in her? Or worse, does he not want her to focus her admiration on another professor?

"Wow," she says. "All this time, I thought you let me in because he asked you to."

Douglas is steely when she says, "How about I agree to never underestimate you? And you never underestimate me?"

"Deal," she says, still processing this new piece of information.

"Good. Then go write."

Spence walks past the science center, up toward the language lab. There's a bench there with her grandfather's name on it. She always has a flash of him when she passes the bench, but she's never *really* thought about him. Until now. Mostly she's thinking about how different the experiences of her two sets of grandparents were.

She writes furiously about her ancestors. On her dad's

side, a long line of wealth and privilege. On her mom's side, grandparents who were part of the first wave of immigrants to leave India for the United States in the 1960s. Doctors who worked their way from Delhi to Jackson Heights to Long Island, and who battled their daughter as she defied them by becoming a model. And now there's Spence, who dreams of breaking barriers like her mom did, but who knows the odds are stacked against her unless she leaves this country. Her mom told her once that instead of feeling like she paved the way for more Indian models, she sometimes feels the opposite. "I know the fashion industry. They feel like one Indian model is enough," she told Spence with a sigh. "I sometimes worry I haven't opened doors for girls like me; I've closed them even tighter." Spence hates that her mom feels this way, when she's not the one closing those doors. But as she writes, she realizes that what her mom told her and what Amira said about Sullivan are versions of the same thing. Is the reason Sullivan didn't cast Amira because one Indian actor was enough for him? She writes about the future she wants to be a part of. A world where there can be more than one Indian model, one Indian story, one student of color cast in the school play.

The hour goes by quickly. At the end of the session, Douglas hands her short story back to her. Then she hands short stories back to Freddy and Brunson. "We won't be reading these out loud," she says. "But they were very good."

Douglas has scrawled notes in the margins. Quick

thoughts like *Necessary?* and *Repetition* and *Perceptive* and *Show don't tell* and *Fascinating, tell us more.*

Douglas zips up her leather jacket. "For next week, I'd like you to attempt poetry," she says. "Write a poem inspired by what you just observed. I'll see you then."

The group lingers for a while when Douglas leaves. "Lunch?" Spence asks.

"Sure," Beth says. "I'm always hungry."

"Yeah, me too," Brunson says. Is she imagining it, or do Beth and Brunson actually seem to be getting along better now? Well, maybe the truth really did set them free.

As they all head to lunch, Spence goes to hold Freddy's hand, and he hesitates. She eyes him, confused. "What?" she whispers.

"No, it's just, we should tell them, so it's not weird." He's looking at Ramin when he says this.

"Yeah, you're right," she says. Then, turning to the group, she says, "Hey, guys, there's something Freddy and I have to tell you."

"You're married!" Beth says.

"You're having twins!" Brunson adds.

"You took a DNA test and you're cousins!" Beth says.

"Ew, no, you can stop there," Spence says, laughing. "We're just . . . you know . . ."

"We haven't really defined things," Freddy says. "But we're together, and we didn't want you to think we were hiding anything from you, so . . ."

"Well, you guys are an annoyingly perfect couple," Beth says.

"Obscenely perfect, it's gross," Brunson adds, and Beth laughs.

Spence feels herself tense up as she says, "Look, I know you guys are joking, but can we not? Because I don't want to be perfect anymore. I want to be . . . I don't know, real."

Freddy takes her hand and squeezes it. "Hey, you never need to be perfect with me," he says softly.

"Or with us," Brunson adds.

Spence feels shy all of a sudden. But she's glad she said something.

Finally, as they get to the steps of the dining hall, Ramin says, "I'm happy for you guys."

Spence feels light that day. After lunch, they all go back to Livingston to pick up her camcorder. They take it to the lake and film themselves dancing and singing and being goofballs. It's not until Mrs. Plain tells the Livingston girls that it's time for lights-out that she even remembers how mad she is at Sullivan. Why didn't he put in a word for her like he promised?

"How does Miller achieve the surreal tone of the play?" Sullivan asks the student scenes class later that week.

"Well," Dallas Thompson says, "the whole play takes place in his brain."

"His brain?" Sullivan asks.

"You know, the protagonist's brain. But, uh . . . it's him, right?" Dallas stammers.

"Yes, it's him," Spence snaps. "The whole play is just

a thinly veiled account of his marriage to Marilyn Monroe. Why are we even reading it?"

Sullivan squints, surprised by her attitude. "We're reading it because Arthur Miller is one of our great voices of the theater, and—"

"Okay, but who decided that?" Spence asks. "Why him? Why not . . ." She remembers Brunson picking at the student scenes syllabus, and says, "Why not Lorraine Hansberry or Lillian Hellman or—"

"Spence, let's not get carried away," he says, and she flinches a little at the use of her nickname. Kids call her "Spence." Teachers call her "Amanda."

She laughs. "Let's not get too *carried away* about theater? An art form that requires nothing but passion?"

"Touché," he says. "But can we get back to the play now?"

"But I *am* talking about the play. Marilyn had just died when the play premiered. She'll never get to tell her side of the story. It just sucks that he wrote this play that portrays her in such a gross way." She doesn't know where all this rage is coming from. Is she really this angry about Sullivan not recommending her to Douglas? Or maybe she just identifies with Marilyn after spending the summer studying where she studied?

Sullivan addresses the whole class when he says, "Every writer is bound to be inspired by the people in their lives. In general, those people won't get to tell their side of the story. Maybe it's because they're dead, or maybe it's because they're not writers themselves. But if we don't write because we're not allowed to tell stories about our ex-wives or our parents or our friends, then there would be no plays in the world. No books. No movies."

"I—I mean . . ." She wants to say something, but she's not sure how to phrase it. She wants to say that there's a respectful way to write, and a shitty way to write. But she doesn't say anything. She feels checkmated by him, and she can already feel the rest of the class nodding in agreement with him.

"Okay," he says. "Let's get back to the structure of the play. What do you think about Miller's use of nonlinear storytelling?"

The rest of October feels nonlinear to her. She falls deeper into her relationship with Freddy. The Circle has more and more fun together. She discovers poetry is definitely *not* her medium when she hands in a silly nursery rhyme to Douglas. She feels her anger with Sullivan grow and grow.

One afternoon, when *Angels in America* rehearsals have ended, Sullivan stops her before she leaves. "Spence, can you stay behind please?" he asks.

She doesn't say anything. She just throws her bag over her shoulder and stares at him.

"It's almost Halloween," he says.

"Oh yeah," she says. Last year, she asked Sullivan if she could raid the costume closet for Halloween, and he said yes.

"You want the keys to the costume closet again?" he asks.

She thinks about how fun it would be to dress Freddy up in some ridiculous Elizabethan outfit. How cute would his Olympic legs look in tights? "Yeah, thanks," she says.

"Spence, is everything okay?" he asks. "You've been . . . testy lately."

She feels herself bristle. She's held on to this secret for almost two weeks now. It's time for her to just ask him. "I'm sorry," she says. "It's just . . . I know that you didn't put a word in for me with Professor Douglas. And it's not that big a deal because I got into the Circle anyway, but it's like . . . why did you lie to me? Did you not want me to be distracted, or were you just humoring me, or—"

"No and no," he says. "The truth is often much simpler than we think."

"Okay, what's the truth?" she asks.

He gets closer to her. "The truth is that I had every intention of putting a word in for you. But one of my fellow faculty members let me know that Professor Douglas doesn't take kindly to anyone intervening in her selection process."

"Oh," she says, feeling silly.

"I thought that if I put a word in, it might backfire," he says. "And I knew you didn't need my help anyway."

She pulls her ponytail tighter. "Well, now I feel like a jerk," she says. "I'm sorry."

"Apology accepted," he says.

"I really am sorry," she says.

"Spence, it's water under the bridge." He holds his

hand out to her, and she shakes it. Then he pulls her into a hug, which makes her feel weird. "Come here," he says, pulling her so close that she can smell his aftershave. She pushes him gently away. "You know where the keys will be on Halloween. Just return everything the next morning."

"Thanks," she says. "I really appreciate . . . every-thing."

Halloween is a very big deal at Chandler. Big enough that Douglas cancels the Circle that Sunday morning to give them time to focus on their costumes for the annual Festival of Frights, a dance and costume contest that the whole school *really* gets into, even the faculty. Last year, Headmaster Berg dressed up as Napoleon, Madame Ardant was Édith Piaf, and Mr. and Mrs. Plain were the couple from the American Gothic painting. Even Doug-las dresses up. She was Gertrude Stein last year. But a student wins every year, and the bragging rights go a long way. Last year's winner was Henny Dover, who somehow dressed up as Bill Clinton on her left side, and Hillary Clinton on her right side. It was a feat of makeup and costuming.

"Where are you taking us?" Brunson asks on Hallow-een afternoon.

"You'll see, it's a surprise!" Spence says, so excited to show the Circle what they all have access to.

She leads them into the Harbor Arts Center, past all the framed programs of old Chandler shows, and toward the costume closet. From behind the framed program for a 1989 production of *Cat on a Hot Tin Roof*, she pulls a key. And then she opens the costume closet for them.

"I don't know if this is a good idea," Brunson says, hesitant.

"We're not breaking any rules or anything," Spence assures her.

"Oh wow," Beth says, entering the closet with wide eyes.

"We can take anything we want?" Ramin asks.

"Well, we can *borrow* anything we want," Spence says. "We have to return it in the morning."

Beth picks up an ornate black-and-white dress that was used in the ascot gavotte in *My Fair Lady*. "Um, this is incredible."

Spence throws an *Into the Woods* Little Red Riding Hood cape around her body. "Right? Sullivan's the best."

"I'm glad you think so," Sullivan says. Spence looks up and there's Sullivan, standing at the door of the costume closet with a smile.

"Hi!" Spence says. "We just got here, but thank you again. We all appreciate it so much."

"You're all very welcome," he says.

"I have to introduce you to my friends," she says. "This is the amazing Circle. Obviously you know Freddy, since he lives in your dorm. And this is Ramin, and Beth, and Brunson."

They all wave, except for Brunson, who says, "We've met."

"Have we? I don't remember," Sullivan says.

"I auditioned for *A Chorus Line*," Brunson reminds him.

"So many students audition for the spring musical," Sullivan says. "I hope you audition again this year."

"I doubt that'll happen," Brunson says coldly. "I can't even sing."

"Well, there's always the winter play," Sullivan says. "Wait until you see your friend Spence in *Angels in America*. She's going to blow you away in a dual role."

"I don't doubt that," Freddy says, pulling her close to him proudly.

"Yeah, I don't think theater's my thing anymore," Brunson says.

"Theater's not for everybody," Sullivan says. "But that's what's so wonderful about Chandler, isn't it? You kids can try everything and see what excites you."

"Exactly!" Spence says.

"Well, have fun finding your costumes," Sullivan says. "I was thinking of dressing up as Che Guevara this year. What do you think? Can I pull it off?"

Spence looks to Freddy, who calmly says, "I think it might be a good idea to pick someone else."

Sullivan shrugs. "You're probably right. Okay, have fun."

"Thanks again," she says as Sullivan leaves.

When he's gone, Spence takes the red cape off, and scours the racks and bins for something *incredible*.

"You guys," Brunson says. "I—I'm sorry. I just

remembered that my mom's supposed to call me in ten minutes. I'll catch up with you at the Festival of Frights, okay?"

Brunson doesn't look at them as she hurries away.

"What just happened?" Spence asks.

"I don't know," Ramin says.

Spence turns to Beth. "You lived with her. What was that?"

"I have no idea," Beth says. "But we should go see if she's okay, right?"

Spence leads the way out of the building. By the time they're outside, Brunson is long gone. Whistler and Connor Emerson, barely recognizable as early-'90s Courtney Love and Kurt Cobain, stop them.

"And the sky was made of amethyst," Whistler screams in Spence's face.

"Oh, hey, Whistler," Spence says, annoyed by the interruption. Turning back to the group, she asks, "Where would she go?"

"She lives at Mrs. Song's," Beth says. "We could start there."

They start walking toward Mrs. Song's residence, when Freddy suddenly says, "Wait, you guys. I know exactly where she would go."

And then it hits Spence. Of course. The lake.

Sarah Brunson

Brunson takes a deep breath, trying desperately to calm herself. She somehow held it together through Sullivan telling her the best thing about Chandler is being able to try what *excites* her.

Once she's outside the Harbor Arts Center, she starts to feel nausea take over her body. The same nausea she felt that night last year. Fuck, she thought she had put it behind her, but now it all comes flooding back.

Whistler and Connor Emerson come down the arts center steps, singing "Come As You Are." She rushes away to avoid them. The last thing she wants is casual conversation right now.

She heads toward Mrs. Song's residence, desperate for a quiet place to vomit. But on her way, she runs right into Laurie Lamott, dressed up as Monica Lewinsky. "Hey, Brunson!" she says. "Where's your costume?"

"I, um—I'm just heading to change."

Brunson feels like the rest of her walk is an obstacle course. The challenge is to avoid all the costumed Chandies and all the awkward conversations. She bolts when she sees Barman dressed up as Father Close, and looks away when she sees Jane King and Rachel Katz strolling hand in hand, dressed up as those creepy little girls from *The Shining*. Children are the one consistently beautiful, innocent, joyful thing in Brunson's life. Why did someone have to go and make them creepy?

But the worst figures on her obstacle course are the endless sea of male Chandies dressed up like Brandon Lee in *The Crow*. A sea of boys in black, wearing creepy makeup. It looks exactly like what it's meant to, a horror movie.

And that's when she turns the other way. She knows a place she can go where she won't run into anyone. But before she gets there, she runs right into Amira and Lashawn, almost knocking them both down. They're dressed as Zubin Mehta and RuPaul.

"Are you okay?" Amira asks.

"I—yeah, I'm fine." The nausea is growing inside her. Her eyes feel hot and angry. She runs away from them, thinking of the years she spent holding her mom as she vomited, cleaning up after her. She suddenly realizes those were the best years of her life so far. She felt needed. She had purpose. And she was distracted from examining herself too closely. She sits down and takes a deep breath when she finally gets to the lake.

"Brunson!" She hears Spence call her name urgently.

She looks up, and there they are. The Circle. Somehow in her mad dash to escape all the Chandies on campus, she forgot that the Circle could find her here.

"I'm sorry," she says. "Go to the festival. Please. Have fun."

Spence crouches down by her side. "Are you okay? What happened?"

Beth sits on the other side of her. "You can tell us anything," she says.

She shifts her gaze from Spence to Beth, and she can't help but laugh.

"What's so funny?" Beth asks.

"Nothing," she says. "Except that you"—she points to Spence—"probably know exactly why I ran away from him."

"I have no idea what you're talking about," Spence says.

"And you"—she points to Beth—"did nothing to help me last year."

"Help you how?" Beth asks. "When?"

Ramin and Freddy sit facing her. "Brunson, it's us," Ramin says.

She wants to tell them. But where does she start? Does she just tell them about that one night? Because that wouldn't capture it. Chandler was supposed to be the place that took care of her. She came here after years of being the caretaker of her family, never knowing what it's like to feel the carefree safety of being a kid, of life being nothing but possibility. That's what she thought this place was, and he robbed her of that experience.

"I was so happy when people here started calling me 'Brunson,'" she says quietly. "It was like a whole new identity. Sarah was sad all the time and took care of everyone, but Brunson . . . Brunson would focus on herself. She'd do it all. Try everything. The school paper and peer counseling and the student judiciary and . . . well, theater." She looks at Spence when she says, "I can't sing, but I love theater. Especially musicals."

"Okay," Spence says.

"I auditioned for *A Chorus Line*. I did a monologue from *Streetcar*, and I sang an off-key verse from 'At the Ballet.'" I told Mr. Sullivan that I knew my singing sucked, but that I could be one of the dancers who can't sing and gets cut from the show. And he told me he wanted to speak to me in private about my potential."

"Fuck," Freddy says, his eyes fixed on Spence.

"Why are you looking at me?" Spence asks before adding, "Go on, Brunson."

"Well, I was a third former," she says. "I was a kid. I mean, I'm still a kid, but—anyway, the point is I went to Holmby House like he asked. It definitely felt weird, but I told myself it was normal. It wasn't any different than being in a meeting with a teacher in their office, or with a dean. Then he leaned in and . . ." She stops herself, the memories too painful.

"Oh no," Beth says.

"I wish I'd left, but I never thought anything would happen. Maybe I figured casting couches were a thing in

Hollywood, but not in fucking high school."

Again, Freddy looks at Spence, and she says, "What, Freddy, what?" He doesn't even need to say a word for Spence to snap. "This never happened to me, okay."

"I'm sorry," Freddy says. "I wasn't accusing. I just . . ."

Spence softens. "It's okay. Can we just . . . focus on Brunson right now?"

"I guess he also made me feel special," Brunson says. "Like, he told me that to be a great actress, you needed to excavate your personal life. And for some reason, I told him all about my mom and . . . well, I don't know. It feels good to have a grown-up listen to you that way."

She waits for someone to say something. Finally, Beth asks, "What about your mom?"

Brunson shakes her head in disbelief that she still hasn't told them about her mom. "Oh, my mom had cancer," she explains. "For a long time." Her voice cracks when she looks into Beth's eyes. "And those hairs all over our room last year . . . well, they just reminded me of her and her hair loss."

"Oh God, why didn't you tell me?" Beth asks sadly.

Brunson's eyes are fixed on Beth, but before she can answer, Spence says, "What about Sullivan? What did he do next?"

She sighs. She looks down as she says, "At some point, he moved closer to me. He only has one couch in his living room—"

"God, that's true." Spence has a look of disgust on her face.

"I was sitting at one end of it, but the more we spoke, the closer he got. And he . . ." She feels shame coursing through her veins.

"That fucking piece of shit," Freddy spits out.

"You don't have to finish if you don't want to," Ramin tells her gently.

"I want to," she says with sudden certainty. "Now that I've started, I have to finish. I have to just, get this all out."

"Take your time," Beth says.

She looks into Beth's eyes. Where was *this* Beth last year? What would have happened if they had opened up to each other sooner?

"He kissed me," she says. "He—I—well, I was in shock, and I think I didn't move at first. I just sat there and let it happen."

"You didn't *let* anything happen," Freddy says. "You were violated."

"Yeah," she says. "I guess I figured that out when he put his hands up my skirt and . . ."

Spence puts her face in her hands. "My God."

"And that's when I ran," she says.

"Back to our room?" Beth asks.

"Not yet," she says. "I ran to the woods. I just wanted to disappear. But even the woods were full of kids. I ran right into a group of sixth formers smoking, and even though I promised myself never to smoke *anything* because of my mom, I took the cigarette and smoked it. And it made me feel even worse. Like, sick and dizzy and well, like I'd just betrayed my mom. And that's when

I ran to our room." She turns to Beth. "And you were there. You had your headphones on. I tried to talk to you, but you wouldn't even look at me."

"I—I'm so sorry," Beth says. "I felt like an impostor in that dorm. I just wanted to drown it all out."

"Yeah," Brunson says. "Well, you definitely drowned me out. I kept trying to talk to you, and you just . . . didn't want to."

"I don't remember," Beth says. "And I could never have known—I mean, you were friends with all the girls in the dorm. I would never have thought you needed me . . ."

"It doesn't matter anymore," Brunson says. "I know you weren't trying to hurt me, and I hope you know I was never trying to hurt you last year. I was just, I don't know, trying to fit in. Make friends."

"Brunson," Beth whispers, "I was your roommate. I should've noticed you were . . ." Beth puts an awkward hand on her shoulder, and Brunson flinches at the unexpected touch. "I should've known something was going on with you."

"You couldn't have known," she says. "I never let you in. I didn't even tell you about my mom. I just—I didn't want to talk to anyone about her sickness. I came here to escape all that."

"Still . . ." Beth bites her lip.

"Anyway, why would you ask me anything when I was a total asshole to you all year?" She lets out a throaty laugh when she says this. "I can see that now."

"Well, I'm sorry," Beth says.

"I am too, Beth. I feel sick about how I made you feel. Whatever pain I was in was no excuse for making you feel like shit about yourself. And Ramin, when I read your story . . . I knew exactly how you felt."

"Is that why you wanted to publish the story?" Ramin asks.

She thinks about this. "Maybe," she says. "Maybe I wasn't ready to take on Sullivan yet, and I thought taking on your prefects was a start to changing things at Chandler. I don't know . . ."

"I can't believe all this," Spence says.

"Wait, you don't believe me?" Brunson asks.

"No, that's not what I said. Of course I believe you."

She realizes how scared she was to say all this to Spence, who seems too close to Sullivan.

"What I mean is . . ." Spence takes a breath. She holds Freddy's hand for comfort. "I guess I'm surprised, because he's never crossed a line with me. I mean, he's hugged me, and he's touched me during rehearsals but only when he's trying to show me some movement for a scene or—"

"Isn't a teacher hugging you and touching you crossing a line?" Freddy asks.

Spence nods slowly. "I guess it is."

"He can't stay here," Freddy says. "If he did this to you, he'll do this to other girls. We can't let that happen."

"Freddy's right," Beth says.

"Oh sure, because me saying he kissed and groped me is going to make a difference," Brunson says bitterly.

"Please. I even wrote a letter to the headmaster about it over the summer."

"You did?" Spence sounds stunned. "Did you send it?"

Brunson shakes her head. "No. I burned it. One fourth former's word won't mean anything. I know that."

"Maybe we should ask Douglas what to do?" Beth suggests.

"No," Brunson says. "She'll feel she has to say something."

"But maybe if it comes from her—" Beth tries to convince Brunson.

"It doesn't matter. It's my word against his."

"But we can't—" Spence says.

Brunson cuts her off. "Please. Drop it. If I accuse him, *nothing* will happen to him. That's how the world works. I'll be the one who's humiliated, and he'll just go on teaching."

"You're right," Ramin says. "This is why I didn't want to publish the story about my prefects."

"I get that now," Brunson says. "I don't know what I was thinking. You were right, Ramin. We can't change the system. The only thing we can do is get through this, and at least I have you guys to talk to now."

They sit in silence, staring out at the lake, like they're waiting for it to show them a different path forward.

Ramin Golafshar

"Hey, what're you doing, kid?" the kitchen manager yells.

Ramin looks down. He's tossing the dirty forks into the bins the dirty knives go into.

"There's a system. You screw up the system and everything breaks down."

"Sorry, I'm tired," he says.

"What do you kids have to be tired about?" he huffs as he walks away.

Freddy, who does his kitchen duty just a few feet away from Ramin, looks over at him. "You okay?"

"Yeah," Ramin says. "I just couldn't sleep. I kept thinking about Brunson."

"Same," Freddy says.

"Is there anything we can do to help her?" Ramin asks.

"I don't know." Freddy wipes chunks of cereal out of

bowls and into a large trash can. "I guess just support her."

"Yeah." Ramin watches the conveyor belt take the bins of dirty plates, bowls, and utensils away. He closes his eyes and wishes they could find a way to put every bully and every abusive teacher on a conveyor belt that would make them disappear.

The whole dining hall is abuzz when he and Freddy make their way out of it. Breakfast smells so much better when it's being eaten than when it's being cleaned up. The scent of maple syrup and baked goods fills the cavernous wooden room, as do hushed gossiping voices.

"I can't fucking believe it," Jane King says to a group of girls. "It's over. It's all over." Ramin gulps down hard. What's over?

At a table in the senior section, Henny Dover says a boisterous "Pay up!" to Marianne Levinson.

"How much did we bet again?" Marianne asks.

"Twenty big ones," Henny says. "You said he'd move back home during Thanksgiving break, and I said November first. To the day."

"Okay, I'll pay you when I have cash," Marianne says. "Or I'll get you a feast at the Tuck Shop."

Connor Emerson stops Ramin and Freddy before they can exit. "Did you guys hear?" he asks.

Ramin feels his throat tighten. He wonders if Brunson said something after all.

"Uh, hear what?" Freddy asks.

"Mr. Plain's homeless days are over. He's packing up his tent and moving back into Livingston."

"Oh," Freddy says, eyeing Ramin. "That's big news."

Henny Dover, still gloating over winning a bet, dances on top of a chair now. "I predicted it to the fucking day, suckers." In the frenzy of her victory dance, she knocks the bag resting on the side of her chair over, dumping its contents on the floor.

"Oh come on!" Toby says.

Ramin looks behind him, and there they are. Toby and Seb, entering the dining hall with Charles Cox and Bud Simonsen. Toby leaps down to pick up the items that spilled out of Henny's purse. "Here, let me help you, Henny," he says. It's the most chivalrous Ramin has ever seen him be. Until he grabs a few tampons, and pretends to smoke one of them. "What a full-bodied cigar," Toby says. "Feels very heavy in my mouth. Must have a heavy flow."

"Shut up, Toby," Henny says. But she laughs as she says it.

Toby tosses a tampon to Bud, who dangles it from his ear. "Hey, what do you guys think of my earring?"

"What do they say about guys with earrings again?" Seb asks, swatting Bud. Then Seb puts two tampons on his head like antennae. "E.T. phone home," he says in a robotic voice.

Toby tosses a tampon to Freddy, who catches it and immediately hands it back to Henny. "I'm sorry for these clowns," he says. He says nothing to the guys as he leaves the dining hall.

Ramin follows after Freddy. He says goodbye to him outside the dining hall and heads to class.

His first class is the Hero Archetype in the Humanitas Building. A crowd has gathered outside, watching Mrs. Plain help Mr. Plain pack up the tent. She carefully folds the sheets he had inside and places the Tupperware containers in a paper grocery bag.

Mr. Plain looks up at the crowd of students. "Okay, you can all go to class now. I hope you learned something about how lucky you all are."

Ramin enters the Humanitas. Outside his classroom is a printed quote that wasn't there last time: "A poor surgeon hurts one person at a time. A poor teacher hurts 130." It's attributed to someone named Ernest Boyer.

"Why a hundred and thirty kids?" Sarah Sumner asks Jane King as they file into class.

"Maybe the teacher in the quote only teaches lecture classes with a hundred and thirty students," Jane says. "I don't know."

As Ramin sits in the back of the class, he wonders how many kids Sullivan has hurt. Is it just Brunson? Is it 130 kids? He listens as all the fourth formers discuss Mr. and Mrs. Plain. "You know what I think," Benji says. "I think Mr. Plain did it just to get away from his wife." That gets a big laugh.

At lunch, Ramin finds the Circle sitting in the back corner of the dining hall and joins them. "Hey."

"Where's your tray?" Beth asks.

"I'm not hungry," he says.

"We had kitchen duty this morning," Freddy explains. "Kind of takes your appetite away."

But it's not just that. Something changed in him last night. It was one thing to know that students bully each other. Knowing teachers are abusing students, too, fills him with a new kind of dread and rage. But he doesn't say any of this. He doesn't feel it's his place to make Brunson relive any of it.

There's still a whole afternoon of classes to attend, but he skips them all. The Wilton Blue Basement is empty when he gets there. The smell of the place fills him with fear.

He closes his door and takes out one of his poetry books. He lies down on his bed, tracing Arya's handwriting. He remembers their last conversation. Ramin begged him not to leave. Arya said it wasn't his choice anymore. His parents had decided they were moving to Turkey. What was he going to do, live in Tehran alone? But that didn't stop Ramin from begging and pleading and crying. He made crazy suggestions. He said they could run away together to France. He said they could apply for asylum because they're gay. He said they could change their identities. But none of it convinced Arya, who knew how to accept defeat better than Ramin. The last thing Arya said was, "I think it'll be easier on both of us if we don't talk again."

There's a knock on the door. Ramin holds his breath, expecting one of those awful prefects.

"It's me," Hiro says from the other side of the door.

"Come in," he says.

Hiro walks in, holding a backpack. "Why weren't you in biology class?"

"Stomachache," Ramin says. Not a total lie. His stomach has been in knots all day.

"Pasur?" Hiro asks.

Ramin nods. He's grateful for the distraction of the card game.

"Did you ever make forts when you were a kid?" Hiro asks.

"No," Ramin says.

"Hold on." Hiro grabs the bedsheet and blanket off Ramin's bed, and throws them over the two of them. There's just enough light seeping through for them to still see the cards. "This is what my sister and I used to do. Hide ourselves under sheets and pillows and blankets so no one could find us."

They play for hours. The safety of their fort is suddenly invaded by the sound of a struggle outside. "I think that's Benji screaming," Ramin says.

"Fuck" is all Hiro says as he throws the sheet and blanket off them, revealing the harsh light.

They run to the common area, where Seb and Toby are viciously tying Benji up with the cord of the vacuum cleaner as the other boys watch, some terrified, some gleeful.

"This'll teach you to clean up after yourself in the common area," Seb says.

"Okay, I've learned my lesson," Benji croaks out.

"Do you think he's learned his lesson?" Toby asks Seb.

"I don't know. Maybe we should give him a pop quiz." Seb pulls the cord tighter around Benji's waist,

236

then moves it up to his chest.

"Question number one," Toby says in a bad British accent. "What do you do when you leave bread crumbs all over the floor?"

"You clean it up," Benji says.

"With what?" Seb asks.

Benji grunts as they both yank the cord tighter. "With the vacuum cleaner. I get it."

"Question number two," Toby continues. "What happens to fourth formers who leave a mess?" Before Benji can answer, Toby turns the vacuum cleaner on. He pulls the circular wand of the cleaner up and presses it to Benji's cheek so it sucks up his skin, making him look like he's in a fun-house mirror. Seb and Toby seem to find this especially funny.

"You look like a Garbage Pail Kid," Seb says, laughing. "Quick, someone take a picture."

"Like we'll ever be able to forget any of this," Ramin whispers to Hiro.

"What was that, Ramoon?" Toby asks.

"Nothing." Ramin's voice is barely audible over the vacuum.

"His name is Ramin," Hiro says, coming to his defense. "And you guys have made your point."

Inspired by Hiro's bravery, Ramin manages to say, "You guys are supposed to be protecting us."

Seb laughs. "Who told you that? We're not here to protect you. We're here to *prepare* you. For the fucked-up world. You think this is a five-star hotel?

You think we're your concierges?"

"No." Ramin's face feels flush. His palms are sweaty.

From the end of the hallway comes the sound of Mr. Court's door closing. In a flash, Seb and Toby turn the vacuum cleaner off and unwrap Benji. "What's going on out here?" Mr. Court asks, oblivious.

Ramin looks to Benji. To his surprise, Benji leaps up and says, "Nothing. I was just cleaning up the common area."

"Good boy," Mr. Court says. "Be sure to get the corners."

Benji turns the vacuum on, dutifully cleaning as the rest of the boys file out.

"You wanna go for a walk?" Ramin asks Hiro.

They walk the perimeter of Upper Campus, breathing in the air, enjoying the silence.

"How do you handle it so well?" Ramin asks Hiro.

"Who said I handle it well?" Hiro asks.

"You definitely handle it better than I do."

Hiro shrugs. "I guess I've learned how to fake it so I don't give them the satisfaction. I don't know if that means I handle things well, or if it means I'm just bottling everything up. That's what Sabrina says. That expressing all my emotions is the only way to be truly happy."

"Yeah, well, you *seem* happy, which has to count for something."

"It does." Hiro smiles. "I'm not gonna let a bunch of insecure bullies rob me of all the good things in my life. Like Sabrina. And my friends. The things I can control, you know. It's not that those assholes don't bother me. It's just, well, I guess I know I can't change them."

"Maybe you're right," Ramin says. "But what if we change the whole culture of the place?"

Hiro smiles. "Isn't that what we're doing by being good to each other? The more of us there are, the faster this place changes."

"Yeah," Ramin says. But he wants it all to change faster.

They get back to the dorm for lights-out. When Ramin enters his room, he finds his bedsheets, usually a crumpled mess, are carefully folded. Atop his crisp pillow is a Kit Kat bar and a few rose petals.

"What is this?" Ramin asks Benji, who's casually reading on the top bunk, his legs dangling below the mattress.

"Toby and Seb," Benji says.

On cue, Toby and Seb appear in the doorway. "Mr. Golafshar, welcome to the Wilton Blue Intercontinental," Toby says. "We are your concierges. So nice to see you've made it back to your room. Before we go to bed, we just wanted to make sure everything is amenable to your specifications."

"If you have any problems or desires, you let us know." The glare in Seb's eyes sends a chill down Ramin's spine. "Room service in the morning, maybe? A bubble bath? Anything for our Persian prince."

"Just leave," Ramin whispers.

"Right away, Your Royal Highness," Seb says.

Toby and Seb both curtsy in front of Ramin before leaving. Ramin looks at Benji and says, "That was strange."

"Yeah, well, at least they didn't vacuum your face," Benji says with a laugh.

"You okay?" Ramin asks.

"Me?" Benji seems surprised by the question. "Yeah. I mean, it was just my turn. Oh, here's your book back." It's not until Benji hands him the book he was reading that Ramin realizes it was his Hafiz poetry book. He feels a brief panic at the thought of Benji reading Arya's love notes, but Benji doesn't seem any different.

That night, he lies in bed, staring up at the coils of Benji's bunk. Benji, usually the soundest sleeper, tosses and turns. Maybe he's not doing okay, but just doesn't feel like he can say anything. Then, he hears Benji's voice from the top bunk.

"So did you have a boyfriend back in Iran?" Benji asks.

"Oh," Ramin says. "I—yeah."

"Sorry, I shouldn't have read your book. I just was curious about the poetry. I wasn't expecting to find . . . you know . . ."

"Does it bother you?" Ramin feels his throat tighten. He's so angry with himself for caring what Benji thinks.

"No, I mean, yeah, I mean . . ." The coils under Benji's mattress squeak. "I guess it would've been nice to know my roommate was into dudes. Just so, you know, I knew, that's all. But it's not like I have a problem with gay people or queers or LGBT, I don't really know what you like to be called."

"I don't either," Ramin says. "There isn't even a word for us in Iran, so any word is, you know, an improvement, I guess."

"Are you into anyone in the dorm?" Benji asks.

"Into?"

"You know, like, do you dig any of the guys in the—"

"No," Ramin says. He knows what Benji really wants is reassurance that Ramin isn't attracted to him, so he adds, "Definitely not."

"Okay, cool," Benji says. "Hey, do you think Father Close is gay?"

"I don't know," he says. "It's not like we can all recognize each other or anything."

"I swear I heard someone say you can. It has a whole name and everything. Anyway . . ."

He waits for Benji to say more, but he doesn't. Not even good night.

Ramin closes his eyes and wills himself to sleep.

"Gaydar," Benji blurts out, long after Ramin thought he had fallen asleep. "It was *killing* me. That's the name of that thing where one gay person can recognize another. You'll probably develop it. Like a dormant superpower."

Ramin doesn't say anything. He just pretends he's sleeping as he thinks about all the dormant superpowers he wishes he could develop.

Amanda Spencer

"This is Amanda Priya Spencer reporting from my room in Livingston," she whispers, knowing her voice will be booming when she plays the video back someday. "I'm here with Freddy Bello, who looks so fucking cute when he wakes up. So let's wake him up. Freddy?"

She puts her bare foot into the frame of her camcorder, gently tickling Freddy's neck with her toes. He laughs. "Stop," he says. Then, seeing the camera, he says, "Oh come on. What are you doing?"

"I need to remember what you look like in the morning," she says.

"Why?" he asks. "I'm not going anywhere."

"We're all going somewhere," she says. Putting on a world-weary voice, she says, "We get older every day. This is the last time we'll be *this* version of us."

He picks up a pillow and swats the camera with it. "Drama queen," he says.

"And proud of it," she says, refocusing on him. "Now shut up and let me film you. The Diwali lighting is perfect."

"You promised me sweets in bed," he says, smiling.

She tosses him the box of sweets her mom sent for Diwali, and films him as he takes his first bite of jalebi.

"Fuck, that's good."

"Try the round coconut balls. They're my favorite sweet," she says.

"I thought I was your favorite." His smile makes her want to drop the camera and leap into his arms. But she keeps filming him, desperate to capture this perfect moment, and fully aware that the camera can only capture so much. Yes, his beauty will be preserved, but what about how her body seems to change temperature everywhere he touches her?

"We have to go to MacMillan," he says, looking at her bedside alarm clock.

"Before we go, can you get in that position you sleep in?" she asks.

"I don't know how I sleep," he says.

"Your body curls in on itself," she says.

He closes his eyes. Pretends to snore. She laughs and kicks him with her right foot.

"Not like that," she says. "When you sleep, your body makes the shape of a question mark. I want that on film."

"A question mark sounds about right." He laughs. "I never thought about it, but you sleep on your back, like an exclamation point." He straightens his body out, turning himself into a rigid line.

She can't stop laughing. It's been a horrible week in so many ways. Brunson's revelation shifted something deep inside Spence. It made her hate a person she used to look to for answers. But it did make her even more grateful for Freddy. And these nights when he sneaks into her Livingston single are heaven to her. "Yeah, well, my mom's *big* on posture," she says. "She insisted I sleep on my back, and I guess it stuck."

Freddy pulls her back into bed. He grabs the camera and puts it down next to them. "Stick to me," he says.

"I will." Spence kisses him. "Okay, we should go, right?"

"Go make sure the coast is clear?" he asks.

She leaps out of bed and throws on a sweater and jeans, with a navy blue peacoat over them because it's freezing out. She peeks out her door. At the end of the hallway, Mrs. Plain waters the sad plant outside her door. Spence waits patiently for Mrs. Plain to go back into her residence. "Now," Spence whispers, and Freddy rushes out of the dorm.

She meets him outside. "Olympic training comes in handy when you're sneaking out," she jokes.

"Take out your notebooks and a pen and write this down," Douglas says as they all stream in. She waits for them to get their materials. *"Not everything that is faced can be changed. But nothing can be changed until it is faced."* Spence scribbles the quote down. "It's James Baldwin,"

Douglas explains. "Before we spend an hour writing something inspired by the quote, I wanted to tell you a little more about Baldwin."

Spence's mind wanders as Douglas tells them about James Baldwin, a Black man, a gay man, who was able to see and write about the United States more clearly when he left the United States.

Spence stares at the quote in her notebook, its words like a dare. She thinks that maybe she needs to leave Chandler to see it more clearly. What else does she not know about this place that helped raise her grandfather, father, and now her? She thinks about Sullivan, about how disgusted she feels when she thinks that he was her mentor, someone she thought she'd count on for the rest of her life. What happened to Brunson could've happened to her, and could happen to countless other girls.

As she stares at the quote, an idea comes to her. *Nothing can be changed until it is faced.* Well, she's ready to face it. And hopefully to change it. She plots out her next move in her head, her thoughts gaining momentum as she goes. It has to work. It will work.

"Pens down," Douglas says.

The hour felt like a minute. She looks down at her paper. She didn't write a word after transcribing the Baldwin quote.

"Amanda?" Douglas asks. "Everything okay?"

"Yes," she says. "Sorry, I—I guess I was blocked."

"It happens to every writer," Douglas says. "I'll see you next week."

"No homework?" Brunson asks.

"Not this week," Douglas says with a smile. "Even writers deserve some breaks."

Outside MacMillan, the Circle lingers together. "I'm gonna go to day care," Brunson says, turning away from the group.

"Brunson, wait," Spence says. When Brunson turns around, she continues. "What if it's not you against him?"

"What are you talking about?" Brunson asks.

Spence gets closer to her. The others follow her. They form a tight circle. "Sullivan," Spence whispers. "What if you weren't the only one accusing him?"

Brunson looks both shocked and moved as she says, "Spence, you have no idea how much it means to me that you're on my side. I thought—I don't know, I thought you'd defend him because you love—"

"I don't love him," she says, her face hot with shame. Did she really act like she *loved* him?

"No, I . . . I know," Brunson stammers. "I just meant . . . anyway, if what you're implying is that you're going to accuse him, too, I can't let you do that. You're not lying for me."

Now she's confused. "Wait, that's not what I meant," she says.

Brunson squints in the sun. "But you said I wouldn't be the only one accusing him. Who else?"

"If he did this to you, then he did it to other girls. One hundred percent. There has to be a pattern. So what if we find those other girls?" She feels her voice speed up with conviction. "What if I ask the other theater girls if any of them have, you know . . ."

"I don't know," Brunson says. "I just—in a way, telling you guys about it was enough for me. It already feels like I'm moving on. But thanks, Spence. Really."

Brunson turns away again. And again, Spence calls her back. "Brunson, wait."

"I have to go," Brunson says. "I have little kids counting on me."

"Yeah, exactly," Spence says. "Think of how long he'll be here if we don't do something. Think of all those young girls who dream of coming to this school. We can stop them from going through what you went through."

Brunson freezes, considering this.

"Isn't that enough to at least see if he's done this to other people?" Spence asks.

"Shit," Brunson says.

"What?" Spence asks.

"You're right. I wasn't even thinking of that. My sister could be here in five years. She could . . ." Brunson lets out a quiet sob. "If you ask people, can you just, you know, not mention my name?"

Spence holds Brunson's hands. "I promise," she says. "I would never do that."

"What if you don't find anyone else?" Brunson asks.

"Then I don't find anyone else."

Spence looks around. On the Main Lawn, Henny and Marianne are trying to perfect the choreography from the ". . . Baby One More Time" music video. On the dining hall steps, Hiro and Sabrina take turns feeding each other from those gross yogurt tubes they sell at the Tuck Shop. She's filled with love for this place. That's why she wants to change it. Because she loves it.

Brunson sighs. "Okay," she says. "Do it."

Freddy walks her to rehearsals that afternoon. "It feels weird," she says. "Staying in the play. Having him direct me."

"I know," he says. "I'm sorry."

"You have nothing to feel sorry for," she says.

"No, I mean, I'm sorry because, well . . . I may have implied that you and Sullivan— And I've heard people joke about you and him. And it's just . . . well, I'm sorry."

She kisses him gently on the cheek. "You're too sweet for this world, Frederico Bello."

In the arts center, she finds Whistler giving Connor Emerson a massage as Dallas discusses his character with Sullivan. Fuad, Wrigley, and Finneas hold their copies of the play and laugh about something.

"I think he's driven by fear," Dallas says.

"Yes, of course," Sullivan says. "But no human being is driven by only one emotion. In order to make the character work, you need to bring more than one emotion to the surface. Otherwise, he's just, well, one-note."

"Okay, I get that," Dallas says. "I just—like, I'm not sure what other emotions to play."

"Well, that's why we rehearse," Sullivan says. Then he claps his hands together, and all the students stand in a circle to begin their breathing and vocal exercises.

They work mostly on the boys' scenes, which gives Spence a chance to go sit in the audience next to Whistler. "He's intense, isn't he?" she says to Whistler.

"Connor?" Whistler asks. "I mean, the character's intense, right? He thinks he's a prophet."

Onstage, Connor says, "I usually say fuck the truth, but mostly, the truth fucks you."

"Feel it," Sullivan says. "Go deeper."

"I usually say fuck the truth, but mostly, the truth fucks you," Connor says, screaming the line, which Spence thinks is different than feeling it.

"I was talking about Sullivan," Spence says, turning her attention back to Whistler. "He's an intense director."

"Oh yeah," Whistler says. Then, changing the subject, she asks, "Did you see Rooney's new haircut? She looks like a ferret." Whistler laughs. "And I said that to her face, by the way. I would never speak behind a fellow Jennifer's back."

"I didn't see it," Spence says.

"Well, you've kind of been in your own world lately," Whistler says. "You don't even sit in the senior section."

"I do, sometimes. I just like to sit with the Circle too."

"Whatever," Whistler says. "The senior section is such a dumb tradition anyway."

She nods, but she needs to get the conversation back on track. "There's so much that needs to change at this school, don't you think?"

"Ha," Whistler says. "Nothing ever changes here. Do you know how many times I've suggested they change the cereals at the cereal bar? Like, what's the point of a suggestion box in the dining hall if you absolutely refuse to take the suggestions? I want Cocoa Krispies!"

This isn't going well. Spence starts to doubt herself. There's no casual way to ask Whistler if Sullivan ever crossed a boundary with her. But she has to keep trying. "Yeah, well, maybe if we change the bigger things, the smaller things will change too."

Whistler puts her feet up on the chair, hugging her knees in tight to her body. "So . . . tell me about Freddy. How's it going?"

"Oh good," she says.

"Just good?"

"I mean, great, but . . . you know, there's been something else on my mind lately." Whistler looks at her curiously. "Does Sullivan ever . . ." She can't find the words. "Like, the other day, he hugged me after rehearsal and it was weird, and I was just wondering, does he ever . . . you know, like, hug you or . . ."

Whistler laughs. "Wait, are you asking me if Sullivan has ever hit on me?"

"Has he?" Spence asks.

"No!" Whistler laughs incredulously. "Has he ever hit on you?"

"No, not really," Spence says.

"*Not really?*"

"No. I mean . . . no, he hasn't," Spence says.

"What even made you ask that?"

Spence feels her heart race. "Nothing important. Just something I overheard." She stops herself before she says too much.

Whistler grimaces. "Gross."

"Whistler and Spence to the stage," Sullivan calls out. They join the other actors onstage. "Why don't we spend some time on Harper and Hannah?" he suggests. "Let's start with Hannah. Spence, any thought about your character before we jump into scene work?"

"Well . . . I mean, she's a Mormon woman who finds out her son is gay, and there's, I guess, a lot of disapproval there. So I'm trying to be all method and think of things I disapprove of."

"That's a great instinct," Sullivan says, smiling. "What do you disapprove of?"

"You know, at Strasberg, we learned that as artists, we have to pull from our personal life, but also that we don't have to *share* that personal life with everyone. Our process belongs to us."

"Okay," Sullivan says, a twinge of disappointment in his voice. He takes his glasses off. Rubs the space between his eyebrows. "Whistler, let's talk about—"

But before he can finish, Spence interrupts him. "The thing is that Hannah just doesn't know better in the beginning. Because by the end of the play, she's changed. And I think maybe we're similar in that way."

"What way?" he asks.

"We both realized the thing we worshipped was deeply flawed," Spence says.

After Whistler, she gets a little better at finding creative ways to broach the topic with other theater girls. After Sandmen rehearsals for the Festival of Carols, she stops Binnie Teel and manages to get her talking about her experiences with Sullivan. But like Whistler, Binnie says Sullivan never did anything to her. "If he ever tried," Binnie says, "I would've called my dad and told him to put the power of the federal government into destroying him." Binnie's dad is a congressman from Florida.

She manages to talk to five more girls about it by the end of the week, but they all say the same thing. Yes, Sullivan's intense. And sure, he treats students like they're his friends. But he's never crossed that kind of line.

She wakes up next to Freddy on Saturday morning. "Good morning, question mark," she says, kissing him.

"Good morning, exclamation point," he says.

"I was thinking," she says.

"You're always thinking."

She kisses him. "There is no pressure to say yes. But since you're not going back to Miami for Thanksgiving, and since my parents have a lot of extra space, maybe you could . . . you know, come home with me?"

He takes a moment to process, then smiles. "Do your parents know about this plan yet?" he asks.

"Not exactly." She smiles sheepishly. "But they'll say

yes. They always want to meet the guys I date and—"

"Can we not mention all the other guys you've dated?"

"Well, you're the first one I *want* to introduce to them." She puts her hands on his cheeks as she says, "A splendid time is guaranteed for all . . . I hope."

He sits up. "What are they like?"

She pulls a framed photo from behind the stack of books on her desk. It's of Spence and her parents at the Met Gala a few years ago. "Well, that's my mom," she says, fondly remembering choosing their complementary Cubist gowns together. "And that's my dad." In the photo, her dad wears a fitted tuxedo and a top hat.

"Yeah, they both look, um, intimidating," he says. "Can I think about it?"

"No," she says, deadpan. She kisses his neck. "I'm kidding. Of course. Think all you want. Just don't over-think."

There's a sudden sadness on his face when he says, "It's just that my last relationship—my only relationship—ended right after I met the parents."

"And aren't you happy about that?" Spence asks, a warm smile on her face. "If her parents weren't assholes, she would never have dumped you and then you wouldn't be here with me."

Freddy laughs. "I never thought about it that way."

"I'm always here for a perspective shift," she says, taking his hands in hers.

She remembers Amira using those words. Perspective shift. Amira said the whole campus needs one. And that's when it hits her. Amira. She auditioned for *Romeo and Juliet* as a third former, then never auditioned again. And she clearly loves theater because she has so many opinions about it and knows plays she herself has never heard of.

"I—I have to go," Spence says.

"Breakfast?" he asks. "I'm hungry too."

"No, not breakfast. I need to go find someone." She doesn't explain. She doesn't have time to.

Amira is a prefect in Shipman, the third-form girls' dorm Spence lived in when she first arrived at Chandler. Walking into the dorm brings back a flood of memories. The smell of the place makes her feel like she's fourteen again. Missing home. Missing her junior high school friends, and the familiarity of New York City. She stops outside the door of her old dorm room. She debates knocking on the door just to see it again. But she doesn't want to slow herself down. Instead, she finds Amira's door, which is covered from top to bottom in pages from books and sheet music. She knocks, but there's no answer.

"Hey." She turns to find that Amira is behind her, holding a huge stack of library books.

"Oh hi," she says. "I just came to see you."

"Yeah, obviously," Amira says. "You're at my door."

"Remember how I lived in this dorm as a third former?" She takes in the dorm again, thinking back. "You were in Redbird with Henny, right?"

"Yeah," Amira says. "She was nice then. I mean, I'm sure she still is nice. We just never talk anymore."

"Yeah, *we* don't talk much either," she says. "We used to that first year."

"Third formers talk to everyone," Amira says. "Then we figure out who our friends are and we keep to our little bubbles."

"That's so true. And kind of sad."

"Is that why you're here? To reminisce?"

"No, I actually wanted to talk to you about . . ." A group of third formers pile out of the common room. They look so young. Did she look that young when she was new to Chandler? "Well, could we go for a walk maybe?"

Amira seems to size her up. "Um, okay. Let me put these books down."

Spence looks at the spines of the books she's holding. They're all about the '70s and San Francisco and cults. As Amira opens her door and throws the books onto her bed, she says, "I'm writing a paper about Jonestown for Song's History of Counterculture class."

"Jonestown?" Spence asks. "Is that the cult that drank the Kool-Aid?"

"Yup." Amira grabs a big woven hat from a futon and puts it on her head. "Biggest deliberate loss of American life. Crazy, right? Imagine that many people doing something that awful and no one saying, *Hey, stop.*"

"Yeah." She looks around Amira's room. There's a guitar in the corner. "I actually *can* imagine that."

"Eighty percent of Jim Jones's followers were Black,"

Amira says. "No one really talks about that. Like, we all know there was this crazy cult that killed themselves, but why were so many Black people under the spell of this white man? That's what I'm writing about."

"That's fascinating," she says.

They're walking away from Shipman now. "Anyway, I'm interested in people who fall under the spell of institutions they clearly don't belong to," Amira says. Then, with a wink, she adds, "I wonder why."

"Yeah, well, that's kind of what I want to talk to you about, actually, so . . . perfect segue."

"We love a perfect segue at Chandler," Amira jokes. "So where are we walking to anyway?"

"The woods?" Spence suggests.

Amira shrugs. "Sure, I love the leaves in November. Best month in New England."

"It's my birthday month, so agreed."

They cross from the manicured campus into the wild woods. "So?" Amira asks.

"Right," Spence says. "Something tells me you're the kind of person who likes people who cut to the chase, so I'll do that."

"You're doing *anything* but cutting to the chase right now," Amira says, laughing.

"Sorry!" Spence says. "Okay, here's what I want to talk to you about." She leans against a tree trunk. Amira stops walking and faces her. "Freshman year, you auditioned for the school play, but you never auditioned again. And I wanted to ask you . . ."

"You want to cast me in your student scene or something?" Amira asks. She strikes a pose, exaggerating her perfect posture.

"No," Spence says, laughing. "We don't even present our first scene until January."

"So . . ."

"So . . . Sullivan . . ."

"What about Sullivan?"

She feels her eyes blinking too fast. She finally asks, "Did you quit theater because he did something to you? Like, you know, something sexual."

Amira's face falls when she hears the question. She doesn't say anything for a few seconds, the steam from her mouth escaping into the cold air. "Fuck. You too," she finally whispers.

Spence's heart breaks as she says, "No, not me. I was spared, for some reason. But a friend of mine . . . And, well, she doesn't want to say anything if she's the only one. And, well, the thing is she's not the only one anymore. There's you now. And there are probably more girls he did this to. But look, would you consider saying something because we can't let him—"

"What makes you think I didn't say something?" Amira asks.

She feels suddenly unsteady when she hears this. She uses one of the tree branches to hold herself up. "Wait, you mean . . . you told someone?"

"Of course I told someone." There's a defiance in Amira's eyes. "I told my mom and dad, and then we *all* told Headmaster Berg."

"What? How is he . . . still here? Still teaching?"

Amira looks at her with something that looks like a combination of pity and envy. "You don't get it, do you?"

"I—I'm so sorry," she says. "Maybe if more girls came forward, that could change things." She talks fast, thinking out loud, desperate to find a solution and fix this. She doesn't know why, but she feels like she's partly to blame for *his* behavior, like she enabled it by being his favorite student and making him seem cool to the other kids or something. "I could talk to my parents. My dad's on the board. If they knew about this, they would insist he get fired. I know they would."

"Sure, go ahead," Amira says dryly. "It's not like the administration doesn't already know what happened to me."

"I can't believe it," Spence says. "I just can't."

"I'm glad you can't." Amira sighs. "It means you got to live at least part of your childhood insulated from the real world. Your friend who this happened to . . . I'm gonna take a wild guess that she isn't a legacy kid or the daughter of a billionaire. It's not Whistler or Rooney or Henny. She's probably a scholarship student, if not definitely on financial aid. Maybe she has some sob story that made her vulnerable."

"Yeah," she says slowly. "You're right."

Amira crosses her arms.

She thinks about Brunson. What Amira is saying makes Sullivan even more evil, like he chooses his victims based on their vulnerability. Spence's whole body feels an intense chill as she wonders if her privilege shielded her from going through what Brunson and Amira did. Not that Sullivan's relationship with her was appropriate. It wasn't. And it's not like her privilege has shielded her from being treated like a sexual object by men who exoticize Indian women, catcalling them and asking to be their maharaja. It's not until this very moment that Spence realizes how vulnerable she's felt all her life, and how her drive for perfection has perhaps been her only method of escaping that feeling. But that's not what matters right now. What matters is supporting Amira.

"Amira, I'm so sorry," Spence says. "I—I'm just really glad you're still here."

Amira smiles sadly. "I wasn't going to let him drive me away from this opportunity. He doesn't have that power."

Spence nods. "No one should have that kind of power. Not anymore."

Sarah Brunson

"I always lose to you," Brunson says, laying down the word *brain* on the Scrabble board.

"You're just distracted, I can tell," Millie Song says, laying down the word *academic*. "I used all my letters. How many points is that again?"

"Fifty." Brunson jots the score down on the back of a Community Day flyer she swiped from the mailroom. Millie's right. She is distracted. It's been two weeks since she told her friends about Sullivan, and instead of feeling liberated, she's just wanted to hibernate since then. She doesn't want to talk about it anymore. She'd much rather play Scrabble with Mrs. Song's eleven-year-old daughter.

"Okay, story time," Millie says when she ends the game with the word *cake*.

This is how every game ends. It's a tradition Brunson started with her little sister. At the end of a Scrabble game, she tells a story inspired by the words on the board.

"Okay, once upon a time, there was an academic with a very big brain," she says. Millie laughs, eating it up. "But the academic was so busy learning all the time that she had never tasted cake."

She hears something and looks up to find Spence standing just outside the open basement door. "Sorry," Spence says. "I didn't want to interrupt the story."

"You came just in time," Brunson says. "I had no idea how to weave the words *xylophone* and *cabinet* and *unique* in there."

"Easy," Millie says. "The academic wants cake, but in order to unlock the cabinet that the cake is in, she has to play a unique melody on the xylophone."

Spence claps. "Of course Mrs. Song would have a brilliant daughter."

"You're pretty," Millie says to Spence.

Spence smiles. "Thanks, but I hope I'm more than that."

"Okay, back upstairs for you," Brunson says, realizing that Spence has never come to see her alone. There must be a reason.

"But I want to hang out with you guys," Millie begs.

"It's just, we need to talk about grown-up stuff," Spence explains.

"Weird 'cause you're not grown-ups," Millie huffs.

Brunson and Millie get into a staring contest, which is always their way of settling an argument. When Millie blinks, Brunson says, "Sorry, you lose. Upstairs."

Millie stomps her way up. "She's so sweet," Spence says.

"Every kid is sweet," Brunson says sadly. "We all start out that way."

"Where does it all go wrong?" Spence muses. "Anyway, want to walk to MacMillan?"

She digs her alarm clock out from under a pile of clothes. "We still have an hour."

"Well, it'll give us time to talk," Spence says.

As Brunson digs a sweater and scarf out of her pile of clothes, she catches Spence looking around her basement room. Spence stares at a framed Brunson family photo on top of Mrs. Song's old piano. Her mom wears a wig in the photo. Brunson holds her little sister, Ginny, in her arms. And her dad's blinking, like he always does in pictures. "Your sister is like a mini-you," Spence says.

"Version 2.0." Brunson throws a fleece sweater on. "Hopefully she'll be an improvement."

Spence rolls her eyes. "Shut up, you're amazing." She attempts to play something on the piano and cringes. "Oh wow, that's out of tune."

Once Brunson has wrapped the scarf tight around her neck, she says, "I'm ready," and they head out into campus.

"Look, I spoke to a lot of girls," Spence says. "And—"

Brunson panics. She's not sure she wants to know the rest. "Hey, your birthday's coming up, isn't it?" she asks. She kicks herself for bringing up Spence's birthday when Freddy told them to downplay it.

"Oh yeah, but I'm not doing anything this year," she says.

Brunson nods nervously, afraid of giving away the surprise, and even more afraid of hearing what Spence came to talk to her about.

"Look, you're not alone," Spence says. "I know of one more student who was assaulted by him."

Brunson corrects her. "*At least* one more student."

They look at each other sadly.

"Yeah, there's some I suspect," Spence says. "Like, there was this really talented singer here when I was a third former. She and Sullivan were very close. And then she abruptly went on a medical leave and never came back. And now I'm pretty sure we know why. Anyway, I can get her contact information. Maybe she'll help us too."

"I thought about that, you know," Brunson says. "Taking a medical leave myself. Or just leaving school. But then he wins, right?"

"Right." Spence nods.

"You know what the hardest part is?" She kicks some rust and gold leaves from the ground. "It's replaying the whole thing in my head and wondering what I could have done differently. Like, why did I even go into his residence? What an idiot."

"You're not an idiot," Spence says. "I go to his place all the time. And to other teacher residences. Brunson, you live with a teacher!"

Brunson laughs. "Yeah, well, Mrs. Song doesn't exactly fit the profile."

"There is no profile. And don't blame yourself."

"Easy for you to say, it never happened to you."

Spence says nothing. She just walks slowly by her side, watching her with sympathy in her eyes.

"I think he knew that I was weak," Brunson says, cracking her knuckles nervously. "He could smell it on me."

"Please don't blame yourself."

"Maybe if I was more like you. You know exactly who you are. You exude strength and confidence. Maybe that's why he didn't do anything to you."

Spence pauses. Then she says, "I actually think it's because of my parents, which is why I want to talk to them about Sullivan. With your blessing."

"I don't—I mean, why them?"

"Because my dad's on the board of Chandler. And he knows all the other board members. And because—well, the other girl, she told Headmaster Berg what he did, but nothing happened."

"Oh shit." This is exactly what she feared. That she could come forward, and nothing would happen to him. She feels a pang of empathy for the girl who reported him.

"Yeah," Spence continues. "So I think—I think we need power on our side. And maybe I can help with that."

"I don't know." Brunson kicks another pile of leaves. This time, Spence joins her. They kick as they walk. "The one thing I don't want is for him to define me. For that one stupid moment to be my whole high school experience. He doesn't deserve that."

"I know," Spence says. "But if we don't try, then he'll keep doing it."

"I don't know," she says again. "Anyway, we should probably get to MacMillan."

"Will you think about what I said?" Spence asks.

"Sure." But Brunson already feels her mind is made up. The thought of Spence telling her powerful parents about Brunson's trauma fills her with humiliation. She doesn't want their pity or their intervention. And most of all, she doesn't want to go through what the girl who *already* reported Sullivan went through. That piece of information changes everything.

As they approach MacMillan, Spence turns to Brunson with one more question. "Do you think I should quit the winter play?" she asks.

"Why are you asking me?" Brunson asks.

"I don't know," Spence says. "Because I don't know what to do. I hate him now. Every time I see him, I think of—"

"Then quit," she says.

"But I love this show, and we don't have understudies, and . . . I'm in his two-semester class and I wouldn't have enough credits to graduate if I drop it now. So it's not like I can just avoid him, so . . ."

"Then don't quit." She feels a flash of resentment at Spence for even asking her this question and for pressuring her.

"Hey, guys," Freddy says when he sees them. He throws his arms around Spence from behind and kisses her cheek.

They head into Douglas's residence. Beth and Ramin

are already sitting on the floor. Brunson sits as far from Spence as possible. She just can't take her energy right now.

"It's our last meeting before you go home for Thanksgiving," Douglas says. "So I thought we could do something different today."

"I'm not going home, actually," Freddy says.

"Me neither," Ramin says.

Douglas corrects herself. "Okay then, it's our last meeting until your break. Freddy and Ramin, I'll be on campus during the break as well, so if you ever want a cup of soup that doesn't taste like yesterday's leftovers, you can always knock on my door."

"You'll like campus when it's empty," Freddy tells Ramin. "Most kids go home, so it's just like, faculty and a handful of international students."

Ramin sighs. "It'll be nice to have the basement to myself, at least. Last night, my towels disappeared."

"Assholes," Beth spits out.

"Hiro had an extra towel. It was okay." Ramin lets out another heavy sigh. "I asked the school to transfer me to a different dorm, but there's no room. Do you know what the headmaster said?"

"What?" Freddy asks.

"He said that as soon as a fourth former is expelled, they can move me." Ramin lets out a sad chuckle.

"That is cold," Freddy says.

"Honestly, how do you answer to that man?" Spence asks Douglas.

Douglas doesn't take the bait.

But Spence keeps going. "Wait, is that why you quit being head of the English Department?" she asks. "Because you couldn't deal with Berg?"

"Amanda, we don't need to discuss—"

"Oh come on, this is a safe space," Spence says.

Douglas sighs. "I quit being the head of the department over an argument about syllabus requirements, that's it. I wanted to . . . update the core curriculum. Add more authors who reflect the experience of *all* the students."

"And Headmaster Berg?" Spence asks.

"He disagreed," Douglas says. "But I choose the syllabus for my elective classes. And I have our Circle. Being the head of a department is full of thankless bureaucracy. Now I can focus on what I love most, which is this. Teaching."

Brunson's not all that interested in why Douglas quit that post. She's still thinking of Ramin and how he's being forced to live in that basement. "You know, statistically, fourth formers are the least likely to get expelled."

"That's true," Beth says. "On average, only one percent of the fourth form gets expelled every year."

Brunson's always amazed that Beth's head is as full of useful Chandler statistics as hers is. "I laid out the *Gone But Not Forgotten* section in last year's yearbook, and the list of fourth formers was tiny compared to the rest."

"Can we talk about that section of the yearbook, though?" Freddy asks. "*Gone But Not Forgotten*. It makes them sound dead instead of expelled."

"The only section that was smaller in the yearbook is the Host Students' section," Brunson says. "There are so few of us."

Ramin's face opens up into a smile when he says, "Wait. That's it. You're a genius, Brunson."

"I am?" Brunson asks.

Ramin looks at Douglas when he says. "I could be a Host Student. Brunson lives with Mrs. Song. And Josie Oxford lives with—"

"There are only five teachers who host students, though," Beth says. "And all those rooms are taken."

"I think he's suggesting moving in here," Brunson says.

Ramin nods to confirm this.

"How many bedrooms do you have here, Professor Douglas?" As soon as Brunson asks the question, she realizes how inappropriate it is. Her face gets hot.

"I—well, you know—I don't think . . . ," Douglas stammers.

Brunson looks over to Ramin, who quickly backs away from his own suggestion. "It's okay," he says. "I'm sorry. It was a bad idea."

Composing herself again, Douglas says, "Faculty homes need to be approved for Host Students. It's a process. And it would need to be approved by—"

"Headmaster Berg." Spence rolls her eyes.

"Yes," Douglas says. "And, well . . . Ramin, if you truly feel uncomfortable, I could ask about myself or any other faculty member hosting you. But it could take time."

"Thank you," Ramin says quietly. "I would appreciate that."

Douglas smiles, probably relieved to end this conversation. "All right, can we begin now? As I said, I thought we could do something different today? Something I hope will be fun." They all look at her with anticipation. "Today, instead of writing alone for an hour, we'll each take turns writing for ten minutes, building a story together." She takes a breath. "It'll be an exercise in listening, because I want you to build on each other's ideas, not negate them."

"Oh, like improv," Spence says. "Like the cardinal rule of improv is that you have to 'Yes and' your scene partner. Which means like, let's say I start a scene at Sotheby's, you can't be like, 'No, we're not at Sotheby's.'"

The whole group laughs at this example, but only Freddy is brave enough to gently mock Spence. "Okay, but only *you* would set a scene at Sotheby's!"

"Shut up," Spence says. "It was just an example."

"You know what," Douglas says. "Before we start, let's do some improvisation exercises. Writing is just improvising on the page anyway. Amanda, why don't you tell us your favorite one?"

"Oh," Spence says. "Well, there's the ABC game where each sentence starts with the next letter in the alphabet. There's the freeze game where two people do a scene and you can yell 'Freeze' to make them freeze. Then you tap one of them on the shoulder and they leave the scene, and you enter and start a whole new scene, building on some physical element of what came before. And so on . . ."

"Let's do that one," Beth says. "It sounds fun."

"Okay, then you're my first scene partner," Spence tells Beth. She and Beth stand in the center of the room. "We just need a location from you. Any location."

"The Tuck Shop," Freddy says.

Spence and Beth sit across from each other, eating imaginary food and sharing fictional gossip, until Freddy yells "FREEZE" and taps Spence on the shoulder. He sits across from Beth in the same position Spence was in, and begins a scene on a spaceship. Beth, playing along, swings her hands into the air. Everyone laughs, and they keep playing the game until everyone—even Douglas— has had a turn. The game changes Brunson's mood. The heaviness she brought in with her has been replaced with the light spark of laughter and creativity.

By the time they get to Douglas's writing exercise, Brunson's really having fun. The story they build together is silly. It's about a teacher and a student who swap bodies. Brunson knows there's probably a pretty painful version of that same story, but that's not the version they write together. And it makes her realize that every story can be written in so many different ways. Just like every life can be lived in so many different ways.

Before letting them go, Douglas says, "I won't see you until December. At least not here in the Circle. And since it's Thanksgiving, I'd like to say I'm very thankful for the Circle."

* * *

They walk to the lake together after the Circle meeting. On their way, Freddy pulls Brunson aside and whispers. "Hey, I saw you and Spence together this morning. She doesn't know about her birthday, right?"

"I don't think so," she says. "She told me she wasn't doing anything this year."

"Good," Freddy says. "I talked to Sabrina again and we're all set."

The lake is still not iced over, but soon it will be. They sit at the edge of the water.

"I'm glad you asked Douglas about moving in with her," Freddy says to Ramin.

As Ramin wonders aloud if it'll ever happen, Brunson stands up and starts walking the length of the lake. She stops at their tree, running her fingers along their initials.

"Hey." She looks up and sees Beth has followed her.

"Hey," she says.

They stand in silence for a moment. "You're really funny," she tells Beth, thinking back to Beth in those improv scenes. "I never knew that about you."

"There's a lot we didn't know about each other, huh?"

Brunson nods. Her fingers are still resting on their carved initials. "Do you think we're the first Chandies to make this lake their spot?"

"Probably not," Beth says. "This lake is probably littered with a century of secrets."

"Yeah, secrets," Brunson says.

Thinking of the students who came before them opens

something up in her. It makes her realize that someday, *she'll* be the student who came before. And she has the power to make things better for the next kids to come to this school searching for answers.

"Spence wants to talk to her parents," Brunson tells Beth. "About Sullivan. Did she tell you?"

"No," Beth says, tilting her head. "What do *you* want?"

"I don't know," Brunson says.

"How does it make you feel when you think of Spence telling her parents?"

"Scared. But also hopeful." Looking at Beth, she says, "Wait, are you therapizing me? You sound just like Dr. Geller."

"And how would you know what he sounds like?" Beth smiles.

"Because I went to see him last year for a bit," she says.

"Another thing I didn't know about you. I mean, how were we so invisible to each other when we were *roommates*?"

"I don't know." Brunson shakes her head. "Sometimes it's hardest to see the shit that's right in front of you, I guess."

"Yeah, well, I don't look at my shit," Beth says.

Brunson laughs. "Gross."

Beth asks, "So why did they send you to see Dr. Geller?"

"They didn't," she explains. "He was a part of my peer counseling training, and I thought he was really smart,

272

and, well, I thought he could help me process leaving my mom and my sister and so we did like, seven sessions, I think. I stopped seeing him before what happened with Sullivan. That was probably a bad decision. Not that I was ready to tell anyone last year."

"Did you stop because he helped or because he wasn't helping?" Beth asks.

"Oh, he helped," she says sincerely. "I guess I figured I didn't need therapy anymore. Like, my mom's in remission. Hopefully forever. I should move on, right?"

"Well, it sounds like she was sick for a long time. There's probably a lot to process."

She nods. Beth is right about that. "I didn't really have parents, in a way," she says quietly. "My mom's treatment was so expensive. And my dad worked overtime to pay for it. So I helped raise my sister. I changed her diapers and mixed her formula. And I watched my mom dying, until suddenly she was living again."

"I really wish we could've talked like this last year," Beth says.

"Me too," she says, an ache in her voice. "You know I was just trying to fit in and make friends, right? I never meant to shut you out."

"I know that *now*," Beth says.

"And the whole thing about your hair," Brunson continues.

"I know. It reminded you of your mom. I get it now," Beth says. "I get *you* now."

Brunson keeps going, saying all the things she

should've told Beth when they were roommates. "The weird thing is that when my mom's hair grew back, when she went back to seeing her own patients instead of being one . . . well, I didn't know what to do with a healthy mom, so I applied here. And when I got in, my mom flipped out. Partly because of the tuition, and partly because I was leaving just when she was healthy enough to finally enjoy me, I guess."

"You must miss her," Beth says.

"Yeah, a lot." Brunson smiles wistfully. "You know what she said when I got in? She said that if someone was going to take her children from her, they should *pay her*, not the other way around."

Beth laughs. "But she let you go," she says.

"I'm hard to say no to when I know what I want." Brunson sighs.

"Somehow I don't doubt that," Beth says with a smile. Then, softly, she asks, "So . . . Sullivan. Do you know if you want Spence to talk to her parents?"

Brunson knows she doesn't want Sullivan to define her Chandler experience. But she also knows that if she doesn't at least try to do something about it, maybe he'll define it even *more*.

Because she'll always look back and wonder, what if?

Freddy Bello

"Happy birthday," he says when they wake up next to each other. It's incredible how easy sneaking into her room is. Or maybe Mr. and Mrs. Plain are just incredibly liberal dorm parents because they see him coming in and out of Livingston constantly, and not once do they remind him about the open-door rule or the three-feet-on-the-ground rule.

"Thanks," she says.

"Do you feel older?" he asks.

"No, just happier." She runs a hand through his hair lovingly. "I could just stay in bed with you all day."

"Exhaustion, definitely a sign of old age." He kisses her in between each word.

"You know *why* I want to stay in bed." She changes tone, speaking more seriously. "But we don't have to do it if you don't want to."

"Of course I want to," he says. "It's just, you said you

didn't want to date most guys because they only had one thing on their minds. And I guess I didn't want you to think that I only want sex or anything like that."

She laughs. "You really are too sweet for your own good, Freddy. I didn't mean that I never want to have sex."

"Well, that's good news," he says, smiling to hide how suddenly nervous he is. The truth is he's never had sex. His last girlfriend broke up with him before it went there. And now he feels a pit in his stomach. Will he disappoint Spence? Will this be the reason she leaves him?

There's a long, strange silence between them. Finally, Spence says, "It doesn't have to be today or anything."

Freddy takes her hands in his. He kisses her fingers. "I'm just nervous, I guess. I, uh, don't exactly have any experience in that department."

"Oh," she says. "Freddy, we can wait. Whatever feels right to you."

"*We* feel right," he says with certainty. "I just . . . I guess I feel like I do before a competition. Doesn't matter how much I practice. Once it comes time to do it in front of the judges, I get so nervous."

"You know what I think?" she asks softly.

He looks over at her, not sure what she's thinking. That's part of Spence's beauty, all those mysteries still left to discover.

"I think you've been trained to see everything as a competition," she says. "But no matter what happens, I won't be judging you. I promise."

276

He looks into her eyes. He knows he told his parents that he wouldn't get distracted by romance, but maybe what none of them could predict is that falling for the *right* person would make him feel more empowered, not less.

His mouth moves as close to hers as it can get without touching her. It's like her breath is coming together as one rhythm. "Let's do it," he says.

"Okay," she whispers. "We can go slow."

"I just . . . don't want you to get your hopes up or anything."

She laughs. "Well, okay then. Now that my expectations have been lowered . . ." She reaches down to touch him, and finds him hard. "Well, my hopes may not be up, but something else is."

Freddy groans at her joke, but he can't help but laugh. They make out for a long time, until Spence turns over and pulls a condom out of a drawer.

"Wow," he says.

"What?" She's suddenly defensive. "You think I'm a slut for having condoms in my room?"

"No!" he says too loud.

"Shh," she says. "There's a whole dorm of sixth-form girls out there who would love nothing more than to find out you never left last night."

He lowers his voice back to a hush. "Honestly, I think you're amazing."

He kisses her and they melt into each other. He's never felt more connected to another human being. All his life, his body has been there to win medals. Now, for the first time, his body is simply there to bring pleasure.

They curl around each other when they're done, just lying there, saying nothing and feeling everything. He realizes something in that silence. The reason he's wanted to quit pole vaulting is to escape that feeling of pressure he hates so much. If he could approach pole vaulting the same way he just approached being with Spence, then maybe he could enjoy it again. Maybe he could experience it with the same wonder he had as a kid who wanted to fly like Superman.

He rests his head on her chest. Maybe he's not going to quit. Maybe all he needed was someone to make him feel safe enough to keep going.

She strokes his hair. "You know that if you ever cut your hair, I'll kill you, right?"

"Wow," he says again, laughing. "I knew things would change between us after we did it, but I didn't think we'd move on to murder so fast."

"What I wanna murder right now is food," she says. "I'm starving."

"Me too." He gets up and throws his clothes on. "Hey, let's go eat in town." He speaks as casually as he can. "I don't want to be around anyone but you today."

She smiles. "Mamma Mia pizza?"

"Sure," he says. "You know I love those breakfast calzones."

They bike into town together. It's a perfect day, crisp but sunny. On their way to Mamma Mia, he slams on his brakes very suddenly. "Oh wait, I left a hat at Sabrina's house when we went to her party. I've been meaning to go ask her if I can look for it. Quick detour?"

She squints, suspicious. "You weren't wearing a hat that night. I have a photographic memory where fashion is concerned."

"You call what I wear fashion?" He thinks fast and adds, "Anyway, it was in my pocket. It must've fallen out."

She shrugs. "Okay," she says.

He breathes a sigh of relief. She doesn't seem to suspect a thing. When he knocks on the door of the Lockhart home, it creaks open. And then the lights turn on, and everyone yells, "SURPRISE!" He watches her take it all in. The Circle is there, and all her sixth-form girlfriends, and the theater kids. She can't stop smiling as she makes eye contact with Whistler and Henny and Amira and Lashawn.

"Oh my God!" Spence slaps his chest playfully. "You tricked me!"

"WE LOVE YOU," Henny Dover screams. "Even if you've been ignoring us to canoodle with your pole vaulter!"

"I—I can't believe this." Spence looks genuinely moved. "I said I didn't want to do anything for my birthday."

"Yeah, but I knew you didn't really mean that," Freddy says. "Did you?"

"You LOVE your birthday," Whistler chimes in. "And this is your last one as a Chandie, so we weren't gonna let you waste it."

"I wasn't wasting it," she says, squeezing Freddy's

back. "But you're right. I *love* my birthday. So let's party like it's 1999."

Sabrina puts on an Ella Fitzgerald CD, and the sixth formers in the room start dancing the waltz, which they learned at their second senior dance lesson.

Spence leads Freddy to Sabrina and Hiro. "Thanks for this, Sabrina," Spence says.

"My pleasure," Sabrina responds warmly. "Freddy said your first kiss was in our garage, so it seemed like a good place to celebrate."

Spence looks at him. "Giving away all our secrets, huh?"

Hiro, his arm around Sabrina, adds, "Love was in the air that night, huh?"

Freddy feels his face get hot. They just slept together, but they still haven't said they *love* each other. "Yes, it was," he says, looking into Spence's eyes. And she doesn't miss the moment, because her face gets warm when he says it.

"My parents said we can have five hours, so enjoy," Sabrina says. Then she pulls Hiro to the dance floor, and he dips her down until she almost falls.

He watches from a corner as Spence makes the rounds. They all love her. After a few songs, Freddy goes to Ramin. "Did you bring it?" Freddy asks.

"Here." Ramin pulls an Iranian CD out of his bag. On the cover is a stunning woman.

Freddy and Ramin head to the CD player and change the music.

"Circle dance," Freddy screams out.

They all roll their shoulders, make ridiculous faces, and wave their hands in the air. And the rest of the kids follow their lead.

Freddy catches the look of amazement on Ramin's face. "Pretty cool, right?" he says.

"Very cool," Ramin says. "I imagined a lot of things about Chandler. And I couldn't have imagined the worst parts of it. But I couldn't imagine the best parts either."

They take a dance break to sit on the porch, where Amira and Lashawn look through an old Chandler yearbook. "Thanks for coming," Spence says to them.

Amira holds up the yearbook. "You guys aren't prepared for this."

"What?" Spence asks.

"The Lockharts had this very old yearbook, and . . ."

"Wait for it . . . ," Lashawn says.

"Boom." Amira opens the yearbook to Headmaster Berg's sixth-form photo, back when he was a student.

"Oh. My. God." Spence squeals.

Freddy leaves her on the porch for a bit. She's still there at three o'clock when he has his next surprise planned. "I need you inside," he yells.

She follows him in. Sabrina futzes with the radio dial until she gets to the right station. An easy-listening song plays.

"What did you pull me in here for?" Spence asks.

"Patience," he says.

The whole party has quieted down now. Finally, the

easy-listening song ends, and the radio host comes on. "Our next song is a request from Freddy."

"No!" Spence says, wrapping her arms around him and squeezing him tight.

"Freddy says, 'Joey, today is the birthday of someone very special to me. Can you play "Amanda" by Don Williams for her? If you do, I know it'll change her mind about something very important.' Well, Freddy, your wish is my command."

The song begins, and Freddy sings along as it plays.

"Wait, are you trying to make me love a song with a proper name in the title?" she asks.

"Amanda light of my life," he sings in a twang.

"You'll never change my mind, never!" she says, laughing.

The rest of the party sings along once they learn the chorus. *"Amanda light of my life,"* they all sing.

Spence collapses into his arms when the song ends. "I love you," she whispers in his ear. "And I've never said that to anyone else before."

He kisses her and whispers, "I love you too."

After the cake, the party starts to thin out. The remaining students pile onto the floor of the Lockhart living room, picking at the pieces of uneaten cake on the coffee table until Sabrina's parents arrive.

Freddy and Spence bike back to campus, and he kisses her outside Livingston. From a few feet away, Brodie Banks screams, "Get a room!"

"Hey, did you see how chummy Hiro was with the

Lockharts when they arrived?" she says. "I mean, they started dating the same night we did."

"Well, she's a day student, so her parents live here."

"I'm just saying." She takes a breath. "If you said yes to my very sweet Thanksgiving invite, then you *could* meet my parents, who will miraculously both be home. And Brunson told me she *does* want me to talk to them about Sullivan, so I could use the support."

"I accept your very sweet invite," he says with certainty. "And by the way, I didn't need Hiro and Sabrina to convince me. I'm not comparing us to anyone else's timeline. I just . . . want to meet the people who created you."

"Hey." She squeezes his face in her hands. "I created myself." Then she kisses him and walks away.

None of the clothes he owns feel worthy of Spence's parents. Her dad probably gets his suits tailored on Savile Row. Her mom, well, she gets free clothes from designers. Meanwhile, he's deciding between packing a Brooks Brothers blazer that's so tight on him now that he can't button it and an L.L.Bean fleece with a hole in the side.

In the hallway, he can hear Charles and Teddy Powers kick a hacky sack from one end to the other. "Get it!" Charles screams.

Last year, he was playing foosball at the SSC when he overheard Henny and Whistler tell Rooney and Marianne about the weekend they spent at the "Spencer Palace," as they called it. Henny was mostly focused on describing the bidets and showerheads. "I've never seen so many bidets," she said. Whistler was more interested in the framed candid photos of the Spencers with celebrities. "I mean, I didn't know Spence went bowling with Liv Tyler!" He stuffs both the blazer and the fleece into his duffel bag, along with every pair of pants he owns. He'll let Spence tell him what to wear when they get there.

In the hallway, Charles and Teddy scream as they kick the hacky sack. Then he hears Mr. Sullivan's door open. "Can you please remember that you're not in the wild?" Hearing Sullivan's voice makes his blood boil. He wants to go out there and show him what being in the wild would really look like.

"Sorry, it's just too cold to play outside," Charles explains.

Then there's a new voice. It's Toby. "Yo Cox," he says. "Is your roomie home?"

"Yeah, he's packing, but—"

Before Charles can finish, Toby and Seb are in the room. They shut the door behind them. It's so stupid that the door is supposed to remain open when a girl comes in, but not when assholes like these enter the room.

"What's up?" Toby says.

"I'm really busy." Freddy keeps packing.

"Yeah, we heard." Seb peeks into the duffel bag. "Meeting Spence's parents. Big step, huh?" Of course they already know where he's going for the holiday. Chandler is a place with endless secrets and no secrets at the same time.

"Guys, why are you here?"

"We're friends, aren't we?" Toby asks.

"Are we?" Freddy tries to sound relaxed, but he hears his voice rising.

"Yeah, of course we are." Seb is about to speak, but Toby stops him. "We're not bad people. You know that."

Freddy doesn't look at them. He focuses on laying out his clothes. Folding them. Stuffing them into the duffel bag.

"Look, we know you're pissed at us, and we don't know what Ramoon is telling you or why he's trying to move out of our dorm."

"His name is *Ramin*," Freddy says sharply.

"Got it, Frederico."

Toby continues. "Listen, we just don't want you to only hear his side."

"What's your side?" Freddy asks.

"You weren't here as a third *or* fourth former. You missed *a lot*."

"I'm sure I did." He tries to figure out how to fold the two ties he owns. Whatever he does, they seem to come apart when he packs them.

"You don't know what we went through." Toby grabs Freddy's arm aggressively. "Can you just listen?"

"Fine." Freddy crosses his arms.

"My prefects my third-form year used to pull our pants down and paddle us with Ping-Pong racquets that they stole from the SSC," Toby says.

"And you know," Seb says, "when I left for Mont-gomery, it was the same. I was a fourth former there when a bunch of seniors made me wear underwear on my head. They took a picture of me. Called it collateral. They said if I ever disobeyed them, they'd post the photo in the mailroom."

"And that was at Montgomery!" Toby says. "You know where I lived my fourth-form year? The Wilton Blue Basement. You wanna know what happened to me down there?"

"No, I really don't," he says.

"All we're saying is that we didn't do anything that wasn't done to us, okay?" Toby nods proudly, like this is the final word.

"Not okay," he whispers. "That's not how it works. It's not like—because someone does something awful to you, you get to do that *same* awful thing to someone else. That's not . . ." He searches for the right word. *Justice?*

"Yeah, well, a little hazing is a Chandler tradition. You shouldn't take it so seriously."

"It is serious, actually," he snaps. "Do you realize what you're doing to people? Are you even sorry at all?"

Neither of them answers the question.

"You know what, I have to go to the bathroom," he says. "I'd really appreciate it if you guys were gone when I'm back."

He feels his heart beating as he heads out to the bathroom, but there's also a smile on his face, because not long ago, they *were* his friends. But now he has so much more.

Charles and Teddy are still playing hacky sack. "Everything okay?" Charles asks as Freddy kicks open the bathroom door and splashes water onto his steaming face. Toby and Seb and Sullivan are all in Holmby House right now. It's enough to make him want to torch the whole place down, but he breathes through his anger.

When he goes back to his room, they're gone. He sighs in relief and finishes packing. He remembers promising Spence he'd show her some childhood photos, and stuffs some old photos in at the last minute. Hours later, he's leaving it all behind on a train to New York City with Spence. He hasn't told her about the visit from Seb and Toby. He doesn't want to relive it. Instead, he listens as Spence describes the Hamptons to him.

"So basically," he says, "it's where people rich enough to drive away from Manhattan in the heat go to get bitten by ticks and party with Puff Daddy."

"I mean, yeah," she says. "But we don't all drive. Some of us take the Jitney."

"What's the Jootney?" he asks, teasing her.

"The Jitney," she says. "It's a bus."

"You take the *bus*?" he asks, incredulous.

"Shut up." She laughs.

The farther they get from Chandler, the lighter he feels. He doesn't care anymore that he doesn't have the right clothes for Spence's parents. He's just happy that he gets to spend the holiday with her, laughing like this. Spence pulls out a photo album she brought to show him photos of her extended family. It's beautiful. There are photos of birthdays and past Diwalis. There are photos of Spence and her dad in matching suits, and Spence and her mom in matching saris. And also so many photos of young Spence with celebrities. There's Spence with Iman and Bowie, with Courtney Love, with Tony Kanal from No Doubt.

He stops at a photo of eight-year-old Spence in the arms of Madonna. "Seriously, Spence?"

"Crazy, right? That was backstage at the Blond Ambition tour in Landover, Maryland, of all places. It was the only date Gaultier could get my mom backstage passes for."

"Your fucking life," he says with a smile. He gets to a photo of Spence in the arms of a gorgeous Indian woman. "And that, I'm assuming, is some huge Bollywood star."

"Nope, that's my aunt," Spence says, laughing. "And now it's your turn. You promised you'd show me photos of your childhood too."

He digs into his duffel bag and feels around for the printed photos he stuffed in there. He pulls a few photos out, and also a piece of paper. On one side of the paper is Freddy's last history paper. On the other side, in big letters, is one word: *TRAITOR*.

His heart stops for a moment. Spence stares at the paper, confused. "What's that?"

He thinks back to when he packed. He left Toby and Seb in his room while he went to the bathroom. He feels invaded and enraged. They didn't come because they missed him as a friend. It was all a stupid trick.

"I feel so stupid for ever being their friend," Freddy says. "Was I just like them? Is that how people saw me?"

She puts her head on his shoulder and says, "I'm sorry. Please forget about those assholes."

"You know," he says, closing his eyes and enjoying the rolling sound of the train speeding down the tracks, "the hardest part of pole vaulting isn't physical, it's mental. It's learning to forget about assholes and pressure and fear and be in the moment."

"And how do you do that?" she asks.

He looks at Spence with a smile. "You meet people who make you feel good about yourself."

George Spencer and Shivani Lal welcome Freddy into their stunning home with open arms. They may have looked imposing in photos, but there's a warmth to them in person.

"Nice to meet you, Mr. Spencer and Mrs. Lal." He offers them a handshake, but they hug him in return.

"Call us George and Shivani. We're not your teachers," George says.

Freddy's eyes widen as they give him a tour of their townhouse. Henny and Whistler were right. There are bidets in every bathroom.

"This is so different from where I was raised." Freddy stares at a Basquiat, like he can't believe it's real.

"And so different from where I was raised too," Shivani says gently.

Freddy smiles. He likes them. And unlike his last girlfriend's snobby parents, they seem to like him.

The whole trip goes so well that neither Spence nor

Freddy wants to ruin it by asking George to speak to the board about Sullivan. They go to museums and to a movie premiere at the Ziegfeld. They go shopping at Barneys. Spence tries to buy him a new outfit, but he refuses.

The evening before their last dinner, Freddy walks down the hallway from his guest room to Spence's room. He loves her room. The walls are covered in Playbill covers from all the Broadway shows she's seen. He finds Spence on her bed, reading the latest issue of *Vogue*. He sits next to her.

"Last night at the Spencer Palace," he jokes, leaning in to kiss her.

"It's been great, right?" She looks up from the magazine. "I think they approve of you."

"Spence," he whispers. "Tonight's your last night to, you know . . ."

"I know," she says. She puts the magazine down.

He kisses her again. "You have to tell them."

"Okay," she says. "Okay."

That night at dinner, they eat puttanesca, and they laugh when Shivani tells them that it means "lady of the night" in Italian.

"Only the Italians," George says.

When dessert comes out, Freddy nudges Spence under the table, and that's when Spence looks up. "Mom. Dad." Her voice is faint as she says, "There's something I need to talk to you about."

Beth Kramer

"So what are we supposed to talk about?" Beth asks.

Dr. Geller smiles. There's a pen in his hand and a yellow notepad on his lap. "The first few sessions can always be a little awkward," he says. "But don't feel any pressure to tell me everything too quickly. We can start wherever you like. How are you feeling today?"

"Fine, I guess," she says.

"Parents' weekend is coming up," Dr. Geller says. "Any feelings about that?"

"Parents' weekend, yay!" Beth's voice is laced with irony.

Dr. Geller smiles. "Do I sense some hidden pain under the humor, Beth?"

"That is such a therapist-sounding thing to say," Beth can't help but respond. "It's not pain. At least, I don't think so." She feels an intense urge to leave, but she doesn't. She doesn't want to disappoint Douglas, so she tries to dig into her feelings. "I mean, it'll be weird, because my parents hate this place. They're going to go absolutely apeshit when they see the construction that started on the new computer lab." She puts her hand over her mouth. "Sorry."

"You're allowed to swear in here," Geller says, smiling. "The only thing I frown upon is dishonesty and deflection."

"Yeah, well, just imagine if my parents knew *how much* Toby's dad donated for the new lab. Then they'd really go motherfuckin' apeshit."

Dr. Geller pushes his spectacles down on his nose.

"Too much?" she asks with a smile. She looks at the clock. She still has forty minutes to go. What's she supposed to talk about for forty minutes?

"Maybe parents' weekend could be an opportunity for you to shift your relationship with your mom and dad. Does that idea resonate with you?"

Beth shrugs. "Maybe. I mean, yeah, it does resonate with me, actually."

"What are some steps *you* can take to make parents' weekend a success for you?"

She can think of so many joke answers to the question, but she's not going to do that. She thinks for a few seconds. "Well, I can be welcoming when they get here, and not like, go into it expecting the worst, right?"

"That's a great start."

"I can include them in my life," she continues. "Like, introduce them to the Circle. Maybe even tell them some of what's been going on."

"I think they'd appreciate that," Geller says.

"I could bring them to a therapy session with you," she says. "Especially since my mom *really* wanted me to get help and is *really* happy I'm finally getting counseling."

"Why do you think your mom wanted you to get help?"

She stammers, nervous to put it into words. "Well . . . like . . . I guess I can be anxious, you know."

"I do know," he says gently.

"And she noticed things I do. Obsessive things. Like I pull my hair out sometimes." She feels herself relax. It feels good to finally admit all this. "Maybe a little more than sometimes. If people knew, they would think I was so weird."

"Beth, everything you're describing is actually more common than you think. And there are tools to help with anxiety and compulsive behaviors."

"Oh good," she says. "Can I buy those tools at the hardware store 'cause I'm ready?"

He doesn't laugh. Just a half smile before he gets her back on track. She opens up, slowly allowing herself to be vulnerable. They talk about her parents, and her compulsive habits, and the Circle, and how much she hates Community Day when the whole concept of it is that Chandies give back to the community. But her family *are* the community. "And it feels really shitty that they rake our leaves or shovel our snow for a day out of *service*," she says.

She tells Geller a lot, but not a word about Sullivan.

It doesn't feel like her truth to tell. But she thinks about it a lot during the session. She knows that therapists need two years of grad school and three *thousand* hours of supervised counseling experience to become a therapist, and wishes to herself that the same was required of teachers. Then maybe the Sullivans of the world would find something else to do.

On the opening night of *Angels in America*, they pile into the front row of the theater. She prays they don't run into Sullivan. Everything is going so well, and she doesn't want Brunson running away again like she did in the costume closet on Halloween. But Sullivan must be backstage because there's no sign of him when the show begins. The whole play is riveting and challenging and expertly performed. But no one commands that stage like Spence. Toward the very end of the show, all the lights go out onstage. The whole audience sits in silence. A few people think the show is over because they start to clap. But then, the lights come back on, except they're not illuminating the stage. They're illuminating the audience, like hazard lights from an oncoming vehicle. A chilling sound comes out of the speakers. Then, in an instant, the sound stops, and a spotlight emerges center stage.

Spence stands in the spotlight, massive angel wings framing her body. In a voice that pierces the room with its clarity, she says, "Greetings, Prophet! The great work begins! The Messenger has arrived!"

The lights go out again, and when they come back on,

the whole cast joins Spence for a standing ovation. They exit the stage, and return for one more ovation, this time with Sullivan standing in between Spence and Whistler. He grips their hands as they take their final bow, and Beth can see the look of disgust on Spence's face as she subtly pulls away.

The lobby of the Harbor Arts Center is abuzz with conversation after the show. Spence and her castmates are showered with praise when they emerge from their dressing rooms into the crowd. Eventually, Spence makes her way to Douglas and the Circle, who are huddled in a corner.

"You outdid yourself," Freddy says, pulling her close.

"It was a beautiful performance. Truly," Douglas adds as Spence accepts their mentor's praise.

Beth looks around the room. So many eyes are on them, probably people wondering what the secretive Circle is talking about. She enjoys the feeling of being on the inside of something instead of the outside. But even more than that, she enjoys the feeling of the different parts of herself feeling like one whole. She's not a townie anymore. She's not a Chandie either. She's Beth.

"I have what I hope is good news for you, Ramin." Douglas leans in closer to Ramin. "I submitted an application to host a student, and it was approved. If you still want to leave Wilton Blue, you can move in with me before the winter holidays."

"Oh wow," Ramin says. "I mean, thank you."

"So that's a yes?" she asks.

"Yes," he says, closing his eyes. "Thank you. I just—I can't tell you what a relief it will be to go to sleep knowing that I'm safe."

"The great work begins!" Beth jokes, and they all laugh.

"Professor Douglas," Sullivan bellows as he approaches them. "I would very much appreciate your honest review of our little production."

"It was magnificent. I was especially moved by Amanda's performance," Douglas says with a smile toward Spence.

When she sees the look on Brunson's face, Spence looks at her watch and tells a perfectly delivered lie. "We're late, guys." With an apologetic look toward the teachers, she adds, "The Livingston girls planned a little celebration for me in the common room."

They all walk away from Sullivan as fast as they can. When the night air hits their faces, Brunson asks, "So has your dad talked to the board yet?"

"No," Spence says quietly. "He said it's hard with the holidays coming up. I'm sorry. He swears he'll talk to them soon."

"What does 'soon' even mean?" Brunson asks, her voice tense.

A few days later, on a cold mid-December evening, they all help Ramin pack his stuff from his room. There's excitement in Ramin's eyes when they're done putting everything into suitcases and boxes, but also a hint of sadness.

"You okay?" Brunson asks him.

He nods. "I'm great," he says. "I thought I was going to be stuck here forever."

The energy changes when Benji enters the room and looks around the half-empty space. "So I've got my own room now," he says. "Cool."

"Good to hear you're happy I'm leaving," Ramin says, a sly smile on his face. Then, staring at the *Hostages* movie poster on the wall, he adds, "And by the way, I never saw your mom's movie, but I'm not sure I want to because even the *poster* is offensive."

"Wait, why?" Benji asks as they head out.

Ramin doesn't answer. They all leave through the side door. Hiro rushes after Ramin. "Hey!" he says. "I know this isn't goodbye, but you know, goodbye."

"Come over anytime you want to play pasur," Ramin says.

"I'll be over tomorrow," Hiro says with a smile. "How much do you owe me now?"

Ramin laughs. "Seven million dollars, I think."

"I accept cash or credit," Hiro jokes.

They stare at each other for a long beat before Ramin says, "Are you sure you're going to be okay here?"

Hiro smiles. "Ramin, you don't need to worry about me. Just take care of yourself. I promise I'll do the same."

"I don't know how you do it," Ramin says.

He shrugs, but there is a sadness to his face. "I guess I just want to prove to those assholes that I'm better than they are."

"I'm not like you," Ramin says. "I can't stay here. But

I know that I would never have made it this far without you. Thank you."

Hiro laughs. "Stop talking like you're moving to Antarctica when you're gonna be just down the hill."

They help Ramin settle into Douglas's second bedroom that evening. She told them she had a faculty dinner to attend and wouldn't be home until close to lights out. "This is so weird," Beth says. "You're going to live with Douglas."

"Why is that weird?" Brunson asks. "I live with Mrs. Song."

"True," Spence says. "But Song is Song and Douglas is, well, she's Douglas. She's kind of an enigma, isn't she? Like, that's her bedroom right there?" She points to a closed door.

"Okay, we're not going in there," Ramin says.

"I didn't say we should!" Spence protests. "It's just weird."

"Everything is weird until it's not." Beth thinks of her whole journey as a Chandie. "Maybe humans just get used to anything."

They all sit on Ramin's new bed as he unpacks his clothes and lays them out neatly in a creaky mahogany armoire. When he's gotten to the bottom of his suitcase, he pulls out a piece of paper and he freezes.

"What?" Beth asks.

Ramin lifts the paper up for them to see. Written on it is one word: *TRAITOR.*

"Toby and Seb were in my suitcase." Ramin's voice trembles. "They—"

Freddy interrupts him. "They did the same thing to me."

"When we went to see my parents," Spence adds.

"Maybe we should go to the lake?" Ramin suggests, clearly desperate to stop thinking about his former prefects. "I'm done unpacking."

"It's so cold," Spence says.

"Scrabble?" Brunson suggests. "When I play with Millie, it makes everything better."

"I don't have a Scrabble board here," Ramin says.

"Like Douglas, the queen of words, doesn't have Scrabble. I'll go look." Brunson heads out.

Desperate to escape the sudden tension in the air, Beth says, "I'll come with you."

They search the living room first, but there are no board games there. So they make their way to the office. The door was left open, so it doesn't feel wrong to enter. They open cabinets looking for games. But all they find are files and more files. They're carefully organized. Beth stops when she sees one marked *Recommendation Letters*.

"See," Brunson says, pointing at the file. "Douglas *does* write recommendation letters. I'm definitely going to ask her to write me one when I apply to college."

"No one says she doesn't write them," Beth says. "Just that she's stingy with them."

"Well, let's see how many she's written." Brunson pulls the file open to reveal a relatively slim pile of paper.

"Okay, maybe you're right. There aren't a lot in here." Brunson grabs the papers out of the file.

"Brunson, we shouldn't—"

Brunson's face falls as she flips through the letters. "Beth," she says ominously.

"We shouldn't be reading her stuff," she says.

"Beth, this isn't a recommendation letter for a student," Brunson says. "It's a recommendation letter for a teacher. And it's not the only letter here. There's one from the teacher. He says he . . ." Brunson can't finish the sentence.

Brunson hands her the letters. She doesn't want to take them, but she does. As she scans the letters, she reads them out loud. "'Dear Headmaster Berg and Professor Douglas, I am writing to respond to the allegations regarding my conduct on the night of March twenty-eighth. I assure you what took place only lasted seconds before I put a stop to it. I had already drunk two glasses of wine when she knocked on my door.'"

"Stop," Brunson begs. "I already know what's coming."

Everything feels hazy around Beth. *Meditate*, she thinks to herself. She feels Brunson take her hand. She closes her eyes, struggling to escape the anxiety.

"Beth, we need to show this to them."

"We had no right to find this in the first place," she says.

"But we did," Brunson says.

Brunson leads the way back to Ramin's room.

"You guys don't want any secrets between us, right?" Brunson asks.

Spence nods.

"Well then . . ." Beth lays the letters on Ramin's bed. "Read this one first," she says, pointing to the letter from the teacher. She watches as Spence, Freddy, and Ramin read it.

"So basically this teacher *also* assaulted students?" Spence asks.

"I've never heard of him," Freddy says.

"That's because he got a job at another school," Beth says. "Now read the next letter."

She watches as they scan the next letter, this one written by Professor Douglas. Spence reads aloud. "'I am writing to recommend Professor Trumble for a position at your school. As head of the English Department, I have seen his passion for teaching firsthand, and have always been in awe of his exceptional knowledge of Homer.'"

"I don't want to read any more of this," Ramin says, turning away from the group. "We don't know anything about the circumstances."

"The circumstances?" Brunson asks. "A teacher assaulted a student. He even admitted to it. And Douglas wrote a letter recommending he teach at some other school."

"I feel sick," Spence says, her hands clutching her stomach.

"How could she?" Freddy asks. "She just sent this teacher to do the same thing to other kids?"

Brunson turns to Spence. "You need to show this to your dad. He needs to show *this* to the board. Because this—this proves it's not just Sullivan. The school's just been covering this stuff up for—forever."

"We need to think about this," Spence says.

"No, we don't," Ramin says. "Douglas . . . she brought us all together. She—she changed our lives."

"We can't hide this," Brunson says. "I'm sorry if it'll hurt Douglas, but—"

"You guys, we don't have to do anything tonight," Spence suggests. "My dad said this can't be solved overnight, and maybe he's right. What if we . . . talk to Douglas?"

"About what?" Brunson says. "You guys, she's just like Headmaster Berg. No, she's *worse*. She pretended to be on our side. But she wasn't. If it were up to her, Sullivan would just, what, go to some other school to—"

"I'm just suggesting we discuss every possible option," Spence says.

"There's only one option," Brunson says. "Telling the truth. I wish I'd had the strength to do it sooner. But I do now. Maybe Professor Douglas breaking my heart is what it took for me to find the courage."

Spence looks like a deer caught in headlights. Beth has never seen her look this unsure of herself. And, conversely, she has never seen Brunson looks so sure of herself.

"Maybe we should sleep on it," Freddy says.

"The school has been sleeping on this for fifty years." Brunson speaks urgently, the words spilling out of her. "There's no time to sleep anymore!"

"Okay, you don't need to scream at Freddy," Spence says. "He's not the enemy."

"Anyone who wants to cover this up is the enemy," Brunson says defiantly.

"Then that's what I am," Ramin says. "Because I would never betray Professor Douglas. If it weren't for her, I'd still be in that basement."

Brunson turns to Beth. "You've been quiet. Please tell me you agree with me."

Beth thinks she agrees with Brunson, but she doesn't feel ready to say so. "It's not you against us, okay," she whispers. "We have to, I don't know, agree with *each other.*"

"She wrote a *letter,*" Ramin says. "That's all. She didn't hurt anyone herself. It was just a letter. Just words on paper."

"*Just,*" Freddy says sadly.

"Beth?" Brunson asks.

Beth only wants to escape the conversation. "I just— we need a break," she says. "Can't we talk about this tomorrow or the next day or—"

"If you do it," Ramin says, "you're doing it without me. And if you don't mind, I'd like my room to myself now." He snatches the papers. "Where did you get these?" he asks.

Beth feels terrible. If she and Brunson hadn't gone looking for a Scrabble board, and then snooped around Douglas's office, they'd still be united. "In her files. There's a folder for recommendation letters," she says apologetically.

Spence stands up. "Well, I'm tired. At least we don't have another Circle meeting until next year, 'cause I don't know how we could all look at her in the same way again."

Spence leaves, and Freddy chases after her. "Spence, wait," he says before he's out of sight.

Ramin stares at Brunson until she, too, leaves.

Beth is the last one left. "I'm sorry," she says to Ramin. "We really didn't mean to find this."

"I know you didn't," he says, his voice quiet.

"Do you want me to leave or, you know, I could stay, too, if you—"

"I want to be alone," he says. "Can you put these back where you found them?"

"Sure," she says. On her way out, she puts the papers back, wishing she could also turn back the clock.

The seven days until winter holidays are the worst week of her life. The Circle doesn't sit together in the dining hall anymore. They don't go to the lake. She's invisible again, except this time she knows what it feels like to be seen, which makes the invisibility feel even worse. When her mom comes to pick her up and take her home, she's actually happy about it.

"Beth, there's a phone call for you," her mom says, knocking gently on her door.

"Who is it?" she asks.

"I don't know, she didn't say." Her mom peeks her head in. She knows what her mom's thinking. It's noon, and she's still in bed. It's pathetic. "It's Christmas Eve, and I've set up the scavenger hunt to end all hunts."

"I'll come down soon," Beth says, though she's not so sure.

"Do you want to talk about what's going on?" her mom asks.

Beth shakes her head. "Maybe later, Mom."

Her mom gives her a thumbs-up and leaves her alone.

She takes a deep breath before picking up the phone. "Hello?"

"Beth, it's me, Brunson."

She sits up, holding the receiver tight to her ear. She's not sure who she was expecting, but not Brunson.

"How are you?" Brunson asks.

"Well, let me think about that." Beth waits a beat. "I'm fucking horrible."

"Yeah, me too," Brunson says. "I can't stop thinking about how we left things."

"Have you spoken to any of them?" Beth asks.

"No."

Beth freezes for a moment. If she hasn't spoken to any of them, then Beth is the only one she's called.

"But I—" Brunson takes a breath before continuing. "Well, I wrote a letter to Professor Douglas. I dropped out of the Circle. I just wanted you to know."

"Oh," she says, surprised at how sad she is to hear this. "Did you tell her why?"

"No," Brunson says.

"Okay." Beth isn't sure what to say next.

The next time Brunson calls, the conversation is lighter. "My sister thinks I'm a superhero," Brunson says.

"What, why?" Beth asks.

Brunson pretends to be offended. "What do you mean, why? Because I'm a badass."

"And so humble," she says, smiling.

"No seriously, it's because I'm Sarah at home and Brunson on campus. She says I have two personalities, like Diana Prince and Wonder Woman."

"Do you?" she asks.

"I don't think so. I mean, I hope not. I think I'm just . . . figuring myself out like we all are. But I've definitely hidden stuff, I guess."

"Like about your mom?" Beth asks. "That's not hiding. That's just keeping private stuff private."

"What about you? Are you two different people?"

Beth lies back, relaxing into the conversation. "I was, for a long time. But not anymore. Now I'm just Beth Kramer, of the Connecticut Kramers."

After that, they talk on the phone every day, sometimes more than once a day, conversations that are about nothing and everything. It's like the distance of a telephone line allows them to finally open up completely to each other.

On one call, Brunson announces, "Beth, there's something I wanted to apologize for."

"Please don't," she says. "Whatever it is, I want to

move past apologies."

"I know." Brunson sighs. "It's just, when I read your copy of Douglas's book."

"Oh, that." Beth feels her body tense. "I definitely overreacted to that."

"Yeah, but I just wanted you to know the reason I did that. It's not because I wanted to invade your privacy." She pauses. "It's because I wanted to read, well, a book about lesbians. Because I like girls."

"Oh," Beth says.

"That's it?" Brunson asks, and gives a nervous laugh. "I just came out to you, and all I get is an *oh*."

"Remember how I said I wasn't two people anymore?" Beth says. "That's because I'm finally ready to admit I like girls too."

"Oh" is all Brunson says, and then they laugh for real. Everything has changed now.

When they've stopped laughing long enough to catch their breath, Beth asks, "Hey, do you think the reason we were scared of each other is because we're actually kind of similar?"

"What do you mean? I wasn't scared of you. Were you scared of me?"

A smile forms on Beth's face. "Yeah, a little. Maybe *scared* is the wrong word. I just thought you were one of those girls everything came easy to. And that scared me. Because I'm so not like that."

"Obviously, you were *very* wrong about me." Brunson laughs. "And I was wrong about you. But I did have a feeling about you liking girls. Recently, not last year. You were a total mystery then."

"Well, we're learning some very important supplemental facts about each other, aren't we?" Beth jokes.

"We certainly are." Beth can hear the smile in her voice. Then Brunson asks, "So are you going to stay in the Circle? Knowing what she did?"

There's a long pause. Beth finally says, "I don't know. I guess I really need the writing."

"We don't *need* her to write."

"I hope that's true," she says. She looks up at her ceiling. The truth is she hasn't written a word over the holidays, and she misses the release of it.

Suddenly, Brunson asks, "Have you forgiven me, Beth? Like, really forgiven me?"

"Yeah," she says quietly. "I mean, looking back, I think I played my own part in our dysfunctional dynamic, you know. Like, I can't shut someone out and then blame them for not including me in things." Beth looks up at all the Chandler memorabilia on her walls. She feels so different from that girl who was obsessed with belonging to the school. "Have you forgiven me?"

"Of course," Brunson says. "I had so much wrong about you, about my family, about everything. Like, I had created a narrative where I was the caretaker. Caring for my sick mom, raising my little sister, like I was some kind of victim. And that made me kind of bitter, I guess. But the truth is that they were taking care of me too. They were loving me into existence, just like you guys all did."

They talk until Beth's mom calls her down to dinner.

And they talk again later that night. They talk about when they first figured out they were gay. And about their families. And about stupid stuff, like their favorite Spice Girl.

"*Baby Spice?*" Brunson asks, incredulous. "Explain yourself."

"I don't know," Beth says. "She's cute, she seems nice, and no one ever picks her."

The next morning, there's a phone call for her. Assuming it's Brunson, she answers in a soft voice, "Baby Spice Fan Club, how may I help you?"

"Beth?" It's Ramin's confused voice on the other end of the line.

"Ramin!" She's mortified. "I'm so sorry, I thought you were someone else."

"Brunson?" he asks gently. "She told me you guys were talking a lot."

"Oh." She feels herself blush. "You spoke to her?"

"I've spoken to everyone."

"About what?"

He pauses. "Being away from Chandler made me realize we can't just look past what Douglas did."

"But aren't you the one who said you would never turn her in?"

"I know what I said." In the background, Ramin's dad calls his name.

"How are things with your parents?" Beth asks.

"Fine, mostly," he says. "It's nice being in London, at least. My parents didn't think I should go back to Iran."

"I've always wanted to see that city," she sighs. After a moment she adds, "So about Douglas?"

"Right. She needs to know everything, and we need to tell her. It's what she taught us. Maybe now it's our turn to teach her something."

"We'll write it," Beth whispers.

"Exactly." He pauses. "Brunson, Spence, and Freddy are in. We'll all write our stories. We'll tell her everything."

Beth finds herself nodding.

"So, what do you think? *Veritas vos liberabit*?"

When Beth arrives back on campus, Brunson is waiting for her on the steps of Carlton House, holding two cups of hot chocolate. "Hi," she says, a shy smile on her face. "Wanna walk?"

"Yeah." Beth feels her cheeks redden from the excitement and the cold. "Let me just put my stuff away."

They walk every day. It's like their phone calls but in person. On a cold January Sunday, they walk toward MacMillan together. Douglas has summoned them, and though Brunson technically dropped out of the Circle, she's still showing up.

On the Main Lawn, Connor Emerson sings "Being Alive" in preparations for *Company* auditions.

"*Company* again?" Beth says. "The school did that show as the spring musical in—"

"1988," Brunson says, finishing her sentence.

"You're such a Chandler nerd," she says.

"Mrs. Pot, meet Ms. Kettle."

"Mrs.? Why am I a married pot in this scenario, while you're some cool feminist kettle?" She laughs uncomfortably at her own joke, Brunson's eyes glued to her. "What, do I have something on my face?"

"No," Brunson says. "I just want to kiss you, if that's okay."

"Oh." She instinctively looks around. The trunk of a sycamore tree hides them from view, although she really wouldn't mind being seen. Turns out being seen feels pretty good. "Yeah, I'd like that."

Brunson leans in. So does she. Time slows down. Or maybe this is how time is supposed to feel, like every second matters.

"The Circle is back together," Freddy says, smiling, when Beth and Brunson finally arrive together and take their places on her floor.

"Not really," Brunson says. "Professor Douglas asked me to be here, but it's just to hear her out. I'm not coming back."

"Thank you for coming, Sarah," Douglas says. "I've read your stories. And whether she chooses to remain a part of our group or not isn't my primary concern at the moment." She looks at Brunson. "Though I hope you do stay."

"Professor Douglas," Brunson interrupts. "Before you

start. The one thing I wanted to say is I'm sorry that we went through your stuff. That's not a part of the story I'm particularly proud of."

Douglas lets out a deep sigh. "I know. Some things happen for a reason. Whatever happens next, I want you kids to promise me you'll remain friends. That's the biggest gift this place has to offer. You *are* each other's family. Do you see that?"

"I do," Beth says, her eyes fixed on Brunson, then on Ramin, Spence, and Freddy.

"Good." Douglas takes a sip of her tea and then puts her cup down. "I'm proud of you."

"I'm so relieved to hear that," Ramin says, his voice shaking. "I was scared of telling you about what we found."

"Before we go any further, I need to say . . . ," Douglas starts. Beth has never heard her sound so vulnerable. "None of this is easy for me. I feel as if I've deeply disappointed you. And disappointed myself. But what I need to say is how sorry I am. I could tell something was going on with Ramin and I thought it was strange that you weren't spending as much time with each other. I should have been more inquisitive. I wish I could've been there for you, all of you."

"The problem is"—Brunson takes a breath—"that you were part of the problem."

Douglas nods sadly. "I know. And before we discuss that, I just want to say that I never liked Mr. Sullivan very much, but I didn't know. And I am so deeply horrified by what he did to you, Sarah."

"Like you were horrified by the other teacher you wrote a letter of recommendation for?" Beth asks.

"I deserve that," Douglas says, closing her eyes. "You *should* be angry with me."

"Why did you do it?" Ramin asks, more sad than angry.

"I did it because I wanted to keep teaching," she says, shaking her head like she knows it's a terrible answer. "I've lived with shame for a long time because of that letter. I've thought about it every day since I wrote it. I know the words by heart. And the worst part is that I know exactly what it feels like when an adult that you trust betrays that trust. Because it happened to me too." She's lost in a memory for a moment. "We didn't talk about it back then. There was so much shame. If a man forced himself on a woman, it was her fault. At least that's what my mother believed. When I confessed it all to her, she told me never to repeat it to anyone else. So I didn't."

They all stare at each other in shock, not sure how to respond.

"I'm not looking for sympathy," she says. "Reading what you wrote, it made me realize that all the justifications I've come up with for what I did are just that. Excuses."

"So what should we do?" Spence asks softly.

"I don't know what you're going to do, but I'm going to contact the school that English teacher teaches at, and make sure they're aware of the allegations against him during his time here." Douglas shifts her gaze across the room. "It's not enough, and it's far too late, but it's something."

"I still don't understand," Beth says. "What does writing that letter have to do with you teaching? Why did you protect him?"

"Because I was afraid," she explains. "I love teaching more than anything. More than writing, even. That's the reason why I stopped writing. That and my shame, I suppose. And I was afraid that if I made those allegations an issue . . . well, let's just say there was a lot of pressure from above me to make the problem go away quietly." She paces the room. "I was already a lesbian teacher, which back then was even harder than it is now. And I didn't want to get fired over a useless stand. I wanted a tenured position here because teaching, it's just . . . well, it's my purpose."

"*Just*," Freddy says sadly.

She flashes them a bittersweet smile. "I do hate that word."

"Professor Douglas, what do we do about Sullivan?" Brunson asks. "Nothing's happened with Spence's dad and the board."

Spence shakes her head, disappointed. "I know. I'm sorry."

"I think you all know the path forward," Douglas says, holding their pages in the air.

"So you think we should show the story to other people?" Beth asks. "Even with all that stuff in there about you?"

"I'm not afraid of the truth anymore," she says.

The cold campus air hits Beth hard when they all walk out of MacMillan together.

"Well, that was weird," Brunson says. "Do you think she'll actually do it? Call the school that teacher works at?"

"I really do," Freddy says. "She seemed . . . different."

Spence stops. "We can't wait anymore. I love my dad and I know he'll do what he can. But enough time has passed. We need a better plan."

They all stare at Spence.

"Okay, but what's the plan?" Beth asks.

Spence looks up at the sky for a moment, then right at Brunson. "Do you still have the keys to the *Legacy* offices?"

"Yeah." Brunson nods, and then it starts to dawn on her. "You want to publish the pages?"

"Yes." Spence nods. "It's what Douglas said."

"But which part?" Beth asks.

Ramin speaks up. "All of it. All of our parts. So people can understand how everything connects. Students who abuse students, and teachers who abuse students, and teachers who cover it up, and how every student isn't treated equally and, well, I'm sick of being afraid. If we publish it all, maybe we can do something about Sullivan and Seb and Toby."

Spence picks up where Ramin left off. "People just accept the way things are, but maybe they'll change their minds when they see it in print."

"I'm on board, but we all wrote parts of it," Freddy

says. "So we all have to agree."

"I'm in," Brunson says.

They all look at Beth, who nods.

Brunson smiles as she says, "The *Legacy* offices will be empty right now. I could log into my email, download the story, and—"

"Are we really doing this?" Beth whispers.

"Fuck yeah we are," Spence says, leading the way to the Humanitas.

They sneak into the office of the *Chandler Legacy* like they're about to pull off a heist. Beth gazes at Brunson in awe as she deletes the cover story she had written over the holidays about the new paint color—Sistine Blue—of the headmaster's house, and replaces it with their story. No photos. Just words. Just the truth.

They sign it as the Circle.

Brunson finishes setting the copy of the paper, then programs it to start printing. "First issue of the new millennium," she says proudly.

"What if Barman sees it?" Spence asks. "Can she stop it from being distributed?"

"It's too late," Brunson says. "The papers will be picked up tomorrow morning."

They watch as the printer spits out copies of the paper. In twelve hours, the whole campus will wake up to a new day.

"It'll be chaos," Spence predicts.

Brunson smiles. "Maybe a little chaos is necessary when you're trying to blow up a century of secrecy."

They walk to the lake when they're done. And they stand in a circle. Spence takes Ramin's hand with her left, Freddy's with her right. Freddy takes Beth's hand, and with a sly smile, Beth takes Brunson's.

"United we swim," Freddy says.

Spence laughs. "Nobody's swimming tonight. That lake is ice, ice baby."

"You did not bring Vanilla Ice into this historic night," Freddy says.

The laughter is contagious. Beth doesn't know if they're laughing because they're joyful or scared. Probably both. "What if nothing changes?" she asks.

"It will," Freddy says forcefully. "Even if Sullivan's not fired overnight. Even if Seb and Toby aren't expelled tomorrow. It'll still be different. *We're* different. Douglas is different."

"So you've all forgiven her?" she asks.

"Maybe it's not about forgiving what she did. It's about . . ." Spence's voice seems to echo over the lake. "Not defining her by her worst mistake. Not defining anyone by their worst mistake."

"Anyone?" Beth asks. "Not even Seb and Toby?"

"If they don't face consequences for what they did, they'll spend their whole lives being assholes," Brunson says. "When that paper comes out, we'll have done them a huge favor. If they get expelled, then maybe when they realize they can't get away with being dicks, it'll be early enough for it to make a difference in their lives. Otherwise, they'll end up like Sullivan."

"Yeah," Beth muses. "Although there are people who will never change."

Beth looks out at the lake and all its hidden depths. Then she walks to their tree, the one with their initials carved into it. She runs her hand over those letters. Letters, words, sentences, paragraphs, stories. That is how they will define themselves.

Spence joins her, leaning against the tree. "You know, ever since I got to Chandler, people called me a legacy kid because my dad went here." Spence runs her hands along the initials as Ramin, Brunson, and Freddy join them. "I never questioned why it bothered me." She leans her head on Freddy's shoulder. "I think—no, I know— the reason I hate it is because it implies that a legacy kid is always going to be defined by their past. Like, my whole identity is about the fact that my dad once walked these same grounds. But that's not who I am. My legacy isn't about living up to my past by trying to be perfect. It's about the future I'll help create by being myself. We make our own legacy, don't we?"

Beth feels her fingers brush against Brunson's. Such a small gesture of intimacy. But it means so much to Beth. It reminds her that there's infinite possibility in the world. Infinite hope and surprise. "You're right," she says. "We make our own legacy."

Epilogue

JANUARY 2008

I wake up around noon. There's a cup of coffee by my bed with a note from Robbie that reads *Love you, baby.* We've been together six years, and he still leaves messages like this all over the apartment. Sometimes I pinch myself to make sure he's real. I take a sip of the coffee. It's cold now, but it jolts me awake.

I had been dreaming of Chandler. Sometimes I wonder if high school will haunt me forever. I've never thought about it before, but the novels that line our shelves and pile up on our floor make the place look a lot like Douglas's residence in MacMillan. Maybe I subconsciously recreated the first space that made me feel safe. Of course, I own signed copies of all her books, the three novels she's written since I graduated and the anniversary edition of *Supplemental Facts*. Looking at these books always brings me right back there. To MacMillan, to her living room, or to the bedroom that became my home until I graduated from Chandler.

I open my computer up to a new document. The blinking cursor stares at me, like a dare. I should be writing a new TV pilot, something commercial. Nothing comes.

Sometimes I think of quitting, more and more often these days. I'm worn down by the constant rejection, and by my inability to write anything that reflects my own truth. The network notes telling me to cut all the gay characters in a script. To change Iranian families to white ones. The meetings where I'm told they love my script, but they already have a Middle Eastern project in development.

I'm struck by a need to see Robbie, so I pack up my things and head to his restaurant. He beelines over to me and gives me a kiss. He's always so happy in this space, a place he created. He leads me to a corner table where I like to write. I don't need a menu. He knows my order. I love that he knows me so well.

I open up my computer and plug it in. The cursor blinks at me again, but this time it feels like an invitation. I realize that I've been running away from telling the one story I've truly wanted to tell. About the friends who first saw me and loved me. I'll write it as a novel. Hasn't that always been my biggest ambition? To follow in Douglas's footsteps?

Then I stop again. Spence is a movie star now, and

she's dating an even bigger movie star. Freddy's a gold medalist. Brunson works with kids and Beth's a therapist, and they're about to have their first kid. Can I really write about them? But then I remember something Douglas once said to us, that writers must learn how to change all the specifics, but keep all the truth.

The smell of the kitchen takes me right back to all those work-study hours I did in the Chandler kitchen. To all the meals I ate with the Circle, and to that one January lunch when we watched as a stack of the *Chandler Legacy* copies were plopped down next to the juice station. Whistler picked one up casually. Madame Ardant grabbed one as she talked to Señora Reyes. Hiro and Sabrina read it together. When he was done reading, he gazed at me across the room and nodded.

It all felt like it was happening in both slow motion and fast-forward. We watched as the voices in the cafeteria fell into a hush while the paper was passed from friend to friend, from teacher to teacher, and finally to headmaster. Eventually, the whole dining hall seemed to be looking back at us. At the Circle.

By the end of that week, three more Chandler students and two alumni would come forward with harrowing details of their own experiences with Sullivan, and he would be swiftly fired and charged. By the end of the month, Seb and Toby would be expelled, not for hazing but for stealing cigarettes from Mikey's. And Douglas, she would stay at Chandler. She's still there, actually.

No matter how many novels she writes, she'll never give up teaching. The Circle, like the seasons, is still going round and round.

But that's where the story ends, not where it begins.

I stare at the blank page and hear her voice, teaching me how to let go.

I feel them all sitting next to me, helping me to accept myself.

And then I open my eyes and begin to write.

AUTHOR'S NOTE

My freshman year of boarding school was the hardest year of my life. I was sent to the school by my parents, who wanted the very best education for me. And this was the very best, a place that had educated a president.

It was 1990, and I had only been living in the United States for four years. I had never had an American friend. I arrived for my freshman year, different in so many ways than the other kids. Browner, more effeminate. The freshman-year dorm I lived in, like Ramin's dorm, was a dark basement. The hazing I describe in these passages is a mild version of what happened there. The shame I experienced that year felt like an ocean I could never swim out of. I attended classes, but for most of the year, I wouldn't leave my room. I was sent to the school therapist, but I told the therapist nothing of what I was subjected to. I would beg my parents to let me come home, but I didn't tell them any details of why. To this day, I don't speak about what happened that freshman year other than to my husband and to the family of friends I eventually made in boarding school. The details belong to me, and as I've grown up, I've discovered that fiction is my preferred method of making sense of the world.

For decades, I thought that what I went through that first year of high school was isolated to me. With time, I felt like I had put it all behind me. And if that first year broke me down to pieces, then the next three years of boarding school made me whole again. They were, and will always be, three of the best years of my life. It was in boarding school that I met the friends who would first accept me and make me feel seen. They remain my best friends to this day, my family and my circle. It was at boarding school that I found adult mentors who first recognized and supported my need to create.

The first person I came out to was a teacher at boarding school. The first friends I came out to were boarding school friends. The person I am today was born on those grounds, and though a part of me still wishes I could have left and never looked back that freshman year, another part of me knows that so much of what is good in my life was born on that same campus in the years that followed.

In April 2017, almost two decades after graduating, I received an email from the school. The email included an attachment to a fifty-page report to the Board of Trustees of my alma mater. Fifty pages that outlined decades of horrific sexual abuse at the school. Twelve former teachers were accused through the years. None were reported to the police. In some cases, the school looked the other way. In others, letters of recommendation were written and the teachers were sent to other schools, no doubt to repeat the behavior elsewhere. I read the fifty pages, feeling sick to my stomach.

That night, I was drawn back to my boarding school family. We texted, emailed, called each other. Some were surprised by the report. Others, myself included, read it with a knowing feeling of dread. Somewhere deep inside me, I knew this was the culture of the school. So many of us did. But we didn't have the words to name it, or question it, or stand up to it. We felt powerless. We were kids back then. We were supposed to be taken care of. I called one of my best friends who lived in that freshman-year basement with me. We talked about how the report didn't even touch upon the abuse that students inflicted on each other. Because when the teachers and the administration set a code of conduct, students will inevitably follow.

As I read about what happened at the school, the parallels to other powerful institutions were obvious. Like the Catholic Church, this school and many others covered up sexual abuse. And Hollywood, the industry I have worked in for my entire adult life, has been revealed to be yet another version of the same thing. Powerful men protected, victims silenced and paid off, predators hired again and again. The problem is universal. It touches any institution that believes itself to be more powerful than its individuals.

This book is my way of confronting the many complicated emotions I have about four of the most impactful years of my life. I hope that by telling this story, readers will understand that they have more power than they think. But this isn't just a story about darkness. It's also about how friendship, love, and creativity can heal us. And set us free.

The statistics about sexual abuse and hazing are heartbreaking. One in nine girls, and one in fifty-three boys, experience sexual abuse by the age of eighteen at the hands of an adult. Almost half of all students coming to college have already been hazed. Students who are bullied are between 2–9 percent more likely to attempt suicide. These problems are pervasive and are all around us.

If you have experienced or are experiencing abuse of any kind, there is help, both personal and professional. There is therapy, and the support of friends and family and mentors, and so many organizations devoted to being there for you.

Below is a list of organizations that can help:

RAINN is the nation's largest anti-sexual violence
organization.
www.rainn.org
800-656-HOPE

The Trevor Project is devoted to saving young
LGBTQ+ lives.
www.thetrevorproject.org
866-488-7386

The National Suicide Prevention Lifeline
800-273-8255

ACKNOWLEDGMENTS

When I was young, I loved to write, but never dreamed that it could become a career. That started to change in boarding school, when a special group of people helped me see myself in a new way. I'd like to thank all the friends and mentors I met at Choate in the 1990s. I arrived as a shy, depressed freshman hiding in my room. I left as a confident, bold senior voted best dressed and most likely to have my own lounge act (still working on it).

I would never have become that person without a very long list of people. I can't name them all without writing another book. If we laughed or cried or danced together in Wallingford between 1990 and 1994, just know I love and appreciate you. Special thanks for life-changing friendship and support to: Lauren Ambrose, Sarah Blodgett, Veronica Bollow, Tom Collins, Jennifer Elia, Stephen Farrell, Amanda Frazer, Ted Huffman, Erica Kraus, Trina Meiser, Amy Rabinowitz, Conley Rollins, Melanie Samarasinghe, Sarah Shetter, Serena Torrey, Sara Upton, Kate Wilson, and Lauren Wimmer. Sophomore year water tower friends, Sonia Tribe, and *Baby with The Bathwater* cast and crew, those are moments that birthed me.

Too many people I went to boarding school with are gone. Two in particular—Fred Torres and Natalia Roquette—were people I shared impactful experiences with. We carry you with us.

Alessandra Balzer at Balzer + Bray is directly responsible for pulling both this book and *Like a Love Story* out of me. I don't know how I'd do this without you, Alessandra. Thanks to you and the whole Balzer + Bray family (Donna Bray, Caitlin Johnson, Michael D'Angelo, Jackie Burke, Patty Rosati, Kattie Dutton, Mimi Rankin, Nicole Moreno, Andrea Pappenheimer, Kerry Moynagh, Kathy Faber, I appreciate you all). And big thanks to the BookSparks team for helping start my journey as an author and coming onboard again for this one.

Corina Lupp and Natalie Shaw, thank you for the beautiful cover. It takes me right back to those boarding school lawns.

John Cusick at Folio, thank you for supporting my desire to tell stories that challenge me creatively. I'm so grateful for the support and I can't wait to see what's next.

Mitchell Waters, I'll forever be grateful that you saw something in me when no one else did. Once an agent, always a friend.

Brant Rose and Toochis Rose, thank you for working so hard on my behalf, and for always doing it with genuine warmth and care.

I'm so insecure when I write a new book, and am so grateful to superfriends Susanna Fogel, Ted Huffman, Erica Kraus, and Erin Lanahan for being early readers of this novel and offering me guidance and support. And huge thanks to Rashmi Kashyap for the illuminating conversations.

I have too many friends to thank, but a few who have been especially supportive to me and my family are Mojean Aria, Jamie Babbit, Alexa Boland, Jennifer Candipan, Tom Dolby, Jazz Elia, Lauren Frances, Nancy Himmel, Rachel Jackson, Mandy Kaplan, Ronit Kirchman, Ali Meghdadi, Joel Michaely, Julia Othmer, Busy Philipps, Jessica Rhoades, Mark Russ, Joyce Song, Jeremy Tamanini, Amanda Tejeda, James Teel, Lila Azam Zanganeh, and Nora Zehetner. To everyone in the writers' rooms I've been in, the laughter and camaraderie of building stories together has kept me going and taught me so much about storytelling.

I love being a part of the community of book writers and book lovers. Thank you fellow author friends, and special thanks to Taylor Jenkins Reid for not only writing the best books, but being the best human. Your kind words about my writing truly mean the world to me. And massive thanks to Leah Johnson, Adib Khorram, E. Lockhart, and Laura Ruby for your generosity in reading an early draft of this novel and supporting it with your always-powerful words.

I'd like to take a moment to acknowledge all the readers who have written to me about *Like a Love Story*. The words I've exchanged with readers from all over the world have moved me, healed me, helped me feel the power of art and community. During the pandemic, you all helped me feel less alone. *E a todos os leitores brasileiros, eu te vejo e te amo. Você não tem ideia de como tocou profundamente minha alma com seu belo espírito. O amor é nosso legado.*

Thank you Tori Amos. You were my muse as I wrote this book. Your music helps me navigate life's most difficult emotions. I love you, my goddess of catharsis.

LA FAMILLE IS GOLD: Maryam, Luis, Dara, Nina, Mehrdad, Vida, John, Lila, Moh, Brooke, Youssef, Shahla, Hushang, Azar, Djahanshah, Parinaz, Parker, Delilah, Rafa, Santi, Tomio, and Kaveh. Aubrys and Kamals! Jude, Susan, Kathy, Zu, Paul, Jamie, and company. My parents Lili and Jahangir, and my brother, Al. I love you all.

My new author photo was taken by my mom's cousin Mandy Vahabzadeh in Central Park on a crisp pandemic day. Mandy is a brilliant artist, and one of the people who first introduced me to the power of great art. Every young teen should have someone in their family taking them to see Kusturica and Wong Kar-Wai films on the big screen (and sneaking them into *SNL* to watch Madonna's only performance of "Bad Girl"). I'm so grateful for you, Mandy.

Jonathon Aubry, one way to know you married the right person is to go straight into quarantine when the wedding and honeymoon are over. You're the one, my best pal and my partner in all aspects of life. We're a hell of a match. Thank you for letting me bask in the glow of your life force, and for always bringing out the best in me. I'm so lucky to love you and be loved by you. We're writing our own legacy.

Rumi and Evie, you are my heart and my soul and my everything. I hope that when you look back on this wild time we're still living through, you remember the beauty we found in being isolated together: the laughter, the movie nights (and sometimes movie mornings), the dance parties to Cardi and Megan and Madonna, the pasur and backgammon games, Dottie catch and the-name-of-the-game-is-speed-speed-speed, bringing Disco home and loving him, the endless splits, the delicious sweets that will someday launch the Right Mama Bakery, the *Drag Race* viewings, the splits, the yoga, our magical Bolognese, Gilda are you decent, and yes, sometimes math and Spanish homework 'cause I'm your parent even if I act like a kid sometimes. You both inspire me so much. Rumi, your humor and curiosity are magic. Never stop laughing and learning. Evie, your passion and empathy are boundless. You always sparkled, and I know you always will, my Sparks. There is no love in the world bigger than my love for you both.